THIS IS MOSTRIM

~ ~ ~

THE FAMINE

MARK CASSIDY

Copyright © Mark Cassidy, 2024
First Published in Ireland, in 2024, in co-operation with
Choice Publishing, Drogheda, County Louth, Republic of Ireland.
www.choicepublishing.ie

Paperback ISBN: 978-1-917242-14-1

The moral right of the author has been asserted.

All rights reserved. No part of this publication may be reproduced, stored in a retrieval system, transmitted in any form, or by any means, electronic, mechanical, photocopying, recording or otherwise, without the prior permission of the copyright holder.

OTHER TITLES IN THIS COLLECTION

This Is Mostrim 2 – The Exile

This Is Mostrim 3 – The Homecoming

To Mam and Dad

also

In remembrance of those who lived and died
during the Great Hunger

Map of Ireland:
- Parish of Mostrim

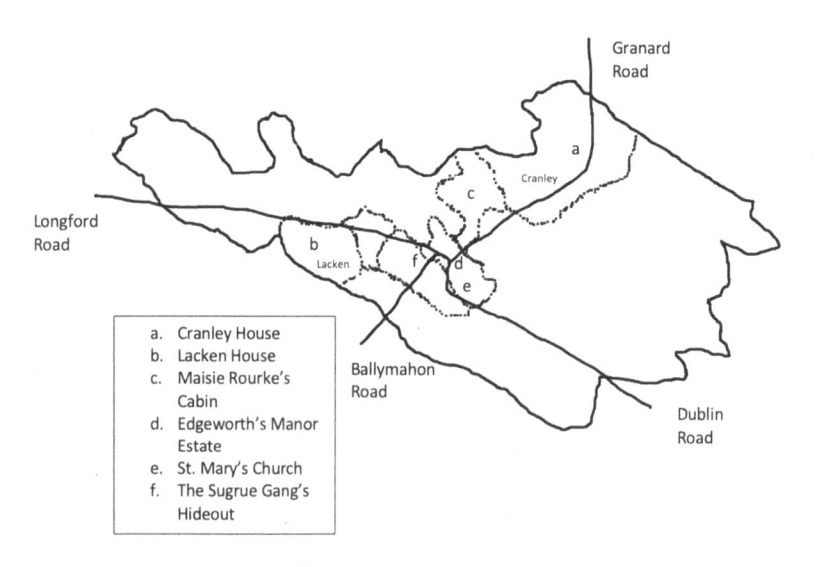

a. Cranley House
b. Lacken House
c. Maisie Rourke's Cabin
d. Edgeworth's Manor Estate
e. St. Mary's Church
f. The Sugrue Gang's Hideout

Parish of Mostrim/Edgeworthstown

One – Cranley House

It was a nice distraction from the stones, watching the old woman and the girl go up the avenue. They were pulling and pushing. It was clear that the girl didn't want to go, but the old lady was having none of it. It distracted the woodcutters too, as axes ground to a halt in the distance. I lifted my hands out of the mud. I stood up straight for a better view and immediately felt the rush of blood to my lower back. Sugrue was already leaning on the fence, a dislodged rock momentarily forgotten in all the excitement.

'She's one of ours,' I said, as the old woman got closer.

'I know that,' replied Sugrue.

'How do you know the crowd out my way?'

'Haven't I spent the best part of sixty years looking at her. I knew your neighbours before you were born,' he said.

The stately lawns of Cranley looked magnificent in the midday sun, but not to the old woman or the girl. The tug-o-war continued up the avenue towards a house of perfect balance. Two granite lions guarded the entrance. The finest windows Gandon ever designed watched over a hundred workers. Three white pillars stood either side of the great red doors. On the rooftop, directly above, shone the crowning glory – a large unicorn, a coat of arms, and two swords crossed before the colours of the British Empire. The lions roared their disapproval as the old woman passed nervously, the girl now snivelling and unable to stop the tears from coming.

'There's one for the kitchens. Come on James, I hear the bells. Lunch time.'

There were no bells – or at least no bells in Cranley. The church in Mostrim was in the village, some three miles away. Sugrue couldn't possibly hear the bells, yet he always begged to differ.

I knew the girl crying in the avenue. I knew her very well. She and her family lived in the same settlement as I did – a place known locally as the clachan of Lacken. Her name is Constance Ryan. The old woman who was pushing her towards Cranley House is her grandmother. I also knew why Constance was crying. My heart went out to her that day when I saw those tears. There was a story going around the parish and I hoped for her sake it wasn't true.

'She's not much older than our Maggie,' I eventually said to Sugrue.

'Whisht about it. My sisters were working by the time they were ten. Isn't Tom McAndrew's young one doing well in there,' he returned, nodding in the direction of the house. 'Head woman now, or so they tell me. Ah, the Lacken crowd always looked after their own.'

He gave a little smile then.

'She's not Lacken no more, Sugrue.'

'Will you go on out of that,' he said. 'We'll leave it to God, my auld son of Eireann.'

The McAndrews were from Lacken too, one-time neighbours of ourselves and the Ryans. They had gone to a new house in a different part of the county. My daughter Maggie would be taking the same trip up that avenue over my dead body. Myself and Mairead had discussed this at length. The stories going about may have been a pack of lies, but why take the chance. I had it on good authority that the Edgeworth estate in the village was the right place for a girl starting out in domestic service.

'Any sign of her father these days,' asked Sugrue. 'Is old Tom still in the land of the living?'

'He's grand, the last I heard. He's a while gone out of the clachan now.'

Tom McAndrew was Sugrue's old comrade-in-arms, dating back to the days of the rebellion. I had heard all the stories. The man I was helping pull rocks out of the ground all morning was a living legend in Mostrim. Tom McAndrew was another. However, to some people in the parish, Tom's star had begun to wane. His daughter Sheila had worked for a couple of years in de Bromley's kitchens. More than that, she was now in charge of the other Irish girls. She was supposed to be militant like her father. They claim she wasn't liked by the younger ones. I had the good sense to say nothing about either of them to Sugrue.

In 1845 the immediate trouble began and, long before the second harvest had failed, lunch packets were already getting lighter. Sugrue's lunch was noticeably worse off, but I knew to thread carefully. He still indulged in a slice of wheaten bread, two oatmeal cakes, and a bottle of buttermilk. But lately his potatoes were missing.

'Oh God, I'd kill for an oat cake, Sugrue.'

The days of Sugrue voluntarily sharing his oatmeal cakes were over. He looked concerned as he studied his lunch.

'These potatoes have me bound so tight, it's like there's a cork stuck in my arse'.

'Enough with that language', he snapped, eyeing the potatoes – or praties, as he always called them.

Sugrue was a fine old gentleman – with old-fashioned manners to match. He was impeccably clean. He wore a moustache, even in his youth. In the *Times Past* section of the *Freeman's Journal*, there was a sketch of a sixteen-year-old Sugrue with baby fluff above his lip during the 1798 Rebellion. But, thankfully, he had ditched the cropped hair. These days, he kept it neither long nor short, curling at the butt of his ears and at the nape of his tanned neck. His face aged well for a man who had lived so many of his years out-of-doors – his strong wide nose and high forehead not much ravaged by his sixty-three summers. He hated bad language. He got that from his mother – an islander from Kilronan in Inismor – along with a first-rate home schooling and a love of music and song. He was talented too, even though he would never admit it. I heard him do a decent version of Malone's new tune, *The Croppy Boy*, after a flask of homemade one night. You couldn't see his scar unless the wind swept his hair in a particular way. The deep trace of a vicious wound snaked down the left side of his head, from his hairline to below his earlobe. Curiosity nearly sent me crazy, but I couldn't bring myself to ask him about it.

'Would you mind trading one of your oat cakes for the spuds?'

Four big potatoes sat before Sugrue's eyes. I could hear the old man's belly rumbling in anticipation.

'I'll take two,' he agreed.

'And what about my constipation,' I said, 'they're no good to me.'

I made out to throw the rest in the ditch.

'Don't you dare. I'll take them so, but you better have another cake. There's nothing better to loosen your bowel.'

That was the way it was with us then and I had it down to a fine art. I could never force Sugrue into taking the potatoes, but I could always rely on a bit of tact to see me through. It was good to have him on that old work scheme – eating praties, gulping buttermilk, and giving his interpretations on life and the wisdom it had brought him.

'Hold on,' I said, breaking one of the spuds with my fingers, 'there's not much point giving you this.'

A thick, black puss oozed from the middle of the potato and I threw it over the hedge.

'Picking stones and building walls, day after day – it's a pity these schemes the Brits so generously provide for us don't involve the cultivation of the land,' lamented Sugrue. 'It would be nice to grow something to eat besides rotten praties. That's what has the constipation on you, me lad, this disease that's come into the praties in the last couple of months. But don't worry, it shouldn't linger long. When I was a young fella there was a disease in the praties too, but it lasted no length.'

Back at work, the conversation turned to more light-hearted banter. I was telling Sugrue all about the day I got married when the old woman reappeared in the great avenue, this time without her granddaughter.

'The year of our Lord, eighteen and twenty-nine,' I stated, 'the glorious year the counsellor delivered our greatest triumph – sixteen years ago this October. What about you, Sugrue?'

Before he could answer, old Missus Ryan stood before us. She stared at Sugrue. It was a stare that was hard to read – a complete nothingness in her swollen eyes.

'Hello, Missus Ryan. How's Finbar beyond in Scotland,' he stammered.

She didn't reply, only held her stare on Sugrue. Then she spat on the ground and moved off again.

'You knew Finbar, didn't you,' he said, when Missus Ryan was out of range.

'Of course. We attended school at the one time. He was a year or two younger than me,' I replied.

'The best foot soldier in the thirty-two counties. She blames me for his leaving.'

Sugrue lived where he worked – on Cranley estate. It stood on the Granard side of the parish. Mine wasn't such a short walk home. Lacken was a four-mile trek, a townland on the Longford side of the village. That evening, as I turned into the lane that led to the settlement, I could see a large crowd gathering outside the cooper's shed. Making my way over, I noticed a man on a makeshift platform. There was shouting and cheering as the few wooden boxes under his feet threatened to capsize.

'Empty promises, my friends,' the man on the platform bellowed, 'and what has he delivered. He promised you an end to the Act of Union and then jumped into bed with Peel. And now, after lining his pockets with your hard-earned money, him and that son of his have gone and done it again – this time with the Whigs.'

Pitchforks were hoisted amid roars of approval. The man on the platform was on a roll now.

'Smith O'Brien and Duffy won't let you down. They're loyal to Ireland, not loyal to making up a government in Westminster. It's time to stand together for *our* land and *our* national issues, not John Bull's land and John Bull's issues.'

And then there was more cheering and pitchfork waving. The speaker wasn't from the clachan. I didn't know him and I didn't like his attitude. He was badmouthing the counsellor in the wrong. I was an O'Connell man, always had been. But lately, a new breed had come in with their big ideas and their newspaper and were trying to take over. I looked across and saw Mairead at our cabin doorway. Suddenly my anger disappeared. It was nice to be home.

Two – The Saving of Henry Teale

Lord Harold Teale was owner of the land in the part of Mostrim where we lived. He was also known as Lord Lacken and, unlike some of his landlord associates, he loved the peace and quiet of his Irish estate. He owned two of the three biggest buildings straddling the border of Mostrim and Longford – Lacken House and the grain mill, a stone's throw from the menacing sight of the Shroid workhouse. According to some people, many of whom had never actually met him in person, Lord Teale was said to be of an agreeable disposition.

I had met Harold Teale. We bumped into other while he was out hunting and I was tending my ridges. I didn't like the look of him, prancing around on a white horse and nursing his gun on his free arm. And I didn't like what he stood for – a foreign ascendancy that ruled with an iron fist. We didn't speak, which was grand by me. After all, what could you say to a pig but a grunt. Besides, we had nothing in common – except where we lived and the makeup of our conjugal homes. We both had what is known as a gentleman's family – the wife, a son and a daughter.

Each summer, Teale threw a party for his family, friends, staff, and tenants. Everyone was welcome – or so he said. Mairead used to bring the kids to it. I couldn't be bothered rubbing shoulders with a shower of toffs. On a particular day each year, a cavalcade of carriages brought excited Lacken people, young and old, over the Westmeath border to Lough Owel on the outskirts of Mullingar. Bianconi's omnibus and horse-drawn carts would be loaded up until everyone who had assembled on the great lawn in front of

Lacken House was catered for. Once there, tables of food greeted the revellers as a day of relaxation and sport stretched out before them. The guests would remain within their own groups. The young clachan girls cavorted beneath trees and pretended not to notice the boys, who played at hurling and rings and swimming.

Constance Ryan greeted this day in 1845 with a tinge of sadness. She knew that this was to be the last time she would enjoy the outing. Her sadness was short lived; our Shay met her gaze with a smile and she blushed and looked away. The boys who were home on holiday and the gentlemen of the big house arrived on horseback, shattering their tender moment. Some of the older men took to a hunt amid the excited barking of dogs. The boys in their public-school blazers divided out coloured sashes, which they asked their favourite young ladies of the manor to tie at the shoulder. Sometimes, the tying of this sash was accompanied by a kiss on the cheek for good luck. These were all the preliminaries of the polo match, the pinnacle of the day's events for those who considered themselves the more privileged in society.

Lady Jane Teale, the Lord's wife, underwent her annual ritual. She donned her parasol while walking about, welcoming the different groups in turn and engaging them in pleasantries – offering a knowing smile and nod of approval in the direction of Constance along the way. She received many compliments, especially with regard to her son Henry's prowess on the sports field. The young man is a talent on the cricket ground, they would say, or Henry is a master of croquet. Lady Jane was embarrassed by all the attention, but Henry certainly was not.

Henry Teale was no different to any young fellow of his age. He was driven by testosterone around the manor girls, whom he had just begun to notice in a different way. He was in awe of his polo teammates – older boys with crests on their blazers from places like Eton, Oxford, and Cambridge, who had ridden the whole way from

Lacken on their own horses. He craved the attention and adulation of both and spent his time on a mission to impress. And young Henry certainly made that big impression. He excelled at the polo match and then at croquet. He was flying in confidence.

The clachan boys had no horses. Their activities were low-key compared to their more illustrious neighbours. After their field games were finished, they set up for the swimming races.

'Henry, I should think you do a jolly sight better on dry land than you could ever manage in water,' quipped one of Eton's finest, as they watched Shay and his friends mark out the hundred-yard dash.

'Nonsense,' replied Henry, 'I am quite the swimmer.'

'Stop teasing him,' said a boy in a Harrow blazer, adding to the repartee, 'it's not Master Henry's fault he's too weak to take on those farm boys. They're quite brutish. Isn't that right girls?'

'I could lick them,' stated Henry, as the manor girls egged him on.

His friends dismounted and tied their horses. The girls clapped and cheered as Henry declared his intention to enter the swimming competition.

This late entry did not sit well with the clachan boys. It felt strange and intrusive. Shay was a strong swimmer. He would never have minded a challenge in the water. Nevertheless, he also felt uncomfortable about Henry's inclusion. But the spectators certainly didn't mind. Suddenly, a rather drab affair was transformed, capturing the attention of both ends of the social spectrum. Lady Teale loved the idea. She was forever encouraging interaction among her diverse groups of guests. They built the excitement with drum rolls and blasts from a trumpet that someone had bothered to bring along.

A hundred yards away, on Lough Owel's marshy shoreline, a boy waved a rag and four competitors took their marks on an old creaking jetty. They were soon off. Henry tore into an early lead, streaking up the outside with his flailing arms. Shay glided silently through his slipstream. At the half-way stage Henry still led, although he was splashing wildly and fighting to stay in front. Shay was only biding his time. He was toying with Henry, building the excitement of the occasion for those who cheered from the bank. Suddenly, with the finish in sight, Shay decided he had given the audience enough of a show and clicked into top gear. Henry tried to respond, but he had nothing left. Shay pulled away with ease and, at first, when he heard the cries for help, he was sure it was a prank. He powered on towards the finish, turning to breathe on his right side. It was then he caught sight of the boy who had started the race, waving his rag furiously and yelling. Shay looked back to see Henry in trouble. The two other competitors were a long way off and of no help. Instinctively, Shay flipped into reverse and propelled his way to the distressed youngster.

In the carriage on the way home, Shay could remember very little about the incident. He wasn't being modest. It was all one big blur, except for the kiss he had received at the end. As relief washed over the onlookers, Constance Ryan forgot herself, put her firm tanned arms around Shay's neck and kissed him tenderly.

Thoughts of what might have been put a premature end to the merriment of the day. Henry was feared dead. His mother had long since fainted by the time our Shay scooped young Henry from the water and was pumping his chest and breathing furiously down his throat. For Mairead, the seconds passed as if in slow motion. There was no sign of life and then Henry erupted in a frenzy of watery vomit. Shay remembered nothing as well as the next moment – his first kiss with Constance.

A gala event was held in Shay's honour at Lacken House. Well, it was a party in the parlour among the workers. But it was arranged by Lord and Lady Teale. It was a source of great pride in the

Gorman household, but also the source of a great argument. I downright refused to go. What would the neighbours think of me, lording it above in the big house with the local gentry. What would Sugrue or the old command think. Besides, I had nothing suitable to wear. As far as I was concerned, manors were reserved for ladies in splendid frocks and men in dinner jackets. I didn't think it proper to be around such finery in my old work boots and dustcoat. Mairead nearly drove me mad about it until I finally exploded.

'No Protestant is going to look down their nose at me, I don't care what he owns around here,' I growled.

'That's you all over, Jim Gorman,' she shouted, 'always seeing it the wrong way around – the *us versus them* mentality will never be finished with you. It's good of the Teales to acknowledge what Shay has done. They've gone to great expense to show us their appreciation. But you can't swallow your pride for one night and enjoy it for what it is. Well, at least I have the manners to attend. You can go over to Sugrue's place and glory in the long-forgotten past for all anybody cares.'

I didn't go to Sugrue's cabin that night – I sat on my own and drank a few flasks of homemade poteen. What I really wanted to do was go over to Lacken House, where Shay was being presented with a beautiful Saint Anthony's medal on a gold chain. I wanted to join in the applause of everyone in the servants' quarters. I wanted to offer my congratulations and look on as Lord Teale shook Shay's hand and Lady Teale hugged him tenderly. I wanted to share the pride I felt with my wife and daughter. I wanted to hear the story of how Lady Teale picked out Shay's prize – on the advice of one of her kitchen staff, who informed her that Anthony was the saint the locals turned to when things were lost or missing. To Lady Teale, her only son had been lost. But Shay had brought him back to her.

'Henry, have you something to say to Master Shay,' asked his mother.

But Henry was embarrassed and made for the stairs and a speedy descent.

'Well, the little vagabond,' said Lady Teale, 'all I wanted him to say was thanks. If it wasn't for Master Shay the young whelp was destined to be drowned.'

'Please, let the boy go,' said Shay. 'After all, I don't believe in destiny. Faber est quisance fortunau suae, that's what I say.'

'Here, here,' shouted Lord Teale excitedly. 'Every man is the architect of his own fortune. I like the cut of that young man's jib.'

I also wanted to join in the fun, pretending not to notice when Constance stole a kiss from Shay and they whispered and giggled in corners. But I just couldn't do it. The way I saw it, there was no middle ground – you were either on one side or the other.

Three – The Arrival of Turk

One day at work there was serious trouble with a new kid. Myself and Sugrue watched it all unfold. A bearded man, a giant from Cranley, who was working on a drainage system, started to roar and hit out with a shovel at the new kid. The kid was lucky; his nimble feet saved him from a sore back. The incident sparked more ugly scenes. It wasn't long before this row caught the attention of Walter Pollach, the number one at Cranley estate in the viscount's absence.

Pollach was a menacing figure, the type of person you didn't want in your business. He kept a horsewhip in his belt and only spared it on the orders of de Bromley. However, with the viscount away in England, those orders didn't amount to a hill of beans. He loved his work and hated his workers. We hated him back and dreaded the clipping sound of his black, studded, riding boots.

Pollach had the whip out then and was intent on making full use of it. He was getting it hard to make himself heard over the bearded giant's shouting. He cracked the ground and ordered the man to be quiet. By this time, everyone had stopped working, the sense of danger causing an unscheduled break.

'I want answers quick-smart or heads will roll,' warned Pollach.

He singled out the bearded giant.

'What's the meaning of this stramash?'

'This is the meaning of it,' replied the giant.

He held the new kid by the scruff of the neck, lifting him up like a pup.

'Mind your place,' snarled Pollach, newly flanked by two musket-wielding men from the big house.

'I'm not working with this spailpin, he talks in gaelic and the stablehands are saying he has the westerners' disease.'

At this, Pollach turned his attention to the new kid.

'Should you not be at school,' he quipped.

The kid was so thin he looked like something out of Master Hogan's classroom. Yet, despite his scrawny exterior, he was strikingly handsome.

'Well, what do you say, is there any truth in this? You're not going to infect my workforce, are you? Identify yourself at once. I don't remember seeing you before.'

The kid stared at Pollach's hanging purple jowls and straight black hair. He made no reply.

'Answer me now, laddie,' continued Pollach, and he cracked the whip off the dusty ground once more. 'Where are you from?'

Nevertheless, the kid kept his silence. Pollach extended the whip, about to lash out. Quick as a flash, Sugrue turned to the kid.

'An as an iarthar thu?'

The kid turned and nodded.

'Sea. Gaillimh,' he answered.

'He's from Galway,' said Sugrue to Pollach.

'Is that all he can speak – that peasant mumbo-jumbo? Or has he any understanding of a civilised language? Ask him has he any diseases.'

Sugrue spoke with the kid again and told Pollach he had no disease that he knew off.

'Well, who let him on this plantation without a word of the Queen's tongue?'

Pollach threw an angry look in the direction of his recruiting officer, who was now double-jobbing as one of the musket-wielding bodyguards.

'We don't want him here,' said the bearded giant, 'we have enough diseases of our own.'

Without warning, Pollach lashed out and gave the giant three hard cracks of the whip, enough to have him down on his knees.

'You will want him if I say you will want him,' replied Pollach.

'We'll take him,' said Sugrue.

'Since when did you become one of my recruiting officers?'

'We could do with him,' replied Sugrue, 'we're strangled over here as it is.'

This was music to Pollach's ears. He was delighted to hear that the work was hard and the old freedom fighter was struggling.

'You're responsible for him,' warned Pollach, pointing the fat end of the whip at Sugrue.

The new kid's name was Turk O Nuallain. I was annoyed with Sugrue, at first, for taking the chance on him. I needn't have worried. Turk was as healthy as a tinker's dog. He was great fun – the kind of company that shortened the working day. He spoke Irish in the family home but he was fluent in English too; his father taught him, in case he had to emigrate. But Turk had already found out the hard way that it was better to deny all knowledge of the English language in certain situations. He would never have to talk to Walter Pollach or any of the superiors on the estate. Sugrue was impressed with the young man's tactical mindset. He would surely have adopted a similar approach, had he thought of it back in the troubled times.

Turk repaid Sugrue's faith with diligence and hard work. Despite his frail appearance, we soon found out that he was as strong as he was good-looking. Although aware that many in the estate still viewed him with suspicion over the westerners' disease, it wasn't long before Turk was comfortable enough in his surroundings to allow the full expression of his good humour and kind nature to shine through. He was really the life and soul of the place, especially at lunch time. But he could be serious – and mysterious – too.

He told us that his ancestral home was in Munster and the origins of the name O Nuallain; he was, no less, descended from the high king, MacCarthaigh Mor. I thought this was great fun, but Turk wasn't laughing. His father told him that centuries earlier the family had been dispossessed after Cromwell and his model army had taken the land, driving his descendants out of Munster and forcing them to take refuge in the hungry hills of Connaught. Unemployment due to a surplus in farming labour had eventually taken its toll on Turk, enticing him to travel east in search of work in Dublin. So, in reality, he was only stopping off in Longford along the way.

Turk's story of dispossession and flight took its toll on Sugrue too. It brought back to him the bad old days after Emancipation, when there was legislation introduced disenfranchising the forty-shilling freeholders. As a result, Sugrue's family suffered greatly. The landlord cut them loose because they had no voting power to give him. They stayed in makeshift accommodation and, despite destitution, his father refused food in exchange for religious conversion. He also forbade the rest of the family from doing so. Despite the atrocities of 1798, I reckon his family's eviction was the greatest influence on Sugrue's political motivations and in his conflict with the British establishment.

Four – The New Curate

The hour before Sunday mass was always quiet and peaceful. I sometimes took a walk around the clachan. I enjoyed the solitude. Most of our churchgoers would already be on the three-mile trek to Saint Mary's, to be in good time for confessions. If there was one thing that really annoyed Canon Reidy it was stragglers, as he called them – members of the flock who tarried so much they arrived late to his confessional. He said he wasn't standing for it anymore. If they wanted absolution then they'd have to be punctual. I rarely went to confessions – but Mairead, like most people in Lacken, went every single week. She refused to receive Holy Communion without first levelling with the Almighty. She always brought Shay and Maggie with her.

Therefore, on Sunday mornings, I was free to stroll around the twenty-four cabins that made up the clachan. They were thatched, detached and semi-detached – dotted about here and there, making up a labyrinth that I could walk through blindfolded.

One particular Sunday I bumped into Micheal Mooney on my rounds. Micheal was a chatty, agreeable sort of fella. He was collecting eggs in a large white cloth at the back of the house.

'God forgive you, Jim Gorman, but what are you doing here at this hour and benediction beyond in the church.'

'Careful now, I could say the same about you. Collecting eggs won't get you into Heaven, Micheal.'

'Well, what do you think of her,' he asked, pointing out the gable wall, 'do you like the colour?'

The Mooneys were grand people, but they were always very house-proud. They had recently succumbed to the new craze sweeping the countryside – the whitewashing of cottages.

'They say the paint keeps diseases from the doorstep. God knows after the year we've had, Jim, we could do with all the help we can get.'

I was house-proud too, and why wouldn't I be. Our place was spacious enough compared to some in the clachan. We had two rooms back then – one for the ladies, the other for myself, Shay and the pig. I, too, had been meaning to get the cabin whitewashed before the year was out, but the bad harvest meant it would have to wait.

'Ah, don't be annoying me – auld superstition. I thought you'd have more to be doing than listening to piseogs, Micheal.'

'Say what you like Jim, we've had it hard with the spuds.'

'Maybe if you whitewash the lazy bed, Micheal, it'll get rid of the blight.'

I knew by his face that Micheal didn't appreciate the joke, so I tried to put him in good humour again.

'You've a nice big dung heap at the back of the house, Micheal.'

'Not bad at all, but it'll be smaller next year. If the pig isn't eating, he's not shiting. It's a vicious circle. Besides, a good-sized dung heap doesn't count for much nowadays. The Maguires had two huge heaps last year – at the front *and* the back. But they still had the same bad crop as the rest of us.'

'It doesn't matter how much you fertilize the in-field, Micheal, blight is the only winner. But they say it'll be gone by the end of the year.'

'By God it better be, Jim. The Maguires aren't relying on the in-field but, by golly, the rest of us sure are.'

The Maguires were coopers for generations. Once a month, a large horse-drawn coach would show up and take away their barrels. They worked for the Teales of Lacken House. They had a workshop on the estate, but they always had barrels hanging around the homeplace too. They made their money from coopering full-time and could afford to buy their potatoes.

'They're not worried about the out-field either,' continued Micheal, pointing to an old wall separating us from the bog. 'They haven't crossed those stones to turn a turf all year.'

'Maybe they're warm enough as it is,' I quipped, as Micheal examined a part of the wall about to collapse.

'And they've moved well up the church, I see,' he said eventually. 'They're a lot nearer the priest now than they were a couple of years ago. Meanwhile, the rest of us will have Franno Wilks over here if we have another harvest like this latest one.'

Franno Wilks was the notorious moneylender in the Longford area and dealing with him was considered a very short step from the workhouse.

The thing about Micheal Mooney – a thing I liked about him – was that he was too honest for his own good. Everyone noticed that the Maguires were making progress up the church pews. But not everyone was prepared to say so, at least not in public.

'We'll have to patch her next year,' said Micheal with concern, surveying Davern's roof.

The Daverns were the family on the other side of Micheal's party wall. For his job to look right, the Daverns would have to do their bit as well.

'Will they come in with you on that,' I asked.

'Begod and they better. I'm not able for the full work, or the full expense of it.'

'I'm okay for now,' I said.

We both knew what I meant by this – mine was a single house and I could thatch when I wanted. There was an uncomfortable silence then. It was a bit of my own back after his boast about the whitewashing.

Micheal handed me four eggs wrapped up in a cloth. He said he'd accompany me to mass, but to come into the house first.

'I want to show you something very special. You could call it my prized possession.'

Curiosity gave way to confusion when we stepped into the parlour and Micheal showed me a coffin.

'Well, what do you think of her?'

'Think of her?' I replied. 'It's just a coffin!'

'It's not *just* a coffin, Jim, watch this.'

Micheal flicked a small latch on its underside and the coffin floor fell open.

'She has a trap door on her, Jim – a clever piece of equipment. Reusable. This coffin has been in my family for generations. It's already buried my four grandparents, and my parents. And, with the help of God, it'll bury me and maybe herself and the kids as well.'

I didn't know what to say. But I could understand what Micheal was getting at. Appearances are important, especially when a person is being laid to rest. We had both been around long enough to see many of the older – and some of the younger – neighbours being tumbled into pauper graves, wrapped up like mummies in the absence of a coffin.

'With the grace of God, next year we'll have a good harvest and I'll be able to buy a nice varnish. I'll have her looking as good as new,' Micheal declared, caressing the coffin's lid as he spoke.

Sugrue sat on the church wall, its black bars and the Edgeworth estate at his back. He warmed himself with a nip of homemade. He always carried a bottle of poteen in his Sunday coat. He drank it at leisure, sometimes at the stile near the porterhouse gate, or while walking home on the Granard Road. He liked to put up his feet at the stile. There, he could see the length of the village and, with a quick turn of his head, out his own road too. The stile was a local meeting place, so nobody could accuse him of being nosey.

Sugrue looked away when he heard the rattle of keys at the parochial house door. Canon Reidy was all business, emerging with a folded soutane on his outstretched arm. As he passed, he cut the old warrior with a vicious look.

'Patrick Sugrue, it would be more in your line to be inside in the chapel, praying for a happy death'.

'I'll leave that to God. I'm out here enjoying a happy life instead'.

'Don't get smart with me, you bowsie. It's not one of your toy soldiers you're talking to now. Where's your salute?'

Sugrue sat coolly where he was.

'I won't ask you again. Where is your bow? You're not too old to be taught a bit of manners.'

'No disrespect to you, Father, but I'll reserve my bow for the Almighty.'

Canon Reidy made a rush and Sugrue got down from the wall to face him. He steeled himself. He had learned that lesson as a boy; never turn your back on the clergy – be they Catholic or Protestant – and always steel yourself when facing up to them. Sugrue wasn't trying to be disrespectful towards God. He had his own sort of respect. But he didn't believe in prostrating himself before any man, priest or not.

The trouble was about to start when the canon noticed myself and Micheal Mooney sneaking in the gate.

'What time do you heathens call this? We're not running some sort of public house here, where you can come and go as you please.'

Caught out, we bowed reverently before the canon while muttering our apologies. This was the sort of respect he was used to. Canon Reidy liked his parishioners to display a certain awe in his presence.

'Rise,' he said, lifting his free hand. 'Jim, a word please – on your own.'

A greatly relieved Mooney scooted into the haypenny place, and I – embarrassed at Sugrue watching on – followed Canon Reidy to the front portal.

'What's going on at home, Jim?'

I was totally confused by the question.

'Yes, at home. Why are you not performing your Catholic duties? Why have you left your young wife so long without a child? It must be ten years since your daughter was born.'

I was burning with embarrassment. Thank God we were too far away for Sugrue to hear.

'May I remind you that your duty as a married Catholic is to produce as well as to provide. It's just not good enough. I'll have to call around to the house and have a word with you both.'

The canon continued towards the sacristy, leaving me to my thoughts and Sugrue's heavy gaze. I couldn't believe I had been interrogated like that. Worse still, I couldn't believe I had let it happen. What I wanted to say was that I'm barely able to provide for the two kids I already have. And I wanted to state that I downright refuse to bring any more into this hungry, horrible world. And that my father did his duty as a married Catholic and brought eight children onto a farm that could scarcely sustain himself and my mother. And I wanted to point out to the canon the inevitable consequences of my father's dutiful behaviour as a married Catholic – three sons and two daughters scattered to the four winds when they were barely teenagers. I also wanted to point out Mairead's refusal – to allow herself any sort of marital pleasure because of the guilt she would no doubt feel as a result of strict Catholic Church laws. Only I didn't say anything at all, just rolled over and allowed Canon Reidy to talk down to me like a dummy yet again.

These were exciting times for Father Murtagh, a young priest fresh out of the seminary in Maynooth. He landed his first job in the parish of Mostrim, where his boss, Canon Reidy, welcomed him with open arms. However, as the weeks passed, it was a welcome that showed no signs of dissipating. The new curate had grown weary of the canon. Eight Sundays in and there was still no chance that his superior would stay away and allow him say mass in peace. Since his arrival, his parish priest had presided over everything. In the end, the young curate had to intervene. He felt bad about it, but he told Canon Reidy, in no uncertain terms, that he was setting boundaries. He finally had the sacristy to himself. Father Murtagh still felt the butterflies in his stomach after two full months. Suddenly, amid the rush of pre-mass adrenaline, the sacristy door swung open yet again.

'Here, you can keep this. I've too many of them,' growled the canon, leaving down the soutane.

The young priest inspected it, then asked Canon Reidy to thank his housekeeper for its pristine condition. He could sense that his parish priest was in foul humour and asked him if there was anything the matter.

'Patrick Sugrue, that's what's the matter.'

Father Murtagh didn't yet know all his parishioners, especially by name, and looked puzzled.

'Oh, just some upstart who hasn't the manners to come into the church. He perches himself at the railings during mass.'

Father Murtagh thought this odd behaviour.

'The very man could do with marching up to the front pew in sackcloth, begging forgiveness for his many awful sins and all the men he murdered during that bloody rebellion.'

Then came the moment that was to change the relationship between the two priests, when Father Murtagh turned to Canon Reidy and said, 'Murdered? What do you mean by *murdered*? Did you not say it was during the rebellion? I take it you mean the Ninety-eight Rebellion. It's not murder to kill your enemy in battle.'

The canon was rocked, but gathered himself sufficiently to lay into his understudy.

'Watch your tone, young fella, or I'll have you removed as fast as you got here.'

But Father Murtagh paid no heed the old priest's threat.

'It's not murder to kill your enemy in battle,' he repeated.

'Battle, my foot,' hissed the canon, 'a crowd of blagguards throwing stones and running in behind the bushes.'

'The only ones who could be accused of murder during the uprising of ninety-eight were the British – firing their canons at a bunch of farmers who were only trying to look after their homes. Freedom fighters like this Sugrue fellow were sent out like sheep among wolves. In certain cases, war can be a sanctifying thing.'

'Listen, sonny, if you want to remain the curate of Mostrim parish you won't talk to me in that tone. I don't know what they're teaching ye in that fancy new college in Maynooth. But I was educated on the Continent, where all the wise bishops of this country were taught – taught to turn the other cheek and love thine enemies. Do not bite the hand that feeds you because, when all is said and done, there's British state intervention in the appointment of our clerical positions.'

'Yeah, and British state finance. Money talks alright. It's all geared toward the interests of the upper-class. What about the majority of the people – the ordinary Irish people,' shouted the enraged young priest.

'Keep your voice down, we don't want the whole parish knowing our business. You heed me very carefully now, you young scut. The ordinary Irish people, as you put it, are out there sitting in those seats. Now do you mean to tell me the few bob collected from them every week is going to run this parish efficiently? It's time to leave that seminary of yours and step into the real world, before I have you sacked for insolence. Get this through that thick skull of yours – the British are our friends. The likes of Patrick Sugrue and his band of renegades are the real enemy.'

Father Murtagh adjusted his cassock and had a last look in the mirror. There was no point in arguing with this dinosaur, he was too set in his ways. He had only one thing to say as he turned and looked Canon Reidy in the eye.

'I'm about to perform my priestly duties, so there's the door. Get out and don't disturb my preparation for the Holy Eucharist again.'

Five – The Hedge School

Peter Hogan was a local schoolmaster in Mostrim. He taught the clachan children in a hedge school. From the early 1840s – since the new national school had been built – he and his classroom could expect a call from the inspector. *An cigire*, the pupils called him. This was a new initiative with the full backing – and full blessing – of Canon Reidy. An inspector toured the schools of the parish annually – Monadarragh, Kilsallagh, the new school on the Ballymahon Road, and Master Hogan's hedge school. The inspector assessed the competence of the tutors and the ability of the pupils of each school, making sure state funding was being put to proper use. It was a curious arrangement, especially as Peter Hogan was not in receipt of any benefits or funding. Nevertheless, the inspector – acting on the sound advice of Canon Reidy – afforded a courtesy call to the hedge school. Master Hogan hated when the inspection time drew near. He was supposed to have everything in order. He was expected to showcase the ability of his pupils. Except, on a balmy day at the start of June in 1845, Peter realised things couldn't have been more out of order. For a start, there was only a handful of pupils present at rollcall.

He arrived in early, greeted by the same five hungry little faces he had been looking at for weeks. Instead of taking out his slate and chalk he dismissed class, sending them home with strict instructions for the following day. There was no point in asking them to wear their best attire. They were already in their only attire. His pupils walked home barefooted in the dust and heat of the morning sun. They didn't know whether to feel happy or sad.

The master needed the day off to put things right. He looked around his summer residence and nodded with approval. Thirty-three slates lay on the grass. He checked under one to make sure there was an assortment of coloured chalks. Then it was time to visit a nearby farmer's field, and a barn he sometimes used.

On his short walk, the master thought about his pupils. He understood why attendances had been so poor. The bad potato harvest for the first half of the year and the good bog weather meant that children were needed at home. Whatever strength they could muster had to go towards earning for the family. He thought about the house calls he would make later that day. He felt disappointed that he wouldn't be making a call to the Ryans. Constance Ryan was Peter Hogan's best student of English Literature and Irish Folklore – or *bealoideas*, as the inspector so fondly called it. Facing him without Constance was a problem. She was definitely gone now, to a job in Cranley House. When the master thought about her it saddened him. Constance Ryan's potential was immeasurable. If circumstances had been more favourable, she could have been anything she liked. For the poor kids who Peter Hogan taught, potential was nothing but a dirty word.

The master had another problem, one that gave him many a sleepless night. It was a problem that was growing by the day. In 1840, Canon Reidy took control of the board of management of a brand new Mostrim national school – a beautiful, two-storied building on the Ballymahon Road. Since then, the canon was steadily recruiting hedge-school pupils. With the winters as cold as they were, Master Hogan just couldn't compete. The new school was dry and warm. The children brought sods of turf for the classrooms' large fireplaces. There was a proper blackboard for the teachers to write on. Peter Hogan felt the pressure. He was up against it. But he wasn't about to give in. He couldn't just stop fighting and allow his hedge school to close up forever.

In good times the children had always paid their way – and Master Hogan's *wages* – by bringing an assortment of foods to school. Some brought an egg or two; some brought a head of cabbage. Someone would have a bottle of milk or a pot of blackberry jam. Peter had always been careful to watch out for poverty. His was a clear policy – children were never compelled to bring food in exchange for education. This policy changed with the bad harvest. He ordered them to bring nothing but themselves to school. Food was to be kept at home. This was the freedom that being single afforded the master – he didn't have the pressure of a wife and family. He only had himself to look after, a job that was easily done by working on farms in the evenings.

When he reached the farmer's barn, he unhooked the door and looked inside. It needed tidying up, but everything else was in its place – thirty-three wooden stools lined up in five rows, thirty-three slates and chalks, and the teacher's table at the head of the classroom. This was his winter or bad-weather residence. As the master cleaned up, another fear came over him. Could there be any truth to the rumour concerning his other star pupil. There was hardly another boy in the whole of the north midlands as proficient in Latin and Greek as Shay Gorman. There couldn't have been. It was time for Peter Hogan's house calls. First on the list was a short journey to the clachan in Lacken.

Mairead was delighted to meet the master again. He blushed and asked her not to call him master, but Peter instead. She wanted to give him something cold to drink, but he respectfully declined. He was on business and couldn't stay long.

'I am extraordinarily busy, Missus Gorman. I have a great many houses to get to.'

'Enough with the *Missus Gorman*. If your name is Peter, then my name is Mairead.'

I came in from work. I was surprised to see the master. I insisted that he stop rushing around, sit himself down, and eat some griddle cakes with us.

'The world will be after us,' I pointed out, 'or why are you in such a panic?'

'Unfortunately, I find myself in a bind,' he replied. 'Despite being offered a number of teaching positions, including a well-paid job with the Erasmus Smith Foundation, I have always enjoyed the challenge of running my own school. Yet, I still find myself obliged to meet a certain standard in education. I have an inspector calling tomorrow to assess my teaching competency.'

'How is that fair? They're not funding you, yet they're still assessing your ability,' said Mairead.

'Yeah, that doesn't make a lot of sense,' I added.

'Canon Reidy is at the back of these inspections – he knows I will not conform to his idea of educating children. He is such a meddling busy-body, it is his way or no way. He has suggested that my syllabus be more in line with church teachings. But, to me, education is all about teaching children to make their own informed decisions.'

Peter's face was flushed with annoyance. Mairead patted his arm to comfort him.

'The English are not the sole beneficiaries of our ignorance in relation to education,' he continued, 'but the political and religious hierarchies of this land too. They always want to keep the working class ignorant so as to keep themselves in power. But the education I aim to give every boy and girl who crosses my path will become like bullets – the real bullets by which Ireland will eventually be set free. The education I will give them, not shaped to any particular view, will do more damage than a million muskets.'

I was impressed with the man's sincerity.

'You're a man of great principle, Peter,' I told him.

'I second that,' said Mairead, 'a great principal. And no underhanded attempt to put you out of business will ever change that.'

'We have made great strides in the past few years,' added Peter, 'two-thirds of all males between the ages of eleven and twenty-one, regardless of their religion and background, are now able to read and write. Imagine telling that to someone before Emancipation – a mere twenty years ago. That is why I had to take the proper job for me, not the job that pays the most money. I got offered both the National Board and Kildare Place Society. I turned them down. Stanley and the Kildare Place are turning their scholars into roaring loyalists. And the diocesan colleges are not much better. They are making theirs into nationalist madmen. But I will do neither. I will give my pupils the education to use as they see fit. That is why I need the hedge school and that is why I need to pass this inspection.'

'You're an admirable man, Peter Hogan. But what can we do to help with this,' asked Mairead.

'I came here looking for Shay. He is my best pupil in Greek and Latin. I need him for the inspector, to show how much my classroom can offer. I also need a full attendance. I hope I am mistaken, but I fear he has left school for a job in Cranley estate. He has been seen quite a lot on their manor grounds lately.'

'That can't be right,' I said. 'You must be confused. I work at Cranley estate, on the new wall-building scheme. What on earth would take Shay to Cranley estate?'

Mairead smiled to herself before speaking up.

'There may have been a bit of a mix up, Peter. Rest assured, Shay has not left for a job on Cranley estate. I can guarantee that he will be at school, bright and early, tomorrow morning.'

This put the master's mind at ease and he thanked us both.

'By the way,' said Mairead, as the master was about to take his leave, 'did any of your other pupils quit school lately for a job on Cranley estate?'

'Yes, as a matter of fact,' returned the master.

'Here's a wild guess. Would that pupil's name be Constance Ryan by any chance?'

Six – Sugrue and the American Wake

Music was playing in the Cranley cluster – the group of cabins on de Bromley's land to the north of the village. Its inhabitants were proud of the name *cluster*, a definition distinguishing them from the settlement on the Longford side of the parish. In Lacken, we called it a clachan, but in Cranley it was known as a cluster. It contained more houses than the clachan – Cranley boasting thirty homesteads, six more than where we lived.

A bodhran drum and bagpipes were in full swing – the atmosphere buzzing. The people were buzzing too, their work in the bogs or the estate or the kitchens at an end for yet another day. Wives were busy preparing themselves and their husbands for a gathering. Husbands were busy preparing too – topping up flasks of homemade poteen for their jacket pockets, the secret friend in times of need. There was a party for young Kathleen O'Dwyer, heading for America the following day. She was bound for New York. We call this party the American wake. Kathleen will never be seen in the parish again. It's a strange sort of affair when one thinks about it. Some see it as the celebration of a life beginning abroad. Others view it as the mourning of a life ending forever in dear old Ireland.

Sugrue straightened on his stool and grimaced. He could hear the music, but it did nothing to soothe his black humour. His daughter-in-law, Ella May, was tending to her son. She washed his head and neck with an old rag. She had planned to go over to O'Dwyer's for a short while, just to say goodbye and wish Kathleen good luck. She threw an eye on Sugrue every now and then, sensing the heavy mood upon him.

'Ellie, I wish now I hadn't persuaded you to hold on to that blasted yoke.'

Sugrue was referring to the handloom perched on the windowsill. It had been annoying him since he came in from the estate. Ella May had noticed him eyeing it. She knew exactly what was bothering him. The O'Dwyers used to spin yarn too. They had been successful weavers, just like Ella May used to be.

'If it bothers you that much, I'll put it out of your sight,' she snapped. 'God but you're like a bag of cats this evening.'

'What's it doing there anyway – good for nothing but gathering dust. I'm sorry we didn't sell it when the going was good.'

'The going was never good, Sugrue. Well, one time maybe. Handlooms are finished now. They're gone and that's the end of it.'

In the past, Ella May Sugrue's handloom had been a goldmine. She was a magician when she put it to work. There was a time, not that many years before, when she had headed for a fair day in Longford's Market Square laden down with handwoven linens and woollen pieces. She brought back nothing but a bag of coins, all her products negotiated and sold to the highest bidders. Those days were gone now – gone forever.

'That's the way of the world, I suppose. The Brits did their job well,' said Sugrue, as much by way of apology than anything else.

He lobbed a spit onto a turf. It hissed in the fire. Ella May scolded him for teaching young Padraig bad habits. He thought back to the Act of Union and how, at the time, it seemed like such a great deal for Ireland. The protection it afforded Irish businesses was a comfort. Then, after a number of years – Sugrue couldn't remember how many – the markets opened. The protection ended overnight. Ireland slowly realised it had been tricked all over again by its nearest neighbour. Once British products came pouring into the country, free from excise duties and taxes, Ella May Sugrue and her colleagues could hang up their looms. Their spinning days were over. They couldn't compete.

'I mightn't bother with the O'Dwyers at all. Sure, won't you be going, Ellie?'

Ella May looked up from grooming her son's hair.

'You're coming over, Sugrue, and that's all there's to it. I've baked a soda for them and we're all going together.'

That was the thing about Ella May and her father-in-law, time and familiarity hadn't thrown up any pet names. She called him Sugrue, and he still called her Ellie, the same as the first day they had met.

The handloom was still in his head. Sugrue turned and fixed his gaze on it again. The real reason for its intrusion came rushing to his brain. It reminded him of Arthur – Kathleen O'Dwyer's husband. Arthur O'Dwyer had been best friends with Sugrue's son, Padge. They made their First Holy Communion together and attended Master Hogan at the hedge school. They had taken the ship together to America. Money was scraped from all quarters to send them out. Now here was Kathleen O'Dwyer, with her American money, heading for New York. And there was Ella May Sugrue, without a shoe on her foot, staying where she was.

Ella May knew the real reason why Sugrue had wanted to shun the gathering. But she wouldn't bring it up. Eventually it got to him.

'It's been almost three years now, Ellie.'

She left what she was doing, crossed the floor, and stroked the hair away from his scarred forehead.

'I know how long it's been, Sugrue. But don't you worry, Padge will come through for us. I know he will.'

'Whisht out of that. Arthur O'Dwyer has already come through, Ellie. And he left on the same ship. What if Padge has forgotten us? We haven't had so much as a letter. What if he's ...?'

Sugrue stopped before he said it. He looked at Padraig. It was just as well his grandson hadn't the sense to understand. He didn't feel his father's absence; he was only just born at the time. Sugrue had stopped because he didn't want to say it in front of Ella May either. It was a thought that had been going through his head for a while. Padge might be dead. Was this the reason they had heard nothing.

Sugrue remembered something from the day of Padge's departure – something strange. He remembered feeling a huge debt of gratitude to Master Hogan, who had worked so hard to ensure that Arthur and Padge were proficient in the English language – writing and reading it as good as any of the shopkeepers' or strong farmers' sons. He remembered this strange feeling more than the sorrow of seeing Padge go, or the relief of watching him leave a wasted country behind. And then, not a word for the best part of three years.

'If he was dead, Sugrue, then surely Arthur O'Dwyer would have sent word.'

'What if they're not together anymore, Ellie? What if they got separated by work or something else?'

'Don't be annoying yourself, Sugrue. Come on, pull it together. They survived the trip, didn't they? Well, there you go. My Padge will come through.'

'I can't go to O'Dwyer's place. I can't face them. I know exactly what they'll be thinking about us – and about Padge. I'm afraid, Ellie. I'm so afraid of the worst. How on earth can we survive if there's another bad harvest? All I want is for you to be safe and well and away from this unfortunate country. I look at Padraig and wonder what sort of future he has in a place like this.'

Ella May squeezed Sugrue's hand. She looked into his eyes with sincerity and love.

'You are *not* afraid. The Paddy Sugrue I know, and the boy who faced down the Redcoats at Ballinamuck, is afraid of nothing.'

It was the first time Ella May had ever called him by his first name. She was almost right. Sugrue was not afraid of death, nor the British, nor the landed gentry who had dominated his whole life. But he *was* afraid that his son Padge had forgotten them. This, to Sugrue, would have been a fate worse than any death.

'You've never really cared what people think, so don't start going soft in your old age.'

Ella May was fully right then. It was time for Sugrue to stop this nonsense and start being himself again. He took out his battered powder flask, uncorked it, and filled it to the brim with homemade.

'You don't still have that old relic,' she quipped, 'I wouldn't let a dog drink out of that yoke.'

'It may be a relic, but it's also a badge of honour from the killing fields of Ballinamuck. And frankly, my dear, I wouldn't let a dog drink out of it either.'

He put on his best smile and walked proudly out the door, hand-in-hand with his daughter-in-law and grandson. It was time to wish Kathleen O'Dwyer the best of God's good luck in the brave new world of America.

Seven – Turk and the Manor Girl

The potatoes may have failed but there was still turf to be saved. Sugrue and Turk made the trip to Lacken bog to give me some help. Two weeks had flown past since Sugrue had cut the turf with a slane that had been in his family for generations. The sods were heavy with water and as black as his boots before being spread on the bank. It was amazing what a few windy days could do. They were soon solid enough to put into reeks.

My old friend, Jabber Farrell, joined in. A well-built and ferociously strong man, you'd stand to watch him at work – such was the speed and skill at which he cleared the bank. He was jovial in the right company. Like the rest of us, he got on with Turk from the start. Work was heavy going, but they still found time to clown around the bog.

Jabber lived near us on what was called the stone-wall side of the clachan. We were the same age. We had attended the same hedge school as kids – under old Master Mulligan, who has been dead for a long time. Despite his good-natured approach, Jabber's home life had always provided the locals with plenty of gossip. It was said that his mother hadn't spoken to him in over twenty years. I never believed that bullshit. To me, it was just another tall tale in the fabled existence of the man.

Milly Farrell was the happiest woman in Longford county the day her only child set off for the seminary. That much is no fable. Maynooth wasn't long open and it was her pride and joy to have another priest in the family. Her brother had been ordained on the Continent, thirty years before. Her blissful state was not to last.

Milly's husband died suddenly while organising a monster meeting, a few months shy of the Emancipation Act. Jabber – or Joseph as he was then known – quit his studies immediately and returned to Lacken, much to his mother's dismay. The story goes that once he came home and joined in the daunting task of building the workhouse in Shroid, his mother gave up speaking to him. When it was finished, Jabber got a job inside the workhouse. He spent some of the unhappiest years of his life there before it all became too much.

I often wondered whether or not it was his father's death that made Jabber quit Maynooth. Without him, Milly was left all alone and fending for herself. It was a great shame though – Jabber would have made an excellent priest. It wasn't the education that got to him anyway. If Mulligan's old hedge school is anything to go by, Jabber was first class in Latin and as bright as a button at everything else. I always liked him, and I never entertained those neighbours who badmouthed him. Once they knew he had taken a job in the workhouse, all sorts of stories went around – he beat the kids senseless; the shed around the back was his torture chamber; he buried illegitimate babies in Lizzard Forest when it got dark. I heard it all – and what a load of nonsense it all was. I knew Jabber as long as I knew anyone. I liked the respectful way he treated those who weren't busy judging him.

One time I asked him why he hadn't settled down and got married.

'Ah Jim, will you quit with that auld talk. Isn't one woman enough for any house,' was his reply.

Even though he didn't say it, Jabber wouldn't marry out of respect for his mother. He wouldn't bring another woman in on top of her. That was just his way.

Turk was on campfire duty. While the rest of us stripped to our waists and felt the sunshine on our backs as we worked, he volunteered to do the cooking. He wanted to display his culinary skills and give us all a treat. Sugrue thought he was scheming – trying to get out of the hard slog of stacking turf.

'Treat us to what? Unless he's going to boil the heather and serve it up,' said Jabber.

But Turk wasn't just talking fancy. When he called us over, four clay bowls of tea – all laced with sugar – sat steaming before our eyes.

'Where on earth did you get all this, my auld son of Eireann,' asked Sugrue.

'Ara, sit down and enjoy, old man. Don't be bothering my head with your questions. It's not important where I got it.'

'What's going on, Turk,' I said. 'We're in the middle of a food shortage and you're making us all tea with sugar. I hope everything is above board here.'

'Upon my oath, James Gorman, I promise you. It's just a little luxury – my way of saying thanks for all the help you lads gave me since I got here. And it will be stone cold if you don't shut up and drink it soon. The tea and sugar were given to me as a present. That's all I am willing to say on the matter.'

As unlikely as it sounded, Turk *was* telling the truth. The tea and sugar were presents – presents of love. During the first week of his new job in Cranley, Turk spied a beautiful manor maiden from the distance. She was on a leisurely walk – taking the air, as they say in the big house. She was turned out just like all the other manor maidens on a fine summer's day, in a bonnet with long strings and gloves to her elbows. Her floral dress was long and her pretty pink boots peeped out from under its low hem. She held a parasol, now and then twirling it absentmindedly, as she looked out into the fields beyond the workers. Turk was instantly smitten with her cascading golden ringlets and white-powdered cheeks. He noticed too the outline of her voluptuous breasts, and the curve of her hips on the flowered pattern. This sort of maturity belonged to no girl.

She was a young woman. She was ripe for picking – with the sort of ripeness that had young Turk O'Nuallain bristling with anticipation. But what chance had a wall-building apprentice from a Public Works' scheme with such a haughty princess straight out of de Bromley's mansion. Turk dropped the rock he was holding and cleaned his hands on the arse of his trousers. It was time for action.

He gave out a whistle. She looked in his direction. He straightened up and smiled. She seemed to take no notice. She was looking right through him. He pushed a black fringe behind his ears. She was unmoved. It was time for a different approach. Making sure the coast was clear of Pollach and his supervisors, Turk walked straight over, bold as brass, and plucked the parasol from her grasp.

'Allow me, madam,' he said in the lowest voice he could muster.

A look of anger flashed in her eyes. Turk offered a smile. Her features softened at once. He knew he had her then. She was succumbing to his charms. It was like a reflex action. Instantly, she knew it was wrong – but she just couldn't help herself. He was only a field-hand. She was the daughter of a baron. Where she had once been so strong, she now felt herself slipping. A year or two earlier, she would have dismissed him instantly – with a clout of the parasol for good measure. What could she do – she may have been a future baroness like her aunty, Lady Veronica, but she was also a young woman. She had wants and, more than that, she had needs.

Turk began meeting the girl in the evenings. She only agreed to see him in secret. She said she didn't want her cousin finding out – in case her cousin felt lonely or jealous. The girl's name was Clarissa Lyndsay and she was from Essex in England. She was holidaying in Ireland with her family. Her father owned a plantation outside London. Turk loved her accent. She spoke in a soft English tone that seemed a million miles from the Irish Midlands.

She may have been shy in public but certainly not in private. Clarissa was a first-class kisser. Out of Turk's many romantic conquests, she was his champion kisser. She had full-bodied, luscious, blood-red lips. And she wasn't about to spare them. If she could, she would have kissed his beautiful face forever. Sometimes, Clarissa's face powder came away with their kisses. It would make Turk sneeze. They spent those first romantic evenings walking in the forest at the back of Cranley House. They paddled in a pond. The more Clarissa saw of Turk, the more she fell in love. She doted on him. That's when the presents started. She began by giving him fruit. She was worried about his health, and worried that someone would find out about their liaison.

Turk found it easy to impress Clarissa. She always believed whatever he said. He told her stories of Galway that other girls wouldn't find interesting. But not Clarissa – she couldn't get enough. She wanted to know every little detail about her man of mystery. It wasn't long before he regaled her with stories of his true lineage.

'I have a confession to make,' he admitted, as a worried look broke out on her face. 'I'm a direct descendent of the MacCarthaigh Mor, the High King of Munster.'

'Munster? What, pray tell, is that,' she asked.

'Ara, it's a place in the south of Ireland. More like a region than a place.'

'I knew as much. There's something regal about you. Are you a prince?'

'No, Clarissa. Not exactly.'

'A duke then,' she said excitedly. 'Why do you stay in a hideous cabin on my uncle's land. You should be living in your family's castle.'

'Castle? Ah nix, there's no castle. Not anymore. Unfortunately, we were dispossessed and scattered during a plantation of Munster.'

'Dispossessed and scattered? By whom? Who would do such a beastly act? Were you very young when this... this plantation thing occurred?'

Turk didn't want to bring up Cromwell and his many ills, so he left his tale of woe at that. Clarissa whispered *poor baby* and hugged him tightly. She showered him with kisses and said that she had something for him. Producing a gold bracelet from her left wrist, she begged him to wear it as a sign of his true lineage – gold being a symbol of kings. Turk said he would be honoured, but asked Clarissa to hold it for him – in case he lost it. The last thing he wanted was to be caught with expensive jewellery on the manor grounds.

That's when the tea and sugar started. Clarissa treated it all like a game. They crept into Cranley House through the cellar's double doors – a concealed entrance towards the back of the estate – at the pathway to the forest. Turk looked on as Clarissa peeled away large sods of grass, carefully laid down as camouflage. All that kept the cellar doors fastened was a rusty metal bar and a loose chain. Once inside, they stole along a corridor until it split in two. Turk offered to take the passageway to the left.

'No, that extends to the kitchens,' whispered Clarissa.

She had obviously been there before. She was taking the passageway to the right. The storage room was down there. Clarissa was excited by the naughtiness of it all. Turk wasn't. His heart was firmly in his mouth. If anybody – especially Walter Pollach – found out about this, it would have been the end of the line. They came to a room with all sorts of wooden boxes. Bags were hanging up, suspended from the rafters. Clarissa produced two cloth sacks, as if by magic, and began to fill them – one full of tea, the other with sugar. She wanted to stay and explore some more but Turk wasn't for hanging around. He couldn't relax until the double doors were firmly bolted and the sods of grass back in place, concealing the entrance. It was time to go. He gave her a hurried kiss, promised to meet her the next evening after work, and vanished into the forest.

Eight – The Ecumenical Meeting

'I know it's for peace but, all I'm saying is, why does the service have to be held on Catholic grounds. Why has everything to ultimately end up there. It would make a nice change if, just once, we had it on our lawns,' said Reverend Smyth, too loudly for Canon Reidy's comfort.

The canon fixed his gaze on the pope's new position. He thought it looked ridiculous. There was a large white square where Gregory XVI used to be. All it did was draw attention to the moving of the picture, from where it had hung for almost fifteen years. It had been altered in Reverend Smyth's honour. Now, he wouldn't see it as he engaged Canon Reidy at the head of the table.

'So long to home advantage,' joked Father Murtagh, much to his boss's annoyance.

It didn't matter in the least. Even the sight of the white square brought out the fight in Reverend Smyth. Young Reverend Charmers was surprised by this side of the old vicar's temperament.

'Of course, I blame us for spoiling yous in the first place. As far back as I can remember, long before my ordination, we've been giving yous one thing after another – Gardiner's Relief Acts and, after that, Hobart.'

'Your Reverence, with all due respect, these were acts concerning land. What on earth have they to do with religion,' pleaded Canon Reidy.

'What about Maynooth seminary in ninety-five? We were looking for a new place ourselves around about that time. But, oh no, everything has to be geared towards Catholicism. There was never a word about what my flock might want or think or feel. If memory serves me right, there wasn't a hand's turn done by your lot for King George's visit.'

'George's visit? George the Fourth? That was years ago,' exclaimed the canon.

'And what does it matter when it was. The point I'm making is yous boyos never think of anyone but yourselves. We're not called the Church of Ireland for nothing, you know.'

Father Murtagh sat at the foot of the table. He was shocked at the way Canon Reidy allowed himself to be chastised with such force in his own home. He was also at pains to witness the pathetic attempts to pacify Reverend Smyth.

'What do you think, Father,' asked Reverend Charmers, clearly embarrassed and seizing an opportunity to break from Reverend Smyth's ranting.

Finally, the moment had come. Father Murtagh had listened to these Neanderthals for long enough – and cave men from the earliest Stone Age would have made as much sense. It was time for the young men to take control. He cleared his throat in anticipation. Just as he was about to speak, Canon Reidy went on the offensive.

'All I suggested was that we have the post-parade prayers here, Your Reverence, simply because of numbers. It is, after all, an ecumenical service. Our prayers shall be carefully chosen so as not to offend the members of your congregation. But if you would like to have the service on Church of Ireland grounds....'

The canon swallowed hard. It was as if the words were caught in his windpipe.

'...I'm sure we could come to some arrangement.'

A parade for peace was being organised. All religious denominations within the parish were to walk side-by-side. It was supposed to be in opposition to the death of Major Munroe, who had been murdered in Ballinalee two weeks earlier.

'If it wasn't for your secret societies, we wouldn't be having this parade in the first place. It's a terror but a man can't go about his normal business in comfort, without being strung up by a crowd of cold-blooded murderers.'

Canon Reidy nodded in agreement. Father Murtagh glared at the vicar, but kept his counsel. The new curate would never condone a murder of any kind but, as far as he was concerned, Major Munroe brought a lot of trouble on himself. He was known for his heavy-handed approach, a man who treated his tenants in the same manner as Walter Pollach treated his. What Father Murtagh wanted to say was that if you live by the sword you will eventually die by it – Major Munroe was a violent man who suffered a violent death. He was found on his Lisameane estate, five miles from the Mostrim border, hanging from an ash tree by the side of a gripe. It sent shockwaves through the county, causing further hardship for its tenants.

Father Murtagh couldn't hold back any longer.

'They're not *our* secret societies,' he snapped.

Reverend Smyth almost spun off his chair in surprise. Canon Reidy was ready to have a stroke.

'Shut your mouth,' ordered the canon.

'No, let him speak,' said the vicar, 'if the young man has something to say, let him spit it out. These secret societies – Catholic, are they not?'

Father Murtagh had come to this ecumenical meeting wanting to talk about a particular issue. Up to this point he had been disregarded and disrespected. Finally, his moment had arrived.

'I want to know about your church tithes. Why should members of the Catholic Church have to pay these taxes? It's not right. Some of my parishioners are little better than destitute after a bad harvest.'

'That's enough out of you,' shouted Canon Reidy. 'I must apologise, Your Reverence, that was totally uncalled for. Please forgive my understudy's insolence. That's what they're being taught now in these new Irish seminaries – how to be disrespectful to your elders and betters.'

'No. I'm glad young Father Murtagh has an ability to speak his mind. You want to know about our charging of tithes. Well, these taxes have been around long before any of us. And they'll be in place when we're dead and gone, I should hope. I suggest you lobby your local politician and see if he can do anything for you.'

'My local politician is a Protestant member of the Anglo aristocracy. He lives and works in London. What does he care about the plight of a starving, *Irish, Catholic* people, the vast majority of whom haven't even the right to vote in their own country.'

'We are getting completely off the point of this meeting,' said Canon Reidy, maddened by Father Murtagh's determination to have his say.

'By the way,' argued the vicar, 'that same starving, *Irish, Catholic* people – as you put it – are not as starving as you may think. They can afford to bolster O'Connell's Tribute until it's bursting at the seams.'

'O'Connell's Tribute is a separate matter,' shouted Father Murtagh. 'Beware, Reverend Smyth. Beware you and yours are not counted among the Pharisees and the tax collectors on the last day.'

Reverend Charmers smiled when the young curate said this. Canon Reidy's cheeks were flushed with anger.

'I'm not wary in the least,' returned Reverend Smyth. 'After all, Jesus sat down with the tax collectors too. When you get a moment,

I suggest you look up Zacchaeus in your catechism. Even Matthew, His own disciple, was a former tax man.'

The parochial house fell silent for a time. It was uncomfortable and awkward. Eventually, the door sprang open and in stepped Canon Reidy's housekeeper. She had pots of tea and coffee, cream buns and cakes. She returned a second time with twinkling china cups and saucers. Canon Reidy helped out, serving Reverend Smyth a large slice of cake from a sparkling silver tray.

'I really pity you fellows,' whispered Father Murtagh to Reverend Charmers, 'all those Catholics to clean up after when this parade is over. That lovely lawn at the vicarage will be destroyed by them.'

After tea, Canon Reidy suggested a walk through the grounds. He joked that he wanted to bring the reverends on a little tour of his humble abode. Only it was no joke. He had prepared this little tour weeks in advance, ordering his housekeeper and Milly Farrell – his trusted sacristan – to have the church finery shining and on display. Reverend Smyth couldn't have cared less what the canon had prepared. He was more concerned with what was going on across the road in the Edgeworth estate. The canon found it difficult to usher him down the pathway and into Saint Mary's Church. The interior of the church looked awesome. The canon bristled with pride as the vicar looked about, first at the splendid colour of the stained-glass windows and then at the studded diamonds on display beneath each Station of the Cross. The smell of polish and lavender intoxicated the senses. The candleholder threw out its golden hew. The gleam of silver and red from the sanctuary lamp dominated the centre of the main aisle.

Then, as the four clerics continued their way from the aisle to the altar, came Canon Reidy's *piece-de-resistance* – his chalice. It stood in full view in front of the tabernacle, without its paten or a purificator to shield its radiance. Speckled with an intertwining of green emeralds and white diamonds, it had a gold cup and a pair of silver doves flying skyward from halfway up its stem. Twelve sparking rubies formed a perfect circle around the wide base. Two freshly cut vases of red and white roses flanked its magnificent presence. Even the old vicar, who had been doing such a wonderful job of looking unimpressed, stopped and marvelled at its elegance.

'I've never seen anything the like,' he conceded.

'Neither have I,' agreed Father Murtagh, who had just figured out what the wily old canon was up to.

'I say, George, isn't it something else again,' continued the vicar.

George – or Reverend Charmers – didn't answer. He was staring blankly at the ambo. He was thinking about what Father Murtagh had confided in him earlier. The curate was right, it would be a shame for the beautiful little garden at the vicarage to be ruined by a stampeding pack of Catholics. Excusing himself, Reverend Charmers took Reverend Smyth aside for a quick word.

Such was the cosy sense of achievement that pulsed through his veins, Canon Reidy failed to even notice the Protestant clergymen's private deliberations. He stood with his hands clasped, staring at his chalice with a beaming smile. The old vicar was soon back. He roused the canon from his daydream, much to the amusement of Father Murtagh.

'Excuse me, Canon, but I may have been somewhat hasty with respect to our decision on the peace parade. Perhaps it should take place on your church grounds. After all, the interests of the majority of the people in the parish should come first. In light of this, I think the Catholic Church lawns would certainly be the more appropriate venue to hold the post-parade prayer service.'

Canon Reidy's smile grew wider still. He would remember this day forever – the day he put his Protestant counterparts firmly in their place.

Nine – The Foxhunters' Ball

Sugrue sat in his favourite place – the stile facing onto the Granard Road. He was joined by Turk, the youngster persisting until he finally got the old man to hand over the poteen. They sat quietly, looking down the village, passing the time and the drink back and forth.

'This is a strange-looking hipflask,' said Turk, examining the many dents, 'it has seen better days. I think it's time you got a new one.'

'It's not a hipflask, it's a powder flask,' answered Sugrue. 'There's not many of them left I can tell you.'

'What's the difference,' asked Turk, 'it still does the same job of holding homemade, doesn't it?'

'Ah, but a powder flask was used for storing gunpowder, until someone came up with the bright idea of putting drink – or homemade, as you say – in it instead. I took that flask from around the neck of a certain gentleman on the battlefield in Ballinamuck.'

Turk was amazed at this.

'Be the hokey! So, what you're saying is, this thing's almost fifty years old,' he replied, holding the flask aloft with both hands.

'Probably a lot more,' said Sugrue. 'It was fairly beaten up when I got it.'

Turk was fascinated and had loads more questions when suddenly a cavalcade of horse-drawn carriages sped by, shooting the early summer dust into their faces.

Forgetting the flask, Turk moved into the bushes. Sugrue took up a vantage point behind the wall separating the porterhouse from the dirt road that we called main street.

The carriages slowed and swung left into the Edgeworth estate. Then, more carriages – this time coming from the Granard direction – thundered up the long lane bound for the manor house. The mystery of the flags and buntings – a cause of much debate among the townspeople for the previous month – was slowly unravelling.

There was a celebration of some sort about to begin. The horse-drawn carriages were stopped here and there in front of the neat lawns. Footmen awaited, attending the carriages on the say-so of the drivers. They opened doors. Gentlemen alighted, dressed in their finery. The footmen helped the ladies descend, taking their gloved hands and then their hatboxes, while servants directed guests around the winding avenue to a partially-secluded front entrance.

Three peasant women appeared in the driveway. It was clear that these women had been foraging for potatoes. Their bare feet were soiled and one of them still had the foot-iron attached to her leg. There was a wrap of cloth between it and her skin. Despite the cloth, her ankle still bled. The smallest woman kept a basket close to her chest. The contents of the basket were visible; small nettles peeped out from one side. Two of the women – the ones without the foot-iron – had large green stains around their lips and on their chins.

Sugrue knew the women to see. They lived a few miles away on the Dublin Road – a place called Kilsallagh. They tended a potato ridge in the field next to the Edgeworth estate. Everyone knew it as the clover field. They made their way up the avenue to where the carriages were parked, then started begging from the gentlemen in the top hats. Turk looked over the wall at Sugrue. He could tell this scene was going hard on the old man. One of the green-stained women – the one without the basket – started to grab at the ladies, who were trying to ignore her. She was shoved away by one of the footmen, who pointed his finger and started to shout. She tried to return to her begging. He gave her a poke of one of the gentlemen's walking canes and made an attempt to chase her away. More horses galloped up the avenue and their carriage gave the three women renewed hope. Before the doors were even opened, the driver took his whip and threatened them with it. He cracked the side of the carriage. The women scuttled away and down the avenue towards the bushes where Sugrue, who had joined Turk, looked on painfully.

'Would ye not have a bit more respect for yourselves than all that,' said Sugrue, stepping out of his hiding place.

The women got a shock from his sudden emergence.

'Than all what,' said one of them – the one with the leg iron. She was clearly the most senior of the trio.

'You shouldn't be reducing yourselves to begging off that lot,' continued Sugrue.

The woman laughed through her rotting teeth. The two younger ones looked at each other, unsure whether to laugh with her or what to do.

'Would you listen girls, God has spoken. Aren't you the grand old man now – the man of great pride.'

'Look lady, we didn't spend our lives fighting the English so you could shame us. The sacrifices of ninety-eight weren't made so you could lie at these people's feet and beg like some sort of family pig.'

Turk appeared from the bushes. The grass-stained women looked at him with indifference. The older woman didn't notice him. Sugrue's face was red with rage.

'Ninety-eight! Do you hear him girls? We have a big brave soldier here, telling me off for shaming him. A gallant man, no less. A hero in our midst. Well, let me tell you something, mister, and let me make it very clear. We don't care about your pride or your heroic past, because pride and heroic pasts are as good to us now as the rotten potatoes beyond in the clover field. Your pride isn't going to feed my baby grandson, is it mister?'

There was no more to be said. The women nodded in agreement. A disgusted and disillusioned Sugrue started for the comfort of the Granard Road stile.

Turk was in pursuit of Sugrue when the door of a carriage opened and out stepped a girl onto the avenue. She wore a long, flowing, red ballgown. From behind, she looked like Clarissa. But this girl wore pleats in her hair. Then, the slow realisation rooted Turk to the spot. Another girl, about the same age, followed her from the carriage. They walked in the direction of the front entrance.

'What's wrong, you look like you've seen a ghost,' said Sugrue, stopping to look back. 'Come on and we'll have the rest of this poteen.'

Turk didn't answer. He wasn't listening. It was like he was in a trance.

Sugrue stormed off in the direction of the stile.

It really was Clarissa. She looked too good to be true. In his excitement, Turk got carried away and began calling out to her. Instinctively, Clarissa turned around. Her smile evaporated. A look of horror took its place.

'Who is that creature,' asked her friend. 'How on earth does he know your name?'

Turk was walking in her direction. Clarissa felt trapped. There was nowhere to hide. Everything about him screamed *peasant*. His clothes were little better than rags. And to make matters worse, he was coming towards her with a silly smile plastered all over his beautiful face. What part of *keeping it a secret* did he not understand. Clarissa was defenceless, in the company of her cousin, and with her father and mother about to pull up in the next carriage.

'Wahu Clarissa, it's me – Turk.'

She linked her cousin tightly and, staring at the ground, ignored him with every drop of willpower she could muster. After walking quickly past, she denied all knowledge of this boy – swearing that it was obviously a trick that someone from the manor was playing.

'A ghastly trick at that. But why are you walking so fast,' her cousin inquired, struggling to keep pace.

Turk was confused. He called out her name again as he watched her hurry away. Clarissa's cousin had just about heard enough.

'Listen, you. Go back to wherever you came from. You've nothing to do with us. If you don't get off this estate at once, I shall have you forcibly removed.'

Clarissa kept her eyes fixed firmly on the ground. She felt so awkward. She burned with indignation. Turk said no more. He stood and looked after her as she went around the avenue to the front entrance. She wanted to run back and smother him in kisses. But she couldn't do it. She couldn't let herself down in front of everyone. Her parents' carriage had arrived. She was relieved that they hadn't travelled with her. She would have had no way of explaining this to them.

'How did that filthy lecher know your name?'

'I really don't know,' stuttered Clarissa, 'perhaps he toils at Cranley estate.'

'Cheeky article,' replied her cousin. 'Boys like him should know their station.'

Clarissa was relieved to get indoors. Turk was relieved too – relieved that Sugrue was back at the stile and had not witnessed his total humiliation.

Lady Jane Teale sat in the carriage with a book on her lap. Lord Teale looked across and gave her a reassuring smile. She listened to the rumble of the wheels on the dirt road, trying to control her nerves. There was a rumour going around Lacken House that Maria Edgeworth would be present for the evening's annual Foxhunters' Ball. She was supposed to be home from Oxfordshire, accompanied by Francis Jeffrey. Lady Teale was to recite a passage from *Helen*, her favourite Edgeworth novel. How wonderful it would be to deliver the reading in the presence of the author herself. The very thought of it made Lady Teale's mouth dry up. But would she do the passage justice. She felt she wasn't ready. She wanted the journey to last forever, dreading the final turn into the avenue.

Lady Teale considered the building a little like Lacken House from the outside. A row of flowered pillars flanked an entrance hall which was dominated by two large portraits – one on either wall. Richard Lovell Edgeworth cut a dashing figure. On his proud head sat a crown of impressive grey hair, curling like a judge's wig. She didn't know much about the man, except that he was said to have accompanied Louis XVI of France to the guillotine. On the other wall, a young woman by the name of Anna Maria Elers peered out with a half-smile. She reminded Lady Teale of the Mona Lisa. Under her name it read: *1743-1773*. Lady Teale thought about the unrelenting, and sometimes unnoticed, march of time. She had been married almost as long as Anna Maria Elers had spent on God's earth. She was feeling sorry for the lady in the portrait when a servant girl came out to take their coats. Lord Teale was whisked away to the smoking room, leaving his lady wife to enter the great hall alone.

The first guest Lady Teale had the honour of meeting was Lady Carrington, a spinster who lived on a large plantation in the parish of Clonguish. She introduced herself as a next-door neighbour to the esteemed Lord and Lady Forbes. They lived a mere two miles apart, as the crow flies, in the west of the county. Lady Carrington was slightly eccentric. Lady Teale was familiar with the stories. Her husband had met Lady Carrington before. Finally, it was nice to put a face to the name. They were alone by the cocktails stand. Lady Teale doubted that they were alone by accident. While the gentlemen mingled in the upper-room – sipping pre-dinner drinks and puffing cigars – the ladies socialised in the great room, drinking sherries and cocktails. Only the ladies weren't prepared to socialise with Lady Carrington. She was loud and brash and outrageously forward, especially for a woman in the market. In an odd sort of way, Lady Teale took to Lady Carrington at once. She saw in her an innocence and was refreshed by her lack of propriety. Lady Teale was also amused by the skilful manner in which the other ladies veered off in opposite directions from Lady Carrington, as if by total accident.

After the bell, the great hall seemed to fill instantly. Serving girls appeared out of nowhere. The gentlemen arrived, nursing their brandy glasses and locked in conversation. They continued to look at the floor as they walked, finding their seats as if by instinct – the way a swallow might find its nest after a sabbatical in Africa. Lady Carrington pulled up a chair beside Lady Teale and winked across at her husband who was sitting opposite.

'How's it going, Harry?'

'Very well, my dear,' answered Lord Teale, returning the wink with a smile.

Then came the starting course – lobster and carrot soup. A Scottish gentleman beside Lord Teale pointed out that it was indeed a daring feat to include lobster on a midland's menu. There was a great guffaw at this and Lady Teale pretended to laugh too, even though she didn't get the joke.

Then someone complained that carrot was an entirely unsuitable match with lobster and that the chef was a candidate for Bethlehem.

'Get that man a drink,' shouted Lady Carrington, 'if you ask me, it's a darn waste of good carrots. And believe me, gentlemen, us single girls know a lot better uses for a big thick carrot than chopping it into a posh soup.'

The gentlemen maintained a dignified silence while the ladies patted their mouths with their napkins to hide their disgust. All except Lord and Lady Teale, who were too busy trying to keep their sides from bursting.

After pudding and tea came the speeches. It had taken some minutes to get over the disappointing announcement that Maria Edgeworth and Francis Jeffrey, who had been expected at the banquet, unfortunately couldn't make it. Something had arisen to keep them back in Oxfordshire. Nevertheless, Lady Teale read her passage in *Helen* to perfection. Afterwards, the chairman of the Foxhunters' Association, Lord Colehill, took to the floor to make his annual address.

'I am privileged to announce that this year we intend to bestow a very special honour on our esteemed hosts, the Edgeworth family. In recognition of their efforts for local charity and their positive influence on the community, it has been proposed and agreed that the parish of Mostrim be renamed. It shall henceforth be known as Edgeworthstown.'

Lord Colehill's announcement was met with deafening cheers and wild applause. The gentlemen gave a standing ovation, as chants of *Edgeworthstown, Edgeworthstown* rang out around the great hall.

Ten – This is Mostrim

'The British parliament is not our friend. It never has been. Its latest regulations on the size of farms, compulsory tillage and the outlawing of tenant labour unions have, once again, left us reeling.'

The voice that rang around the cluster belonged to Pius Mooney, a brother of my friend and neighbour, Micheal. The response was lukewarm at best. He certainly wasn't receiving the energy rush of the night before. He was standing on two old wine barrels – no doubt belonging to the Maguires – conscious that a lean here or a step there could cause him to fall. What could he do; it was all the stage he could find.

Sugrue and Turk were among the crowd. Pius needed to talk fast. His audience knew it. Pius knew it too. He had only a short time. The cabins in Cranley were closer to the big house than in Lacken, where Pius had given his speech the evening before. They were so close, Pius could be seen from the upstairs windows of de Bromley's mansion. Those who gathered around him feared the worst. They threw anxious glances across their shoulders.

'The laws of Westminster have placed a barrier on Irish freedom – our freedom – from further back than anybody here can remember. The seventeen ninety-three Convention Act, suppressing our volunteers, was in direct contravention to Paine's *Rights of Man*. In eighteen thirty-two, they passed a Composition Act making tithe payments compulsory for at least twenty-one years. Two years later, they converted tithe payment into a rent charge – a rent charge you must stump up to an alien church from an alien country.'

Even the most muffled cheers were silenced as two boys from the estate house appeared and stood outside their stone wall enclosure. As they looked on, the crowd was painfully conscious.

'Funny liffle accent, innit?' said one of the boys, as he listened to Pius. 'It's abouf as flat as land around 'ere.'

'It's abouf as shit as land around 'ere too,' replied the other. 'Why 'e decided to come to this kiphole in first place is beyond me.'

The *'e* the youngster referred to was his uncle, Viscount de Bromley.

''e didn't decide anyfink. 'e had no choice. 'e was granfed this land by monarchy for 'is services to justice deparfment.'

'They could have given somefink beffer than this, somefink closer to Dublin. You'd die of boredom around sparrowfarf village like this – no girls nor noffink.'

''e didn't do too bad considerin'. Uncle has a landlord friend in west of Ireland, a place with a funny liffle name on it – Me-You or somefink like that. Anyhows, land is far worse over fere. You're always finking of your 'ole. There's lots of serving girls in big 'ouse if you want to gef leg over.'

'No way, mate. I wouvn't touch 'em wif bargepole. You never know what you'd come down wif. Me-you, indeed. Well, me-you would be beffer off closer to Pale mate, where proper bit o' skirt can be 'ad.'

The presence of the young de Bromleys only served to strengthen Pius's resolve. His voice grew ever louder. Pius was under no illusion, he knew the dangers of making such a speech in the Cranley cluster. He also knew that, despite their apparent lack of enthusiasm, the people of this townland were on his side. They were quiet because they were afraid, with homesteads to protect. Pius was afraid too, but he had a job to do. And this was a job for a single man with no ties – to land or a family home. Pius was the right man for that job. He felt an obligation to speak out. He had always felt an obligation to help the downtrodden. His mother instilled this in him from the very beginning. She named him after Pius VII, who was ordained Bishop of Rome three days before Pius Patrick Mooney was born, on 17 March 1800.

Sugrue and Turk were on his side for sure. Sugrue was fighting the urge to join Pius on the podium. He wanted to stir the crowd, to liven things up. But Sugrue had to be realistic. Such behaviour would lose him his job – as well as his homestead. While sleeping under the stars held no fear for Sugrue, he didn't want Ella May and little Padraig to be homeless.

Turk was also anxious to keep a low profile. Besides the job on Cranley estate, he wanted to mend his relationship with Clarissa – who had been estranged from him since the evening of the Foxhunters' Ball.

'Yes, my friends, alien is the word I use. Everything English in our country is alien in our country. And now they tell us that our little parish is to be renamed Edgeworthstown. This is surely going too far. We cannot and we will not stand for this. It is time that we, the people of Mostrim, stood together to guard what is rightfully ours.'

The fine hairs on Sugrue's neck stood on end. Turk could see it in the old man's face; he was getting emotional. It was the hottest topic at the time – the gentry's decision to rename the parish. Over my dead body, Sugrue whispered to himself.

'He's right you know.'

Sugrue could hold his tongue no longer.

'After all, this is Mostrim. If we don't stand up and fight for it, then what kind of people are we in the first place.'

The de Bromley boys could hear a familiar voice and the familiar clipping sound of studs on stone coming up from behind, breaking their attention on the speechmaking.

'Stand aside, laddies.'

It was the voice of Walter Pollach. He led a couple of estate men, each armed with a blunderbuss, over the stone wall and into the enclosure. They were heading for Pius Mooney. The men pointed their weapons at anyone in their path. The crowd dispersed in all directions. Pollach took out his whip and shook it loose. The clipping sound grew ominously louder. Pius held out his hands to show that he was not armed.

'No need for weapons,' he declared, as Pollach walked towards him, 'this is a peaceful demonstration.'

When he was close enough, Pollach lashed out and caught Pius on the side of the head, tumbling him from the barrels. Women screeched in terror. Pollach walked up to where Pius lay sprawled. He didn't utter a word, just lashed him furiously with the whip. Some of the crowd begged him to stop, but their pleas fell on deaf ears. Pollach was hammering home his message. This sort of thing would be dealt with mercilessly.

Pollach was beating Pius to pulp. His face was destroyed, his clothes torn from the ferocity of the whip. Turk made a jolt forward. Sugrue caught him by the arm.

'Stay where you are, my auld son of Eireann. There's nothing you can do, so leave it to God.'

It was hard for Sugrue to say it. If he was Turk's age he would have charged in too. But time had taught him well. They couldn't help Pius now.

Turk could take no more. He turned to walk away. Sugrue stopped him in his tracks again.

'Don't,' said the old man. 'Don't go. Watch it all, young Turk, every last blow. Stay and watch and *never* forget.'

Eleven – The Eviction Ceremony

Jabber Farrell secured a job on de Bromley's estate in Cranley. His first day was an eventful one. He wasn't working with me or any of our buddies from the bog. He was part of a new drainage scheme, further down the plantation. Jabber didn't mind. It was steady income for the house, supplementing his mother's meagre pay. He made the trip from Lacken on foot, myself in tow for company. As we passed on our way, we called in at the cluster of cabins in Cranley. Sure enough, there Sugrue waited patiently, Turk at his elbow.

'You'll be quiet today, Farrell,' joked Sugrue, 'it's not the soft fellas above in Lacken you're rubbing shoulders with anymore.'

'Oh now, my boxing days are long finished,' returned Jabber, Turk putting up his dukes in preparation for battle.

Turk's show of bravado was all for nothing. Something else had caught Jabber's attention – a piece of paper dangling from the door of Sugrue's nearest neighbour.

'Merciful hour! It's a while since I saw one of these,' he remarked.

'What is it,' asked Turk.

'A warrant of distrain,' explained Jabber. 'It's from the sheriff – not a good sign at all. It means whoever lives here will soon be out in a ditch or in the poor house in Shroid.'

'Ah, that's been there for a couple of weeks now,' said Sugrue. 'I wouldn't pass much remarks at all.'

'I'm afraid I would,' continued Jabber, 'I'm familiar with these warrants from my time at the workhouse.'

'But whoever lives there won't qualify for the workhouse. He's farming more than the quarter acre. Look at his boundary,' I said, pointing to the fence.

'Didn't I say there's no need to get excited,' explained Sugrue, 'that man, Aidan Skelton, and his family have been sorted out. He has made a topping little deal with de Bromley. They've agreed to scale back to the quarter acre so there'll be no need for a certificate of compliance to the poor house. I think Skelton has one eye on convincing the viscount to send them abroad.'

I was glad to hear this. I knew Aidan Skelton and his wife from going in and out of mass. When I say that, I only knew them to say hello to. Nobody liked to hear of eviction, it was a nasty business that had a habit of catching on.

At lunch time – when the front lawn was always fairly full – the big red doors of Cranley House were pushed open. Down the great avenue came Walter Pollach, whip in hand. He was flanked by the two blunderbuss bearers from the Pius Mooney incident. Behind them walked a man in a fine suit, a sheet of paper in his hand, and two more men, armed with long knives and wearing the black jackets and white sashes of the militia. They carried pistols in their broad white belts. The militia man on the left held an oil lamp – peculiar for the time of day.

Sugrue locked eyes on the militia man to the right, a grey-bearded man of his own vintage. As he passed, the grey-bearded militia man caught sight of Sugrue, allowed himself a brief smile, then refocused his attention on the task at hand. Sugrue was concerned. Those eyes – they echoed something from a distant, disturbed past. The smile sent a shiver down the old man's spine. Sugrue was sure he had seen that smile somewhere before. Then again, maybe he hadn't.

There was a buzz among the crowd. Pollach and his men walked the length of the great avenue, where they were joined by a man in a brown dustcoat. He looked weather-beaten. He had a bag of tools, hauling them across his shoulder as he followed Pollach to Skelton's house. The buzz gave way to a dreadful silence. They knocked at the door. Skelton opened the window. He looked frightened. He came out to meet them. Pollach stood aside and the man in the fine suit identified himself as a bailiff. He read from the sheet – a Bill of Ejectment – compelling Aidan Skelton to surrender his holding and all associated crops to Her Royal Highness, Queen Victoria, on breach of the laws as set by Her Majesty's government concerning the renting of lands in the United Kingdom of Great Britain and Ireland.

Skelton was horrified. He pleaded his case to the bailiff. The bailiff didn't respond. Pollach held up his hand, demanding silence. All eyes were on him now. He had deliberately set this eviction for midday. The plan was working a treat, sending out a strong message in the wake of the Pius Mooney trouble. Usually, evictions were more subtle than this – taking place at dawn or when the tenants were away from their holding. But where was the fun in that. If the crowd was going to gather around Pius Mooney, listening to his anti-establishment poison, then they were going to have to bear this sight as a consequence.

The man in the brown dustcoat was poised and ready for action. He held a long-handled instrument of about five feet at the thick end, with two prongs attached at the head.

'What's that, Sugrue, a hay fork?'

'No, young Turk, an eviction crowbar. It's not a good thing.'

'That's new to me, but very professional,' whispered Turk. 'They're less fussy where I come from – they just scatter the houses by hand.'

Skelton began shouting at Pollach and the bailiff, reminding them that he had a deal with Viscount de Bromley. They couldn't do this. His defiance wilted at the sight of the whip. He kneeled and begged for mercy while his wife shielded their smallest in her skirts. The other Skelton children were outside too, wailing in terror.

When the bailiff had dispensed with the formalities, Pollach gave the order and the man in the dustcoat set to work with the crowbar. He snapped the door off its hinges and knocked stones out of the walls. He entered the premises and a table and stool flew out of the space where the door used to be. When the children saw their favourite sugan chair outside in the dirt, they wailed even louder. There were two rooms in the cabin, with long reeds hanging between them for privacy. The man in the dustcoat pulled the reeds down and wrapped them in a ball. He went outside and lit them from the flame of the oil lamp. He returned to the cabin. A clay wash basin came through the window. Aidan Skelton got off his knees and ran inside. Much of the gable wall had been knocked by this stage. We could see parts of the kitchen and a scooped out hallow in the floor. Aidan was pulling at the man's dustcoat in an effort to restrain him. The burning reeds were pointed at him in a threatening manner. The militia men went into the house. They dragged Skelton away. The thatch went from billowing black smoke to a crackling fire in seconds. There was nothing left for Aidan Skelton to do but retreat to his family. They turned away from the blaze, huddled together, and sobbed their eyes out.

I looked at the huddle of stick-thin bodies and whispered a prayer. It was their one last luxury. On entering the workhouse, even the basic comfort of a family huddle would be prohibited. They would be split up and banned from meeting. That's if they qualified for the workhouse. What a place. I looked at Jabber and wondered how he had worked there for so long.

On his reappearance, the man in the dustcoat flung the burning reeds back into the cabin. He cleaned the crowbar and returned it to his bag of tools. He extinguished the flame in the oil lamp and handed it to the militia man with the grey beard.

There were more gasps from the crowd as the cabin roof caved in. All the women were crying. Memories of ninety-eight came flooding back to Sugrue. He told me it was a common scene back then. Be it for fodder or thatch, the British were intent on burning every blade of straw in north Longford that year.

The flaming roof had special significance for Walter Pollach too. It was a first real chance to exercise the extraordinary powers Viscount de Bromley had bestowed upon him. Under normal circumstances, this eviction would not have been allowed. The viscount was the only one with the authority to evict. But de Bromley was either in Essex or Kent. Pius Mooney's speech the previous afternoon had been music to Pollach's ears. It was all he had been waiting for. It gave him the power to evict without consulting the viscount. Pius's speech would be considered a serious breach of security – emergency measures needed to be carried out.

Pollach walked slowly to the stone wall separating the estate from the cluster. He scanned the crowd. The militia men fell in behind him as he addressed workers and tenants alike.

'Many of you present may blame the bailiff, the Lord Victory, or perhaps myself even, for what you have witnessed here today. But you would be wrong to do so. The Skeltons were in arrears with their rent. It is true that the viscount had come to an arrangement to save them from destitution. But an act of anarchy has rendered this arrangement void. The body at fault for Mister Skelton's eviction is none other than Pius Mooney, for the wee stunt he pulled on this estate yesterday evening. If you want to blame anyone, blame him.'

Father Murtagh rushed through the crowd. He had been sent for. By the time he reached Cranley, however, the cabin was already on fire. He marched straight up to the eviction party. He didn't say a word, just eyeballed each one in turn, finishing with a long look into Walter Pollach's sniggering face. Father Murtagh had raised the matter the previous Sunday – how a warrant of distrain had come to be hanging on the Skeltons' door. Canon Reidy didn't want to know. Instead, he warned Father Murtagh against getting on the wrong side of their Protestant neighbours. He told his understudy to mind his own business, pointing out that he already had Reverend Smyth's back up over tithe payments and what the viscount did or didn't do with his tenants was nobody's business but his own.

Eventually, Father Murtagh walked past Pollach and on to the grief-stricken Skeltons. His heart stirred with sorrow to see their cabin roof going up in flames and the walls scattered in single stones, here and there on the grass. He looked at the children and tried to smile. He couldn't do it. The youngest child, covered in tears and snot, ran in behind his mother as he saw the priest approaching.

It was finished with Canon Reidy. Father Murtagh had made up his mind, once and for all, that he would be taking no further instruction from his parish priest. From then on, he would be acting on his own initiative. These people weren't just Viscount de Bromley's business – they were part of Father Murtagh's flock. That made them *his* business. This eviction was *his* business. The Skeltons needed care and attention. They needed love and understanding. Yet all they had received was abuse from the state and ignorance from the church.

Twelve – The Neighbours Fight the Tithe

The Mostrim anti-tithe campaign was in full swing. The tip-off came from the most unlikely of places – inside Cranley House. Constance Ryan had been enjoying a rare evening of leisure after yet another day of taking orders from Sheila McAndrew – from the hour she had been marched up the great avenue by her grandmother, Constance had found herself dancing to McAndrew's tune – when she intercepted the vital information.

At bedtime, as she filled her wash basin, Constance heard tapping at the window. She knew immediately who was there. Having checked that the coast was clear, she rushed to open it. Shay – my son – was crouched behind a bush. He dropped a handful of pebbles and raced over. They embraced through the small window. Constance was becoming bolder, her confidence growing in this nightly ritual. Shay was more at ease too, compared to the start of their courtship. He had been a bag of nerves around the big house, but his love for Constance knew no bounds.

Constance looked troubled. She told Shay he must act with haste. She had news of great importance for the people of Lacken. She had overheard a conversation in the great hall. Two gentlemen were discussing how the tithe proctors were to make a swoop on Lacken the very next morning. The name Mooney was mentioned, but she couldn't get close enough to hear much more.

'Shay, you must warn them tonight,' pleaded Constance.

'I'll go in a while. I haven't seen you in ages.'

'But you saw me last night.'

'A night without you seems like ages,' he answered, leaning through the window frame for another kiss before setting off on the four-mile hike across the parish to the clachan.

The next day, Lachan was wide awake at the crack of dawn. We were all ready. Jabber was sitting in a tree – on lookout duty. His deafening whistle was needed for the front line. Behind him, a hundred yards away, myself and Peter Hogan were busy cutting large branches and hiding them in ditches. The plan was to block the road as soon as the whistle came through. I liked spending the time in Peter's company. His serious nature was pure entertainment.

'You know the way the parish name is being changed by all the hobnobs,' he said, while hacking lumps out of an ash tree. 'Does this mean from now on it'll be known as the Edgeworthstown Ribbonmen, instead of the Mostrim Ribbonmen?'

Those were the sort of questions that stirred Peter's imagination.

Sugrue arrived in the clachan to help Micheal Mooney. Turk was eager to help out too but, if the worst came to the worst, Sugrue didn't want the boy implicated. He despatched him on an impromptu assignment to keep an eye on Cranley House instead – Sugrue labelling it a *behind-enemy-lines-intelligence-gathering* mission. Micheal's pet pig was also despatched – to a friend in the nearby townland of Camlisk. The few healthy potatoes that had survived the blight were buried in a hole in the bog. Micheal was very nervous about his coffin. Sugrue suggested another hole. Micheal wouldn't hear tell of it. Under no circumstances was his treasured coffin, a family heirloom for three generations, going into a hole in the ground.

'But sure, that's what coffins are for, Micheal, to go into the ground.'

'No way, Mister Sugrue. Over my dead body is that coffin going near any hole in the ground.'

'Right, then, we'll cover it with the manure heap instead.'

It almost broke poor Micheal's heart to have to do it, but Sugrue assured him the coffin was safe beneath the pile of shite. The smell would be a great defence against the nosiest of tithe proctors. While Sugrue was checking on all the houses, he caught sight of McAndrew's cabin - a ruin now with brambles and briars climbing out the windows and door. There was no point searching that old shack to see if anything needed saving.

'We're all rushing about the place, trying to hide our belongings before the proctor gets a hold of them. No fear of old Tom rushing about, Micheal.'

'Tom McAndrew? Have you gone mad, Mister Sugrue? Sure, Tom McAndrew hasn't been seen around here for years. You and him were fierce great once upon a time.'

'Yeah, well, the world keeps turning. Once upon a time doesn't always have a happy ending. He won't be worried about tithe – no matter where he hangs his hat.'

The coffin was forgotten about once Pius showed up. He walked in a stooped motion; the injuries to his back were not yet healed. His neck showed the scars from the whipping. Micheal Mooney was delighted to see his brother and, despite Sugrue's presence, gave him a big hug. Pius had heard about the warning too, and he wanted to help out.

'Once a Ribbonman, always a Ribbonman,' Pius proclaimed piously.

But not everyone was as happy to see Pius Mooney. There were side-glances and murmurs. There was a coolness towards him. Pius detected this. He pretended not to notice. Sugrue detected it also. It made him so mad. All the nastiness of the previous few days was finally coming to a head.

Sugrue was as big a hero in Lacken as he was in Cranley. Whenever tales of Ballinamuck were told around the firesides, his ears must have had steam rising out of them. He was a huge part of our folklore. Now it was time to use that fame for the greater good. He overturned a derelict turf cart and stood on it. He brought the people of the clachan out of their homes with a guttural roar. He ordered us all to gather round. Then he began his address.

'Friends and fellow comrades, we all know why we are assembled at such an early hour, and what this day means for the people of Lacken. You are only doing what has been forced upon you to do. You must act with speed and cunning. Your goal is a collective one. Therefore, you should either enjoy a collective success or endure a collective failure. You have been plagued with blight this year and your praties have been badly affected. Why should you give what little you have – your hay and harvests, your praties and other produce – to a foreign and illegal tithe payment? You are here, in your cabins, drinking well water from clay mugs, while those in charge of tithe are above in their great mansions and palaces, drinking wine from golden goblets and afternoon tea from china cups. I see some members of the Tenant Right Movement here among us. What these good people want is improved farming methods and productivity. They seek legal guarantees with regard to fair rent, safeguards against eviction, and compensation for improvements upon leaving a tenancy. Is this asking too much? Is it asking too much to be treated like normal human beings? Alas, I fear it is. When it comes to the welfare of its Irish citizens, Westminster couldn't care less. In 1838, a mere seven years ago, they converted tithe payment into a rent charge and rewarded the collectors with a twenty-five per-cent bonus. Despite the best efforts of Sherman Crawford and William Blacker, English law is, and always has been, unfair to the Irish tenant. London sides with landlord ownership and private land rights.'

Looking down into the people, Sugrue sought out Pius Mooney. For once, he was uncharacteristically subdued – deliberately trying to keep a low profile.

'Among you today is Pius Mooney, a volunteer who has, in no lesser way than Crawford and Blacker or the Tenant Right officers, put himself out for the good of his fellow citizen. He is an honourable man, a man who has suffered physically and mentally for what he believes in. This week he has been cast as a villain. I will not stand for this. I will not stand by and let a good man be ostracised from the society he strives to protect. Who, here among you, believes Walter Pollach's lies? Who believes Pius Mooney was to blame for Aidan Skelton's eviction? Hands up who thinks Pius Mooney is responsible for the tithe proctor's imminent arrival? Hands up high. Let me see them.'

Sugrue scanned the crowd. He waited a full minute. To Pius, this seemed like an eternity. Not one hand was raised.

'That ends it then, once and for all. There will be no ill-feeling towards Pius Mooney or any of his family. We stick together, all of us, it's the only chance we've got. And we'll leave the rest to God. It's enough that we have to fight the injustices of the British, without having to fight each other as well.'

A hand eventually went up in the crowd, and a middle-aged woman vented her frustration towards her neighbours.

'The tithe commissioner has a fixed amount on Lacken. He says if a household fails to meet its obligations, then the shortfall will transfer to the rest of us in the clachan. I'm not paying extra to make up the quota,' she protested.

This caused consternation among the crowd. Heated debate progressed into quarrelling, then into a full-scale row.

'Whisht,' shouted Sugrue, his hands outstretched. 'Stop and listen to yourselves. You are doing exactly the opposite of what I asked. Stand up and fight tithe payments together. Have you not learned anything from our years of fighting the British? They have always relied on the same old trick when it came to dealing with us – divide and conquer! They adopted this policy back in ninety-eight and it worked for them then. They've adopted it against us ever since. Dividing tithe up in this way is just another form of dividing us up before the conquest. But there is one way to fight this tactic. Stand together. Whatever they throw at us, we are stronger if we stand together and fight this as one. That is the only way to stand up to the British Empire.'

The crowd fell silent. Pius Mooney was the first to applaud. Slowly, more joined in until eventually everyone was clapping and cheering and chanting Sugrue's name.

The corrugated-iron sheeting made an awful din from the horses' hooves and the wheels of the stagecoach wagon. Jabber Farrell pulled the scarf down from over his nose. During the long wait he had calculated that the metal sheets gave him roughly a minute. He stuck his fingers in his mouth and whistled with all his might. Then he ran back to myself and Peter as fast as he could.

We were discussing the school curriculum when the whistle came through. It was straight into action. We hauled out a large trunk and laid it across the road. We added to it with bushes, then retreated to the trees nearby. I admit I was worried until I saw Jabber racing towards us. I let a roar to disclose our whereabouts. Peter got off his haunches, his face in his scarf and a rock in his hand. He moved to a tree on the far side of the road. Jabber was safely by my side before any sign of the approaching stagecoach. I felt frightened and excited. I also felt a strange sort of freedom for the first time – the freedom of standing up to my oppressors. I was breaking the law, but I didn't care – and I wasn't sorry. It wasn't our law, just a law designed to keep us down at heel. I doused the first sod of turf in camphine. Jabber lit it and told me to keep them coming.

The horses ground to a halt. The driver got down to inspect the roadblock. Something stirred inside the stagecoach. Walter Pollach put his head out and demanded to know what was going on. A door opened and a militia man got out. I recognised the sash and the grey beard instantly – the same militia man had been at the eviction. The driver was shaking his head at Pollach, explaining how it wasn't his fault. Suddenly the missiles came raining down. Pollach just about got the window shut in time. The militia man rushed back to the stagecoach. The driver put his arms around his head for protection. He tried to get to the rear of the wagon for cover. He was pelted with large rocks. The militia man reappeared with a musket. He steadied it on the rim of a wheel and took aim. He couldn't see anyone to fire at. The stagecoach window had been broken. Pollach was crouched down across the seat. He shouted at the other militia man to protect the proctor in the carriage.

'You, clear the road,' Pollach ordered the driver.

The driver crept towards the roadblock but was beaten back by a ferocious counter-offensive. Myself and Jabber were pegging balls of burning turf from one direction, Peter Hogan throwing rocks from another.

The grey-bearded militia man was waving his musket all over the place. He couldn't get a fix on anyone, his concentration broken from the two-fronted attack.

Pollach and the militia men could only hold out for so long. Turf burned on the roof of the stagecoach. In his desperation, Pollach forgot his fear and began to shield the tithe proctor with his own body. If he was returned to Reverend Smyth with an injury, Pollach would never get the loan of the proctor again. The militia man sat beside them with his loaded musket, just itching to get outside to help his older, grey-bearded, colleague.

'We're on fire, Mister Pollach,' roared the driver.

Pollach hadn't heard the driver. A burning sod of turf bounced onto the seat beside them. The clean-shaven militia man had had enough. Taking the burning turf in his gloved hand, he hurled it back in the opposite direction. He then discharged his musket blindly into the trees.

'Retreat, retreat,' roared Pollach. 'Get in now,' he snapped at his grey-bearded protector. 'Get us out of here,' he shouted at the driver, 'do you ken we're on fire.'

The driver sprang into the box seat. He straightened the reins, but the horses kept jumping and kicking. Finally, he managed to back up enough, turn the horses, and steer the stagecoach in the opposite direction.

There was great rejoicing in Lacken that evening. It was like a fair day. Sugrue toasted the health of Constance Ryan. Without her warning, we'd have all been sitting ducks.

'God bless her hearing,' he said, as he held up a flask of poteen. 'And God bless young Shay Gorman for the late-night warning.'

Myself, Peter and Jabber were feted like heroes of old. We arrived back to the clachan with three dead rabbits and a go of mushrooms. Jabber did a spot of poaching in his spare time. After checking into Camlisk on the way home, he found his traps full.

It was a wonderful evening of celebration. Micheal Mooney took out a fiddle and Pius had one of these new Clarke bone whistles. The youngsters sat around Peter Hogan, their old schoolmaster, at the open fire. They ate rabbit and hung on his every word - about how he had repelled a coachload of heavily-armed militia men with little more than a couple of well-placed rocks.

It was like bygone days in the clachan. Jabber's mother, who was standing by the boundary wall with the older women, came over and gave him a kiss on the cheek. Sugrue smiled and Jabber became embarrassed. So much for the old wives' tale about them not getting on.

Yet, despite all the merriment, I couldn't shake a strange feeling of anti-climax. I wanted that other feeling back – the feeling of power as I watched the stagecoach scurry away. It was the first time I had ever felt that sort of superiority towards those who applied their version of law and order over me. I loved it. Now that I was back at the clachan, I missed the danger of it all. Mairead came over and led me out into the clearing where several other couples were dancing. She kissed me and called me her brave champion as we waltzed to the music.

Then a boy turned into the clachan, limping and out of breath. Nobody, except Sugrue, passed much remarks. He recognised the boy from the cluster in Cranley. While the rest of us laughed at Peter Hogan's swashbuckling tales, the old man rose immediately and went to his youthful neighbour.

'You're a long way from home, my auld son of Eireann. What brings you here?'

'Mister Sugrue, I was sent out to find you. Bad news from Cranley,' he panted.

'Steady on, sonny. Take your time.'

'This evening there were men with lanterns looking for you at your house. Missus Ella May answered the door and said you were abroad at your business. They hit her in the face and forced their way past her. They said they were there for your tithe payment, then wrecked your cabin and took your potatoes. Missus Ella May protested. She told them they were only entitled to a tenth of what they brought. But a man threatened her with a whip and told the proctor to take it all, that you were badly in arrears.'

'Is Ellie alright,' Sugrue asked the boy.

'She told me to tell you that she's fine, Mister Sugrue, and asked that you return with me at once.'

By now, Micheal Mooney's fiddle had fallen silent and the merry mood of the evening was gone. The clachan gathered around Sugrue and the boy as the fire blazed at their backs.

'These men,' said Jabber, 'did they show up in a stagecoach

drawn by two Clydesdale horses?'

'They did for sure, sir,' answered the boy.

'Were there two militia men with them?'

'Yes. It was one of the militia men that struck Missus Ella May. He asked her if Mister Sugrue's business was putting up roadblocks in Lacken. Then he slapped her across the face with the back of his hand and spat on her. That's why I was sent here to find you.'

Sugrue went quiet then.

'This militia man, was he an old fella with a grey beard,' growled Jabber.

'Yes, he sure was,' replied the boy. 'And he had a personal message for Mister Sugrue. When he was leaving, he told Missus Ella May to tell him that Roger Giles sends his regards.'

Sugrue stared into the fire. It was as if he was losing his edge. It all came flooding back with the name. That stare, those eyes – Sugrue should have recognised him instantly at the eviction. But he hadn't seen Roger Giles in so long. They hadn't crossed swords in many decades. The grey beard and militia headgear had thrown him. His mortal enemy was back to haunt him, to finish what they'd started forty-seven years earlier on the fields of Ballinamuck. The old warrior held the powder flask like a baby in his hands. He examined it as his mind drifted.

'Are you alright, Sugrue,' asked Jabber.

'It's going to be war now – war to the knife,' replied Sugrue, as if we weren't even there.

'Don't be upsetting yourself,' said Jabber, 'Ella May is made of stronger stuff than all that.'

But Sugrue wasn't talking about his daughter-in-law. He knew what the rest of us didn't – that while Roger Giles had a breath in his body he would stop at nothing until he had overseen Paddy Sugrue's demise, just like he had done with the Paddy Sugrue before him.

Thirteen – The Threat of Reprisals

Canon Reidy was only getting into his stride on the high altar. He couldn't see Peter Hogan, but he knew he was there. Master Hogan was glad for small mercies; at least the canon was facing the other way. He knew the opening sermon had been directed at him personally. Peter couldn't believe how low his parish priest could actually stoop. The canon already had his victory – the inspector having closed the hedge school and scattered the children. Some of Master Hogan's pupils were now to be found among the eighty-two boys and one hundred girls on the roll books of Master John Hanlon and Missus Mary Gahon at Mostrim's new national school on the Ballymahon Road. The rest – the unlucky ones – were simply kept at home or sent out to the fields. In the five years since the new school had opened its doors on 22 January 1840, it had gone from strength to strength under the astute management of the canon. He now had the resources to pay his principal a salary of £20 per annum. Still, the victory wasn't enough. The old priest had to rub salt in Master Hogan's extremely raw wounds.

'Never again will a child in this parish be expected to concentrate on their lessons while battling the elements of nature. A farmer's shed is no place for a serious student, with its wet and its cold. And neither is the butt of a hedge. From now on, children will be snug and warm while receiving their education.'

I looked over at Peter Hogan. His expression said it all. What a load of bullshite. There was no mention of the poorest kids, those who couldn't afford to bring turf for the teacher. Not one word about the children condemned to sit at the back, far away from the classroom's cosy open fire. How snug and warm would *they* be then while concentrating on their lessons.

Canon Reidy was in bad humour. We could sense it in the pews, especially when he turned to face the congregation. He only ever turned when he was about to lay into us. He wanted to see our faces – to judge our reactions. That's what he told us. But that was bullshite too. The real reason he turned around with a face like thunder was to intimidate and frighten people.

'It is only right that we cherish the children of our parish and give them all an equal chance in life.'

Not a sound could be heard from the churchgoers. Their usual Sunday-morning fear was upon them. It was edge-of-the-seat stuff. Well, most of the churchgoers. Turk O Nuallain slouched in the haypenny place, slumbering on the shoulder of a man who looked set for the gallows. A light snore made its way through the crowd. He was awoken by a poke in the ribs. He sat up and listened then. Sugrue, who was sitting on the wall outside, would be wanting an in-depth report. It was time for Turk to find out what the canon had to say on the latest scandal to hit the parish.

'But how on earth can we cherish our children when we can't even give proper example of how to live like ordinary decent human beings. What happened the other night in the fields of Cranley is nothing short of an abomination. I was out there, on the de Bromley estate, at the invitation of Reverend Smyth. How embarrassing was it for me to have to admit that somebody I may have baptized could actually be so monstrous. I am aware that a large amount of poaching goes on in the parish but, while this is bad enough, it is nothing compared to the deliberate butchery of dumb animals. Poor Reverend Smyth couldn't even walk the estate for fear of getting sick.'

The morning after the atrocity, the canon had spent an hour looking at the carnage. The burning smell wafted through the air. The animals were barely recognisable. It was an awful mess.

Almost all de Bromley's livestock in the field beside the cluster had been burnt black. A cow and a calf had survived. Constance Ryan's heart nearly broke as she scrunched pillows around her ears to drown out their crying. Walter Pollach loaded a pistol to put an end to their misery. Two policemen – or peelers, as we call them with affection – were going around the estate, talking to anyone they came across.

'I felt I had to make a personal apology on behalf of the Catholic people of the parish,' continued the canon in a near whisper.

He went behind the high altar and returned with a large piece of paper.

'This was taken from the great oak on the Cranley estate lawns. I shall return it to the police barracks later. It is a notice stating that the killing of the cattle was in retaliation for the eviction of Aidan Skelton and the illegal seizing of tithe payments. *Should this continue*, the notice warns, *then we will have no choice but to continue with the destruction of the property you have acquired illegally from your Crown.*'

The signature at the bottom of the notice read: *The Whitefeet*.

'The Whitefeet,' repeated Canon Reidy, who at this stage looked ready to burst. 'Many of you will be wondering what I am doing with this notice from the police barracks today. I am showing it to you for a reason. The person or persons who wrote this notice are sitting among you. They are known to you. Your silence in protecting them means you, and I mean *all* of *you*, are as guilty of this terrible crime as they are. You are harbouring evil and protecting anarchy. But I will not have this, not in my parish. I refuse to stand by and allow the haters of the common law to have their way. Private property rights have to be acknowledged here. They are rights that must be upheld and adhered to. Church of Ireland tithe payments must be observed. They are part of the law of this land, a law that I shall protect with every fibre of my being.'

Turk's interest was piqued with the mention of private property rights. He considered that this must have been a new development because the ruling class had forgotten to observe and uphold private property rights in relation to his crowd – the MacCarthaigh Mors. Instead, they were stripped of their lands and their castle and chased out of Munster. He would have liked to have stated this publicly, but he could tell that the canon was in no mood for chit-chat.

'They are the common laws of this land from time immemorial. Yes, my dear people, from the time Strongbow set foot in Ireland. Therefore, whoever wrote this threatening notice are enemies of law and order.'

The canon went silent and sat down. He was dizzy with vexation. He needed a moment to reflect. He said a prayer in Latin and everyone breathed a sigh of relief. But he wasn't finished yet.

'We have let down our Protestant neighbours badly. We have shown ourselves up in an extremely poor light. We must make it up to them, starting today. There is a sale of goods in the parish hall at three o'clock, and I want to see every one of you there. Our Church of Ireland neighbours have kindly given us the opportunity of purchasing certain items at a reduced price.'

An awkward silence fell on Saint Mary's chapel. Turk recognised the problem instantly, and he wasn't about to be bitten twice. Since his arrival in Mostrim, the young Galwegian had already been to one of these sales in the Auburn Hall. He had fallen into excellent conversation with a gentleman who was selling his lot in a chained pen. There weren't many in excellent conversation – and even less buying any of the goods on offer. They were just standing around, watching and whispering in corners. Sugrue came over, grabbed Turk roughly by the collar and led him away. Sugrue was furious with him. Turk had no idea why. Sugrue explained that the man Turk had been talking to was being boycotted for taking possession of eviction property. Sugrue also explained that most of the goods on sale had been previously seized by the tithe proctor and this was an attempt to convert these goods into money. Turk was encouraged to shut his mouth and open his eyes. Sugrue was only at the sale to ensure that no one reneged on the boycott.

'As for these Whitefeet,' concluded Canon Reidy from his pulpit, 'let me assure you these fellows *will* be caught. Then we shall see how white they keep their feet in the cells of Kilmainham Gaol or the bulkheads heading for Van Diemen's Land.'

Fourteen – Pollach Warns the Parish

Missus Ryan stood on the cold clay floor and pulled the headscarf tightly around her cheeks. She had to stand, there was no choice. The only seat in the room was taken by Walter Pollach. The old woman could tell he was enjoying himself. He was making her feel uncomfortable. But she kept up the appearance. She held her head high and refused to show fear. She wouldn't allow him the pleasure.

'Your granddaughter is doing fine over at Cranley House, madam,' he said, after a pause.

He was examining a silver snuffbox. He played with it for a while, using the glint of the sun to create a spotlight on the wall. When he moved the snuffbox in a certain direction, the spotlight moved with it. Missus Ryan didn't need Pollach to tell her how Constance was getting on. She visited her granddaughter every Sunday from six until eight – visiting time in the servants' quarters.

'I hear she's getting promoted from the kitchens. She's going to be Lady Ivens' new nanny, if you don't mind,' continued Pollach, in a tone of fake admiration.

Lady Ivens was the viscount's sister. She had two brats who tore around the big house, breaking everything in their path.

Missus Ryan was only half listening. She was focused on the snuffbox – her late husband's pride and joy. She didn't want Pollach messing with it.

'Let me take that, Mister Pollach. I'm sure you don't want tobacco on your lovely new clothes for your trip back to Cranley.'

Before he could protest, she swiped the snuffbox from his clutches and returned it to the back room. Pollach walked slowly across the kitchen, to the pot hanging on a crossbar over the open fire. There was stew in the pot. He looked out through the top half of the door at the two guards he had brought with him. They were standing at attention, one with a loaded crossbow and the other with a cocked pistol.

'Did any of you fine chaps order some broth? Well, too bad, kitchen is closed,' he joked, and slammed the half-door shut on them.

The kitchen filled with smoke and Missus Ryan scurried out from the back room. She didn't like to see the back door fully closed.

'Is there a Mister Ryan at all, *Missus* Ryan? An auld hen like you must have a clatter of bairns about the place.'

Missus Ryan didn't answer. Instead, she went to open the top half.

'Leave it,' he said in a threatening voice.

He smiled at her worried expression.

'Look, the smoke is nearly cleared. You didn't answer my question. Is there a Mister Ryan?'

He had resumed his playful tone.

'There is, Mister Pollach. My son, Finbar, is in Glasgow.'

'In Glasgow, is that right. I, myself, am originally from Scotland.'

'Yes, I gathered that from the way you speak, sir.'

He was happy to hear Missus Ryan say this. Walter had been worried that the many years spent working for the viscount in Ireland had begun to erode his accent and, worse still, replace it with an Irish one.

'You can still hear the Scottish influence in your voice,' she continued, as Pollach beamed with delight.

'And what, pray tell, is this Finbar doing all the way over in Glasgow?'

'He's picking spuds, sir, and working with farmers. He's doing just fine, thank God.'

'Is he indeed,' growled Pollach, his hand wandering down to the folded whip in his belt. 'He is in his arse. Let me tell you what he's doing, Missus Ryan. He's going about polluting Scottish girls, him and the rest of the dirty Irish cunts, with their low morals and their filthy habits. You see this thing here.'

Pollach pulled out the whip and extended it across the table.

'This is the only thing those buckos understand, and we're the boys that'll dish out lots of it. We've tried reasoning with them before, but you can't talk to animals. They're more ignorant than pigs. Now, I'll only ask this once more. Who burned the viscount's cattle last Thursday night? Don't tell me again that you don't know.'

Outside the closed door, Pollach's two guards were fed up. They felt silly. It was grand when Pollach was delivering his warning to the people as a group – they added to the threatening nature of the speech. But standing like sentries outside an old woman's house was downright ridiculous.

'At ease soldier,' said the guard with the crossbow. 'Let's have a little break while we can. The old girl is hardly going to run amok.'

Laying down his crossbow, he walked over to a nearby cabin and looked in the window. It was dinner time in Micheal Mooney's home. A few dodgy-looking potatoes, some leaves of cabbage, and bits of chopped-up turnip were piled into one large dish on the middle of the floor. Around it sat three children – two boys and a girl. They were soon joined by their mother.

'Oi, soldier, come here. You've got to have a peek at this.'

The guard with the pistol continued his official stance for a few moments before curiosity got the better of him. He joined his colleague at the window. Micheal Mooney had gathered with his family around the dinner dish. He began feeding some cabbage to the family pig. Missus Mooney was trying to keep the dog's snout away from the spuds. Then, the biggest boy shared a piece of steaming turnip with the dog, and gave him a pat on the head. A cock came running in from the other room, but a wave of Micheal's arm soon put a stop to his charge for the bowl.

'Now there's a sight you won't see every day. Imagine inviting that lot to dinner at the great hall.'

'Bloody disgusting, mate,' said the guard with the pistol. 'I wouldn't believe it only I'm seeing it with my own eyes. What's that then?'

'What?'

'*That*,' continued the guard with the pistol, 'in the corner. Is it a coffin?'

'Blimey, I think you're right. They must be having some sort of funeral feast. Hey, maybe it's a kind of peasant ritual, like the stories you hear them talking about in the big house. Funny that.'

'They're always going on about ghost stories above in the big house, and about the curse that's supposed to exist. This is completely different.'

'It's very strange.'

'It's weird is what it is,' replied the guard with the pistol, 'and disgusting. These Catholics and their pagan ways. I can't bear to watch any more. I'll never understand the way they live, not in a million years. Come on, let's go back to our duties, before they open the coffin and start on the corpse.'

Inside the shut cabin door, Missus Ryan didn't break. The anger had risen in her, especially when Pollach was insulting her son and her neighbours who had gone to work in Scotland. But she put her feelings to one side.

'And as for doing just fine – Finbar and his Irish maties – a trusted friend tells me a different story in his letters. They can be seen in their thousands in the filthiest ghettos of Glasgow, down and out from drinking and whoring. Full of the pox, much like the rest of the scum I've had to warn today.'

Pollach took such pleasure in reporting this to Missus Ryan.

'Down and out,' he repeated, 'like O'Connell and his Repeal Movement.'

The tension dissolved from Missus Ryan's face and she broke into a smile. This took Pollach by surprise. He grew even more confused as her eyes brightened and her smile broadened.

'Wipe that silly grin off your puss,' he grunted. 'What has the likes of you to be so happy about anyway?'

'I have a trusted friend too – God the Father in Heaven. And I'm safe in the knowledge that Finbar and his Irish maties – as you call them – have the protection of Jesus and the Blessed Virgin. That's what I have to be so happy about. God help you, Mister Pollach, who is going to protect you – those two young fellas the other side of that door?'

Fifteen – A Day at the Fair

Lord Teale was amazed at how well Shay Gorman could handle the grey pony. His regular stablehands, seasoned horsemen as they were, had trouble with her. But in no time at all, Shay had her munching out of his hand.

'I say, old chap, I think you have a way with animals.'

'What's her name,' asked Shay.

'Quick Silver,' replied Lord Teale.

'Ah, her colour, Your Lordship.'

'Well, yes, in the main. She's a little flyer also. And Quick Grey doesn't have quite the same resonance.'

Normally, Lord Teale would have given the boy anything that he asked for in a heartbeat. But he had been worried about lending his pony to Shay. Quick Silver was a temperamental little filly when she wanted to be – which was nearly all the time. But with Shay she seemed different – very much at ease in his company.

'She didn't mind being saddled up this morning. She goes berserk as soon as any of the coachmen attempt to fit the harness,' said Lord Teale.

'They're fitting the breeching straps too tight,' answered Shay. 'No wonder the poor little girl doesn't like it. The traces are too tight as well. There should be a four-inch gap – the width of a man's fist – between the straps and her skin. Otherwise, the shafts will be rubbing and uncomfortable.'

'I say you have the gift, old chap.'

'More like common sense, Your Lordship. You don't mind me taking her out tomorrow?'

'It must be a special occasion,' quipped Lord Teale, stroking the filly's mane. 'You've been requesting herself since last week. One might assume you are trying to make an impression.'

Ever since Shay had asked to take Quick Silver out, there had been nothing but probes and jibes from his lordship. But that's the way it was between them. They saw each other every day. They worked together and they ate together. Since that fateful day when Shay had saved his son from drowning, Lord Teale had really looked out for the boy. He had a plan for him too. Because Shay was such a good scholar and animal-lover, Lord Teale intended to pay for him to be educated as a veterinary surgeon – Shay's dream job.

But Lord Teale was no fool. He knew Shay was not just taking Quick Silver to the fair in Longford Town for the fun of it. It was all in aid of a young lady, a former member of the lordship's clachan.

Constance Ryan felt uncomfortable as she waited in her summer dress and sandals. All eyes were on her and she hated the attention. She was playing down her imminent trip as *just a bit of a ramble in the countryside* to any of the workmates who winked suggestively or pushed a little comment her way. She had a beautiful new hairband in her pocket, but decided against putting it on until she was well away from Cranley House. It was only Constance's second whole day off from work since she had started over a year earlier. She had given a full month's notice. She could hardly wait until they would be heading for the gates of the great avenue, away from prying eyes. She still didn't know where Shay was taking her. He said it was a surprise.

There was a sudden clattering of hooves outside. It was Shay and Quick Silver. Constance thought her cheeks were on fire as she inched towards the front door. She felt the whole house was watching. The girls were smiling and waving, and some wished her luck as she passed. Sheila McAndrew popped her head around a corner to see what all the commotion was about.

'Remember, curfew is ten o'clock,' she shouted down the corridor, as Constance disappeared out of sight.

Helping her into the trap, Shay could feel her hand trembling.

'What's wrong, darling,' he asked, 'I thought you'd be excited.'

'I am,' she replied, 'but I'm not used to so much attention. I would have much preferred if you had stalled the pony at the gates, as we agreed, away from all the nosey-parkers.'

'By that you mean the McAndrew one?'

'Yes, Miss McAndrew, among others.'

'Inter alios,' said Shay.

'What?'

'Miss McAndrew, inter alios. It's Latin for among others. You haven't forgotten what you learned from Master Hogan already, have you?'

'Well, it's obvious that you haven't. *Latin?* You were the one that was good at Latin, not me.'

Shay stiffened the reins on Quick Silver and she halted.

'Why are we stopping, Shay?'

'I may have been good at the Latin, but you were good at everything else – maths, English, bealoidis ...'

He leaned across and gave her a kiss.

'...smooching,' he continued.

Constance was highly embarrassed at being kissed so boldly in public. He leaned in for another, but she recoiled and said they had better be on their way.

'Now you listen to me, Constance Ryan. I'm taking you to Longford Town to visit the new cathedral, attend the fair, have a picnic, and stop off in Lacken on our way home. I've gone to great lengths to get my hands on this pony and cart, and it's your first day off in ages. I don't want to hear any more about Sheila McAndrew or the giddy chambermaids at Cranley House. I don't want you feeling embarrassed either. We're going to enjoy ourselves and have a bit of fun in our lives. Is that understood?'

Constance nodded. Then Shay gave her a long tender kiss and she cuddled tightly into his arms.

Saint Mel's Cathedral looked immaculate. It had been finished since 1840, but this was the first time they had visited it. Shay said it was worth the five-year wait. It took Constance's breath away and dispelled the black mood that had set in since passing the workhouse in Shroid. They both knew people in that workhouse. The sight of it dampened what was otherwise a thrilling eight-mile jaunt. Quick Silver was as strong as a plough horse and a joy to handle. Shay fed her apples to keep her in good humour.

The entrance to the cathedral was an awesome spectacle of six giant pillars fixed on a base of ten steps.

'Just like Cranley House,' observed Shay.

'Cranley House,' exclaimed Constance.

'You know like – pillars and steps.'

A white marble depiction of the Last Supper looked down from a carving above the giant oak doors. A green dome shone from the top of the tower, just below the steeple's cross. Three saints looked out over the landscape. Under the dome was a bell, partly visible through four concrete panels. Constance looked down at her feet. After five whole years of being walked on, the paving stones still appeared new.

'Come on, let's go in and have a peep,' said Shay.

Even the front porch was adorned in splendour.

'It's not the *front porch*, it's called a narthex,' explained Constance.

'Oh, excuse me,' said Shay, 'I must have been milking cows the day Master Hogan taught us that.'

They went through to the nave aisle. The altarpiece was stunning.

'It's in the baroque style,' Constance gasped, overawed by its magnificence.

'It's like a palace,' said Shay.

There was a beautiful choir area at the edge of the altar. The side aisles were lined with rows of saints, their names illuminated in gold lettering beneath their feet.

'They're called transepts, not side aisles,' joked Constance.

Shay had had enough of her showboating.

'Aren't you the regular little Isaac Newton,' he said.

'What do you mean?'

'A real brain box – and a showy off one at that.'

'Why are brains always associated with men? Why couldn't I be a regular little Mary Shelley? Now there was a true brain box.'

They went back out into the daylight.

'Well, what do you make of it all,' asked Shay.

Constance used to think there was nothing to rival Saint Mary's in Mostrim, with its beautiful stained-glass windows and Canon Reidy's spectacular chalice. But this was something else entirely. It was breathtakingly beautiful.

'It's out of this world,' she gushed. 'How on earth could they afford to build such a place?'

Shay smiled to himself. He could have told her in a heartbeat – the pennies of the great unwashed. But he was determined that nothing was going to spoil this day. Instead, he shook his head in fake disbelief.

'I don't know. But I do know that when it comes to elegance, the Catholic Church really does leave the rest of them in the haypenny place.'

Longford Town was charged with excitement – colour and noise everywhere. There was a man playing pipes on the market square. Every time his cheeks inflated, the pipes erupted in a deafening cacophony which sounded like a molly-cat on a summer's night. Constance had never been to a fair in the county town before. Mostrim fairs were boring, centred around agricultural buying and selling. Here, there were jugglers and singers and other entertainers. Something was happening every few paces. An old man in a straw hat captivated an audience with his three-card-trick routine.

'Can you find the lady,' he asked, as he caught someone's eye.

Shay stood for a moment, looking into a large pen. Its chain was attached to a hook in the wall of the Market Inn on Ballymahon Street. Farmers haggled and deals were done with a spit and a handshake. Labourers handled livestock and fowl. Some were collecting the money when a bargain was struck. Shay noticed their shabby clothes and their hungry eyes. They were enjoying the feel of money for the first time since the last fair day. Even though it wasn't *their* money, you could tell that they loved having it in their hands. Constance tugged at his jersey.

'Come on,' she urged, having her fill of farmers and their pigs and cattle.

Strolling down the town, they met a woman selling alcohol, tobacco and confectionary. Shay bought a bottle of whiskey and a brown bag of chocolate sweets for Constance, who couldn't hide her concern.

'The whiskey's not for me, it's a present for my father,' he assured her, then had a little smile to himself.

After that, Shay bought two linen headscarves – one for his mother and the other for Missus Ryan. Constance asked why he hadn't bought them from the stalls in the Main Street. Instead, Shay had deliberately sought out an old lady in Harbour Row. She wrapped the headscarves in light paper and invoked God's blessings on him and the rest of us. Her bony face made her eyes seem huge.

'Her goods are so expensive,' said Constance, 'you could have purchased them for half that price in the stalls.'

'Very true,' conceded Shay, 'but there's a lot of imported stuff in those stalls. My grandfather used to buy clothes from that lady on fair days, way back when she did a roaring trade. He used to say that Longford linen is so much kinder to a woman's skin.'

Down a lane approaching Camlin Bridge, there was a huddle of shifty-looking fellows. Shay knew straight away that this was a betting ring. No money was on show, but a well-dressed man, sitting to one side, was busy writing in a notebook. He tore out small pieces of paper, which he handed to those around him. Inside the huddle, two cocks squared up for a fight. There was cheering and squawking, as feathers began to fly in all directions. When the squawking had died down, some in the huddle made a beeline for the well-dressed man, to shake his hand in congratulations. Others swore and flung away their pieces of paper. The well-dressed man preceded every handshake with a quick dip in his overcoat pocket.

A little further down the same laneway, Shay was surprised to encounter Jabber Farrell. There were lots of men around him too, and Jabber was issuing instructions to an intense-looking, barechested, youth. As Jabber talked, someone else rubbed the youth's shoulders with a towel.

'That fella will catch his death of cold,' said Constance, 'going about like that. I know it's summer, but it's not that mild today.'

'A rogue day, as the old people would call it,' quipped Shay.

It was clear to Shay what was happening here also, but not to Constance. These were the final preparations for battle and this youth was obviously one of Jabber's boxers.

'How are you neighbour,' shouted Shay.

Jabber looked around hurriedly. He nodded reluctantly in Shay's direction. Then some of the men, who had been focused on Jabber, looked around. They seemed nervous and not at all pleased with Shay's interruption.

The towel was taken from around the youth's shoulders. A green sash was tied at his waist. He looked menacing. There was a scar at the top of his right arm – just below the shoulder. On closer inspection, it looked more like the letters XL than a scar.

Jabber sought out Shay again and beckoned him over.

'No place for your young lady – in case the peelers show up. You know what I'm saying?'

'Loud and clear,' answered Shay.

He led Constance away and watched from a distance. Jabber returned to barking out instructions at the youth in the green sash.

Another bare-chested fighter appeared and the men formed a ring. He was wearing an orange sash and he was very confident, judging by what he had to say about the upcoming bout. An old guy in a beaver hat brought the two sash-wearing youngsters to the centre of the man-made ring and issued some rules. As they shook hands, the men got excited, shouting out things like *don't let the squire down*, and *do it for the Mary's*, and *you're not wearing the orange for nothing*.

It didn't matter to Jabber Farrell what they shouted. He had done his talking. While the men forming the ring waved their fists and roared, Jabber looked on pensively. He used to be that youth in the green sash – the undefeated champion from Saint Mary's, Mostrim. Since returning from Maynooth seminary, he had won a hundred battles – most of them against scrappers from other parishes or, as in this case, other churches. In all his time as a street brawler, Jabber had never tasted defeat. It's how he came by the pet name. It's also how he came to be revered by every bare-knuckled boxer who ever plied his trade on fair days or foul, regardless of station or creed. Jabber was a god in their eyes.

There was a splattering of blood and a loud cheer. The old guy with the beaver hat was talking down at one of the fighters, who lay prostrate in the dusty circle. He was telling him to get up and then asking him if he had had enough. Eventually the old guy bent down, unknotted the sash, and handed it to the youth with the XL on his arm. He held the orange sash aloft in victory, before walking across and presenting it to Jabber. There was more swearing and giving out. The ring broke up and some of the men stamped their pieces of paper into the ground, while others made straight for the well-dressed man with the note book, for more shaking hands and congratulating.

The gloaming was upon them as they returned to Cranley House. Quick Silver trotted up the great avenue, a red sky at her back. Shay's heart beat faster as they approached the big house. Constance was weary and napped on his shoulder. She jolted as Shay brought Quick Silver to a halt.

'Well, did you enjoy yourself,' he asked, as she rubbed her eyes.

It had been the best day ever for Constance, even better than Lord Teale's old Lough Owel summer parties. The highlight had come on the way home, when they stopped to visit her grandmother's and our house. Constance hadn't been back to Lacken in over a year and nostalgia ate away at her as she looked around the clachan.

She answered by way of a kiss, before Shay collected her up in his arms and carried her the rest of the way to Cranley House. For him, the day had been magical – and yet the best part had still to come. He took her around to the servants' entrance. Suddenly,

Constance got spooked as she remembered Sheila McAndrew's parting words.

'What about this new law,' she exclaimed. 'We've already exceeded the curfew. You must go now. It's not safe at this time of night.'

He stood her on the ground, before tossing his head back in laughter.

'What peeler is going to stop a pony and trap belonging to Lord Teale, no matter what time of night it is. Don't worry, my love, I'm lawfully untouchable.'

Walter Pollach was replacing the sods of grass after securing the cellar's double doors. He was going to relax, a bottle of red wine – courtesy of Viscount de Bromley – tucked under his oxter. Suddenly he heard laughter. He barely had time to hide in a thick hedgerow at the entrance to the forest. He looked through a gap and saw Constance and Shay, holding hands and walking slowly past.

'Before you go in, I have one more surprise for you,' said Shay, his voice croaking with nervousness.

He took out a beautifully embroidered handkerchief. It had been given to him by his parents, on the occasion of his Confirmation. It was white, with a majestic Celtic cross intricately designed in green and red stitching.

'Constance, I'd like to marry you. Will you be my wife?'

Constance was shocked. She didn't know what to say. It took a while for her to respond.

'Yes. Yes, I will,' she said excitedly, and kissed him tenderly. 'But what about this place and …'

He stopped her in mid-sentence.

'Don't you worry your pretty little head about this place,' Shay replied. 'I'll see to everything. Lord Teale has given me a plot in the clachan, and my cabin is almost finished. When that's done, I'll take you out of here for good.'

Constance was overjoyed. They embraced passionately again. There was a sudden rustling in the hedgerow behind where they stood. It gave Constance a start. She went to look behind her, but Shay was having none of it. He pulled her head forward and continued to kiss her longingly.

'I almost forgot,' he said. 'I don't have your ring yet. In the meantime, take this handkerchief as a token of my faithful love.'

'I will treasure it more than anything in the whole world. Now you must go before it gets any later,' replied Constance, tiptoeing her way to the entrance leading to the stairs of the servants' quarters.

Sixteen – Turk and the Queen's Shilling

The queues on Friday evenings were long. That was payday at Cranley House. The faces were long also. Everyone had to wait until Walter Pollach and his bookkeeper were ready. They talked excitedly around us. They marvelled at the smell of the hallway.

I didn't share their excitement or their wonder. I couldn't. In fact, I hated the feel of the house. If the exterior looked daunting, then the interior felt even more intimidating. Most of all, I hated the look of the other workers. They were haggard and weary. Their faces showed their pain. I pitied them – their tattered clothes and their unmade hair. If Pollach had told them to wait in line for three days they would have done so willingly. When I thought about it some more, I began to feel guilty. I was ashamed of myself for pitying my own.

The first day Turk queued up to collect wages was an eye-opener. He too was blown away by the splendour, the moment he walked through the door.

'You get used to it,' I said. 'It's only a house.'

Sugrue and Jabber were with us, waiting patiently for their names to be called from the counting room.

'Close your mouth,' Sugrue told Turk, 'and you'll catch no flies.'

'I thought you'd be used to a place like this,' added Jabber, 'you coming from royalty and all that.'

We were waiting for Turk to respond – he had an answer for just about everything – when a clerk came out of the counting room towards us. Sugrue put a finger to his lips and Turk went quiet. The clerk read names off a sheet and the queue pressed on.

'Nearly there now,' I remarked, as we inched our way towards the jingle of money.

'Nearly there, my arse,' snapped Turk, 'what about that line over there?'

'What line,' asked Sugrue, looking around.

'Ara, those bucks there,' replied Turk, pointing to the opposite side of the room.

'That's not a line,' explained Jabber, 'that's us, Turk. It's our reflection. That's a mirror, you eejit.'

Turk didn't realise he had been looking into the giant gilt-framed mirror that hung in the hallway of Cranley House.

'Look,' said Sugrue, 'raise your hand. That's you Turk – and that's me; there's Jabber and Jim.'

'I knew that,' said Turk, his lugs going red, 'I was just getting a rise out of ye.'

Jabber gave me a nudge in the ribs, but nobody said another word.

We eventually made it to the counting room. It was always a lively place. A large wooden desk – with its shiny brass inkwell – dominated everyone's interest. The clerk sat to the right side, the bookkeeper in the middle. They didn't even look up at the workers as they filed past. The clerk simply counted coins quickly and methodically and, as he swept them aside, the bookkeeper dipped his quill in the inkwell and doled out the words: *sign or place your mark here.* There were two women in the background, dipping into a money bag. They were responsible for keeping sufficient coinage on the table at all times. The procedure was fast and efficient.

The standard rate of pay was four pence per day for those of us employed by the Public Works Board – twenty pence per week.

Keeping his mind on his work, the clerk separated five fourpenny bits – or joeys, as we called them. They made quite a din as they clattered together. The workers collected their wages in turn. A quill was dipped in ink and handed to them. They signed or made an X. Then we all moved on. Nobody said much in the counting room. We didn't have to – the procedure was simplicity in motion. Besides, money is a serious business to rich and poor alike – too serious for the intervention of small talk.

Walter Pollach oversaw everything from the chaise-lounge in the corner, his hand propping his chin. He sat cross-legged in his riding breeches, his top hat resting on the table before him. The weekly ritual was in full swing. It was being carried out by an older man sitting opposite Pollach, a British union-flag at his back. The weekly ritual brought a sickness to the pit of Sugrue's stomach, especially when Pollach would catch his eye and smirk deliberately. For an extra two shillings on top of one's weekly wage, any worker who wished could take an oath of allegiance to Her Majesty Queen Victoria. Those who decided to avail, knelt before the Union Jack and placed their right hand on a Bible. Then they recited the oath, repeating the old man's words in front of the whole room.

Every week I had to steel myself against the sight of Irish men and women debasing themselves for the extra two shillings. I may not have agreed with it, but I understood why they did it. There were hungry mouths at home and a rotten ridge of potatoes wasn't going to feed them. They were only words – empty words – if you really wanted them to be. But Sugrue could never see it that way. Every time he went into the counting room, the weekly ritual cut him to the bone. He was no good at hiding his feelings the way I could. And worse still, Pollach knew it. He knew it because he could see the rage burning in the Sugrue's eyes.

It was Turk's turn at the counting desk. The money was flung out, counted and swept aside by the clerk. The bookkeeper's quill was offered. But Turk didn't move. And the money didn't move. And the fingertips suspending the quill in mid-air didn't move. Slowly, the clerk's hand hovered over on the coins a second time and he was forced to look up.

'What's wrong, Pat,' growled the clerk.

'Ah nix, my money's wrong,' replied Turk.

'What do you mean?'

'That's only fifteen pence – you're five short.'

The clerk's cheeks turned crimson.

'It's not wrong, Pat, now take it and get out of my sight.'

The bookkeeper rested the quill in the inkwell and had a look at the coins.

'You're an ignorant cunt,' the bookkeeper said to Turk.

'Not my mistake. Five thruppennies is fifteen pence, all day long,' protested Turk.

The bookkeeper held up one of the coins.

'This is a fourpenny bit, you dirty ignorant cunt. Five fours are twenty – *all day long*.'

Turk took one of the coins in his hand. He was convinced it was a threepenny piece. It was the same size as the threepenny piece. It had the same depiction of Brittania on its face. But, on closer examination, it had a milled edge that was a good bit thicker than the threepenny piece. He had never seen the coin before, at least not west of the Shannon. Turk was embarrassed as he gathered up his wages.

Once again, the bookkeeper was holding his quill aloft.

'Now sign or make your mark, Pat, you dirty, ignorant, Irish cunt.'

There was no need for a mark as far as we were concerned. We hurriedly signed our names. It was time to get out of the counting room as quickly as possible. I was relieved to set foot back in the hallway.

'Thank God for the oath of allegiance,' Jabber muttered, as we waited on the others.

Thank God again. It was our only saving grace. Pollach was busy with the weekly ritual. Only for this, Turk may not have got out of the counting room quite so easily.

'That was a close call. What did Sugrue tell you, Turk, in the heel of the hunt? What was the last thing he said before we went in to collect our money?'

'Ara, I know, I forgot.'

Jabber looked at him and shook his head.

'Forgot?'

'I thought I was being short-changed, Jabber. There's no point trying to argue with those bucks in the Irish language.'

Sugrue was shutting the door into the hallway when he heard the word *stop*. The clerk came out and told him that Mister Pollach wanted a word. When Sugrue went back in, Pollach was standing by the Union flag, a Bible in his hands.

'Mister Sugrue, do you know what this is,' asked Pollach abruptly.

'It's a Bible.'

'It's a Bible what?'

Sugrue did not want to show any sort of respect to Pollach. He didn't think it was deserved. He always maintained respect should be earned. But he had his job and, more importantly, Ella May and Padraig to think about.

'It's a Bible, sir.'

'That's better. Yes, it is a Bible, Mister Sugrue. It's God's good book – but I wouldn't expect you Catholic heathens to know much about that. Let me tell you something about the Bible, Mister

Sugrue. Sometimes the Bible is used to swear oaths, and sometimes the Bible is used to weed out liars. Would you consider yourself a liar, Mister Sugrue?'

'No, I would not,' answered Sugrue, 'I don't tell lies.'

'Och, but I beg to differ, Mister Sugrue. I could have sworn – on this here Bible – you told me, to my very face, that the wee laddie – what's his name, Turk – spoke Irish. Therefore, would it not be reasonable for me to assume that he has no knowledge of Her Majesty's eloquent mother-tongue? Well now, Mister Sugrue, I do believe you were telling me lies.'

'I told you he speaks Irish – which he does. I didn't say he couldn't speak English.'

'Oh now, Mister Sugrue, I think you'll agree that you may have misled me.'

'I'm not responsible for what you think.'

This final remark did not sit well with Pollach. It riled him into action.

'Don't get snotty with me, old man. I don't like your tone or your attitude. So, I've decided, as of now, you are sacked and evicted. I am a fair man, however, and I would be willing to return you to your employment, and your home, provided you kneel down here before the Union flag, place your right hand on the Bible, and swear an oath of allegiance to Her Majesty of Great Britain and Ireland.'

Sugrue was caught and there was only one way out. Ella May and Padraig came back to his mind. It was their home too. He knew what he must do – what Ella May would want and expect him to do. He walked over and took the Bible from Walter Pollach's pudgy hands. As he knelt down to face the old man and the flag, the clerk grinned at Pollach – who was revelling in such a sight. Sugrue put the Bible on the chaise-lounge and placed a big, blistered, right hand over it. Then he started to speak.

'I'm not a religious man but I do have respect for God's good book. I saw it misused already today, and I have no desire to insult it further.'

Then Sugrue arose and faced Pollach defiantly.

'So, you're not going to acknowledge Her Majesty's rule over you,' said Pollach. 'Consider yourself sacked and evicted. Now get off this estate before I have you thrown off.'

'Your Queen has no legitimate power over *me*. I will gladly lie under the stars and starve before I acknowledge her claim to rule my country.'

Seventeen – Court Case 1: Shay

It was pandemonium in Cranley estate. All sorts of stories were doing the rounds. The cellar at the back of the big house had been breached in the dead of night. Several bottles of red wine, among other things, were missing. Sugrue was the chief suspect. He and his family had just been evicted from their home and this was his revenge mission. That was what most people thought. So, when news came through that the peelers had lifted Shay Gorman – as he worked on his new cabin – and placed him in Longford jailhouse to await trial, nobody could quite believe their ears.

Constance was in a state of shock. She was so disturbed; she had to be escorted to her room for a lie down. She cried so much that she could barely see. When she reached for the beautiful handkerchief that Shay had given her, she got another fright – it wasn't on her dresser table. She searched the place high up and low down, but it was nowhere to be found. Eventually, she gave up and sat on the side of the bed, clutching her shoulders and rocking herself back and forth.

The trial was set for the following day and was part of the Longford assizes under government surveillance. Lord Teale's carriage called around at the clachan and picked up myself and my wife. Mairead looked as if leeches had just sucked every drop of blood from her face. Lady Teale seemed equalled distressed, with his lordship patting her hand and issuing words of encouragement. We rumbled on towards Longford Town where Sugrue awaited our arrival at the front of the courthouse.

'What are *you* doing here?' I remember asking, delighted to see him.

'Now that I'm a man of leisure I have to pass my time at something,' he replied. 'Let's get this over with and get your young man back home where he belongs.'

'Lord Teale has instructed his barrister, Mister Thornton, to act on Shay's behalf,' I said, and nodded my appreciation once more at Lord and Lady Lacken.

Sugrue was relieved to hear this. He knew, from previous experiences, that these trials were a lost cause if the defendant did not have the proper defences. As we walked into the court gallery, dozens of people were gathering in the side portals. The police were arriving with those about to face their charges, and a beggar woman with a baby in her arms was warned by a well-to-do gentleman with a cane to refrain from entering Her Majesty's courthouse.

When they brought Shay into the courtroom, he was flanked by peelers with batons drawn. Mairead began to sob. Nobody had been allowed any contact with him in the short time since his arrest. We all stood up as the magistrate walked into the room. There was a British union-flag directly behind the magistrate's seat. I could tell that Sugrue wasn't impressed. The court clerk came out – a little, fat, middle-aged fellow with knee breeches and buckles on his shoes. He unfurled a scroll and read in a loud clear voice: *we will now hear evidence in the matter of Her Majesty versus Seamus Gorman.* He couldn't say the word *Seamus* properly – he left out the *h* sound after the first *s*. The magistrate was a swift-talking, no-nonsense type of man. He wore a white curly wig and, to cut the tension, Sugrue whispered that he was thinking of copying his style.

The first thing Mister Thornton did was call Peter Hogan to the stand. He fired questions at the schoolmaster with regard to Shay's character and dismissed him. After that, Father Murtagh took the stand and swore his oath. He also gave Shay an excellent reference, during which he said the boy would never harm or hurt another or their property, and that these proceedings had been all one big mistake as far as he was concerned.

'I'll be the judge of that,' said the magistrate, who was in an obvious hurry to move matters along.

Mister Thornton made a good defence, summing up by underlining that there was no actual evidence connecting Shay Gorman to the scene of the crime. Then the magistrate called on the barrister for the Crown.

Counsel for the plaintiff was Mister Blythe – a thin, careful-looking man with long bushy sideburns. When introduced by the magistrate, he shot out of his slumber and into action. His questions were fast and to the point. He never mentioned Constance, even when Shay answered that he was seeing her at Cranley House. As he neared the end of his interrogation, he approached the bench and placed upon it a white handkerchief with a red and green embroidered Celtic cross design.

'This, Your Honour, was found on the cellar floor. It was obviously left behind by the thief, as it was not on the premises when the estate manager checked the cellar earlier on the night in question. I believe this to be property of the defendant.'

The magistrate took up the handkerchief and inspected it. He twirled it about, before shaking it loose. When Shay saw the hanky, he got angry.

'What are you doing with that,' he roared up at the bench, 'that doesn't belong to you.'

The magistrate gave the gavel a couple of wallops off the bench and warned that there would be order in his court.

'Obviously,' replied Mister Blythe, 'do tell, young man, who really owns it?'

'That's my hanky. I gave it to Constance – the girl I was telling you about, who lives and works in Cranley House – the night I asked her to marry me,' roared Shay.

'Well, this is fantastic in the extreme,' continued Mister Blythe, 'for in a police interview yesterday morning, the manager of Cranley estate – a Mister Walter Pollach – denied ever seeing Mister Gorman on the grounds, or that there was even a girl of that name working at the house.'

At this, the gallery became unruly. The magistrate almost banged a hole in his bench while trying to maintain order, only this time followed up with a warning that he would give a month to anyone who contaminated his court.

'That's a lie,' shouted Shay. 'Constance does work there. And anyway, how would Pollach have seen me – I used to meet her there at night.'

Mister Blythe smiled as he looked down towards Mister Thornton and then back at the bench.

'The boy admits to meeting a girl at night. Well, this is indeed a new development, Your Honour. Mister Thornton has gone to great pains to have these character witnesses – the priest and the schoolteacher – present. Indeed, they painted a pretty picture of the accused. And now, in your esteemed presence, the boy freely admits to trespassing on private property while breaking the curfew as set out in Sir Robert Peel's Coercion Bill, which alone carries a maximum penalty of fifteen years transportation.'

Silence descended on the courtroom. Mister Blythe folded a sheet of paper and sat down. The magistrate fixed his glasses, pushing them further up towards the bridge of his nose. There was a slight delay. Then everyone stood to greet the verdict.

'In light of the case that counsel for the Crown has furnished before this court, I am left with little choice. Seamus Gorman, I find you guilty as charged and sentence you to twenty years penal servitude in Van Diemen's Land. Take him down.'

Mairead wailed in the courtroom gallery, then collapsed to the ground before Sugrue could get to her. I was dumbstruck in my seat, unaware of my wife's distress. Nor was I aware of the inconsolable Lady Teale across from me. All I remember at that moment was a gnawing in my stomach, as if someone was pulling out my guts.

The Freeman's Journal attacked a judicial system that could destroy a young man's life – a boy's life – on the circumstantial evidence of a handkerchief. It called for change and questioned the sentence, pointing out that Shay could have been imprisoned in Dublin or Wales or London, and not a world away – where the boy had little hope of making it back to his loved ones ever again.

Shay Gorman, my only son, was put on board the *HMS Success* for transportation to Tasmania on August 15 – the feast of the Assumption of Our Lady – in 1845. Before he was banished, myself and Lord Teale got to see him one last time. We followed the prisoners' wagon the whole way to Galway Bay, where the ship was moored and ready to depart for the holding cells on Spike Island. Mairead remained at home. She hadn't the strength for it. Shay asked Lord Teale if Mister Sugrue and his family could keep his new cabin warm until his return. Lord Teale just nodded, unable to say a word, as the tears streamed down his face. Shay made me promise to look after his mother and sister. He also made me promise not to despair, and instead to look forward to the happy day when we would all meet again. He took off the gold chain, with its medal to Saint Anthony, that Lady Jane Teale had given him for saving her son. Calmly, he asked me to make sure Constance received it.

'It will protect her. Tell her not to ramble too far, as I will be marrying her on my return to Mostrim.'

As they led him away in manacles, Lord Teale finally broke his silence.

'Faber est quisance fortunae suae,' he shouted.

Shay turned in our direction and made a fist. Then he bent down and grasped a handful of cool grass, before disappearing into the hull with the other prisoners.

Myself and Lord Teale stood and watched the ship leave.

'What was that you said,' I asked him.

'Just a reminder,' answered Lord Teale, 'of something very important.'

We looked on until there was nothing left on the horizon.

'So that's the definition of justice these days,' lamented Lord Teale, as we returned to his dogcart, 'fill a ship full of young Irishmen, call them convicts, and send them to the other side of the world.'

'That's about the height of it,' I added, 'well, British justice at any rate.'

In Cranley House, Constance Ryan went into the study and stared at the large map of the British Empire. Then she traced a line with her finger – starting at Hobart and finishing in the centre of Ireland.

Eighteen – The Triumphant Return of the Viscount

The girls had been running around all morning, making final preparations for the big homecoming. Sheila McAndrew adopted an all-hands-on-deck approach, which meant the kitchen staff was now doubling up as cleaners and window washers. She even pitched in herself, taking a rug outside and beating the dust out of it.

'Isn't it really exciting,' another girl said to Constance. 'I've never met the viscount, but I hear he's charming.'

She leaned into Constance and winked, before saying: *and good-looking as well.*

Constance felt only numbness. Since Shay had been sent away, all she was interested in doing was burying herself in work. It distracted her mind. She didn't sleep much and longed for the business of the day. She didn't smile like she used to and nothing excited her – especially the arrival of some man she didn't know, and really didn't want to know.

Constance was making a bed in a spare room when Sheila McAndrew grabbed her by the back of the neck.

'You listen to me now, young madam. You've been moping around here, feeling sorry for yourself, for the past three weeks. I don't want to see a long face when the master arrives, or I'll give you something to be sorry for.'

Constance looked blankly into Sheila's eyes and maintained her silence. It was enough to shut McAndrew up. It wasn't a look of hate or a look of fear. It was just a hallow look of nothingness.

Cranley House had been adorned for the occasion. Outside, the avenue looked splendid. There were pots of red roses from the entrance gates right up the great avenue. The garden staff had the lawns looking magnificent. The grass was neat and trees and bushes were pruned. The house was freshly painted – inside and out. A large picture of the viscount on horseback hung at the entrance to the great hall, dominating the view as one walked through the large red doors.

The staff was all outside to greet the procession of carriages. Private workers and Public Works Board employees were lined up behind the flower pots. Kitchen and house staff held a guard of honour, starting at the granite lions. As everybody waited with bated breath, the viscount's management team talked in pockets among themselves, away from the hired help.

Two trumpeters, who had been deployed to the head of the avenue, suddenly burst into life, almost deafening the workers nearby. The cavalcade was in sight. The management had one last inspection – getting men to stand straight and adjusting pinafores on girls – as the carriages trundled into the avenue.

There was no sign of the viscount to begin with. While horses trotted past, the insides of carriages were scanned. The viscountess travelled in one of these, but no Viscount de Bromley was to be had. Suddenly, an open-top carriage approached and there appeared a big man dressed like a king. The viscount wore a long red and white cloak, joined in the centre by a silver chain. His hair was brown – straight, long, and tied in a tail at the back. The crowd went wild with delight and cheered him up the driveway.

Myself and Jabber Farrell were standing in the crowd. We weren't cheering and weren't going wild with delight. We were only standing there because we were told to by the manager of the Public Works' scheme.

The viscount stopped waving and started to gesture at the crowd. As he got closer, we realised he wasn't gesturing at all, but throwing money. As the coins landed, the guard of honour buckled. Workers sprang for the money, fighting each other off in the scramble. Then he passed by us and I got a better look at his face. I remembered seeing the viscount once before – about twenty years earlier. A picture of him had formed in my mind, based upon what I could recall from then. But his face looked nothing like that picture now. He was more handsome and stockier.

'Father Christmas, as the Brits would call him, has come early,' Jabber said quietly.

'He's dressed for the part,' I replied.

Then, a threepenny piece – almost a full day's wages – landed between us. Myself and Jabber looked down. We didn't move an inch. There was a rush from the side and two men fell, wrestling in the muck. Then one of them emerged, smiling with the coin. Neither myself nor Jabber said a word to him. The look on his face said it all. It was disgusting to see Irish people behaving in such a manner. It sickened me even more to think that some of these were our friends and neighbours. They should not have been debasing themselves in such a manner. Moreover, they should not have been debased by the viscount – an educated pillar of society who should have known better.

The viscountess was the first dignitary to reach the front entrance of Cranley House. There waiting for her was Walter Pollach. He helped her dismount. The door of her carriage opened a second time and Pollach was forced to call on one of the servants to act as a makeshift footman. But the door hadn't opened by accident. There was someone else in the carriage – a young gentleman – and he wasn't about to dismount on his own steam. He was helped out of the carriage by hand, just as the viscountess had been. Behind all his finery and mannerisms, I recognised the face immediately.

'Would you look who it is, Jabber.'

He was straining to see.

'Who? The peacock on the steps? How should I know?'

'Come over here, quick,' I said, and Jabber moved to a better vantage point.

'Merciful hour, it can't be,' he said, his face puzzled. 'It's not Burke, is it?'

'Spot on, Jabber. Young Burke from Lisanore, the one and only.'

'Would you look at the get up of him,' said Jabber, 'the scut left Mostrim without an arse in his trousers.'

Pollach didn't know what to make of this overdressed male-floozy travelling with the viscountess, especially when she introduced him as *my husband's right-hand man*. He didn't like that description at all. As far as Walter was concerned, he was de Bromley's right-hand man. He had never even heard of a Shaun Burke before. And now, here was the good lady of the house labelling him as the master's *right-hand man*. This would not do. Walter owed it to himself to take back that title, which was rightfully his in the first place.

Eventually, the viscount's open-top carriage reached the forecourt of the big house. He was obviously glad to see Pollach because, after dismounting, he threw his arms around his loyal servant. This made Walter feel much better. It put his mind at ease, at least for the time being. The travelling party proceeded up the steps and towards the big red doors. The male servants smiled and bowed as they passed. The kitchen maids curtsied. Constance curtsied too. But in her attempt to blend into the background, she stood out all the more. She was truly miserable. Shaun Burke noticed as he passed her by.

'If you look like that now, I can only guess how beautiful you'd be if you smiled,' he said, then took her hand and kissed it.

Sheila McAndrew glowered in Constance's direction. She bowed to the gentleman and snapped her hand back.

'But I do aim to find out,' he concluded, then disappeared through the red doors with the rest of the arrivals.

Walter Pollach could smell the fresh paint as he waited in the viscount's office. It was the only room in the big house he had never been in before. It was always kept locked while the viscount attended his affairs in England. It had only been done-up a few days earlier in honour of the master. Walter expected the worst. Why else would the viscount have summoned him within an hour of his return. With this Shaun Burke around, Walter felt surplus to requirements.

Viscount de Bromley came in with a ledger and sat at his new desk. It was several minutes before he lifted his head in Walter's direction.

'My advisors tell me the last time I was here we had thirty smallholders.'

'That's correct, my lord,' answered Pollach.

'And now we're down to twenty-eight, is that so, Mister Pollach?'

'Yes, my lord. The Skeltons, you know about. And then, just last month, I had to evict the Sugrues as well.'

'Tut, tut, tut. Mister Pollach, what's the meaning of this?'

Drops of perspiration appeared on Walter's forehead.

'My lord, I felt I had no choice. The safety of Cranley House was at stake. I was backed into a corner. I felt it necessary to exercise the power you vested in me to act without your consent in times of danger to the wellbeing and preservation of the estate.'

'What a mouthful! Alas, I fear you've consumed a dictionary while I was away, Mister Pollach? *Vested*, now there's a word. I like it. It isn't every day you get to hear a word like vested, wouldn't you agree?'

The viscount thought that amusing and afforded himself a little chuckle. Walter stood in front of him, fearing the end was near.

'And what was this trouble I heard about – some young scallywag on the estate, making speeches and inciting my tenants?'

'I dealt with him, my lord. I only used the necessary force I felt the situation demanded. It was vital to the law and order of the estate.'

'And the other trouble,' continued the viscount.

'*Other trouble,* my lord?'

'My cellar.'

'Och yes. That matter has been cleared up in its entirety and the culprit, at this very moment, is sailing to a prison in the colonies.'

'Is he indeed. Well, it seems there has been quite an amount of strife going on in my absence. My smallholders are disappearing slowly. I'm wondering are you the right man for the job at all, Mister Pollach?'

'My lord, please don't sack me. I'll do anything. I'll be more lenient. I'll get more tenants in. I'll divide up the land and double your smallholdings. Only please, don't sack me, sir. I've served you loyally for all my puff.'

'Divide up the land? Double my smallholdings? Sack you? Have you gone raving mad? I'll tell you what you should do – and by whatever means possible. Tear down those stone walls. I want no divides on my properties. We're changing the usage of land on this estate from rundale to conacre. We're growing one crop and we're taxing my tenants for it. The Skelton and Sugrue properties will remain vacant. I don't want it any other way. Do you think you can manage that, Mister Pollach?'

Walter was shocked. Were his ears deceiving him. He was still very much in the master's plans – and just when he thought he was finished for good.

'Forgive me, my lord, but conacre will cause a mutiny among the tenants. They're already overstretched with the rent and the tithe. A new tax will break them for good.'

'Precisely. Eventually, we'll have one large farm – not this carved up mess that's bleeding me dry. So, can you enforce these changes or not, Mister Pollach? Or do I have to seek another in your place?'

Walter's mind was now fully at rest – and not just for the time being. He smiled broadly at his master. His hand wandered towards his belt, to where his whip was tucked away. He pulled it out and shook it loose.

'Don't worry, my lord. I think you've got the….no, in fact, I can guarantee you've got the right man for the job.'

The viscount smiled back.

'Glad to hear it, Mister Pollach. Now do sit down and have a drink. I brought you a nice cognac, from my travels in the south of France.'

Nineteen – The American Letter

Sugrue had searched the cabin twice. The handloom was missing. It tore at his conscience. One fair day, some years back, he stopped Ella May from selling it. Sugrue remembered it well – the opening day of Mostrim's summer fair of '39.

'It's worth nothing anymore,' he said back then. 'And besides, the poor woman, God rest her soul, wore her fingers to the bone off that old loom. It reminds me of her, Ellie, and we shouldn't let it go.'

But it was no longer to be had in Shay's new cabin. The handloom belonged to Nell, Ella May's mother. In her day, she had made clothes for half the parish. In fact, there was a time when Nell earned quite a nice living from that loom. Before the turn of the century, while Sugrue was fighting the English on Cairn Hill, stay-at-home hand weavers like Nell Reilly were up to their eyeballs in work. In 1798, as the canons shook the ground in Ballinamuck, linen-produced goods amounted to seventy per cent of all Irish exports – over thirty-seven million yards was sent to Britain that year. Back then, with a woman spinning in the home and a man farming in the field, there was comfort in many Irish houses – despite the rebellion.

Sugrue pondered the sorry state of weaving now. Less than half a century later, the profession had all but died out in the homestead. The Act of Union's protective tariffs, with their bountiful rewards, had long since come and gone. Their absence hurt the business sorely. The Industrial Revolution, with its dumping of surplus linen and other clothing goods on the Irish market, sounded the death knell for the industry.

But what right had Sugrue when he thought about it. Ella May could sell the loom if she wanted. After all, whatever little money she could get for it was more than he had brought into the home since getting the sack from Cranley estate. Not happy with terminating Sugrue's employment, Walter Pollach had to go and blacken his name with the Board of Works, making sure he couldn't get on any of the public-work schemes – not in Ardagh or Ballinalee or Longford. He spent the time scratching around his new surroundings at the clachan in Lacken, trying to pass the time. Since moving in, himself, Ella May, and Padraig were living hand-to-mouth. His grandson had become noticeably thinner, so Sugrue started to skip as many meals as he could get away with. Ella May soon noticed what was going on and confronted him.

'What's the meaning of this self-enforced hunger strike,' she asked.

Sugrue tried to deny it, saying he was sick and had no appetite.

'Don't give me that,' continued Ella May. 'I know what you're at, Sugrue.'

'How can you expect me to eat when I look at Padraig and see the bones beginning to appear through his skin. I brought this on us, Ellie, me and my stupid pride. I should have taken the oath for the sake of us all and left the rest to God.'

'Now you listen here to me, Sugrue, and heed what I say. Nobody in this family has ever bowed the knee to the British Empire before, and we're not about to do it now. What you did, you had to do, and I'm proud of you for doing it. If you had bowed the knee and taken the oath, you would have shamed Padraig and me and Padge in America – and all that you achieved in the past would have been for nothing. The British couldn't break you in ninety-eight, so don't let them break you now.'

When Ella May was finished, she had kissed Sugrue on the cheek. He felt a strange sort of pride. Pride, however – as the woman with the foot iron said – doesn't put food on the table. One day, soon after that, Ella May sat him down. She told him calmly that if things didn't improve, she would be forced to take Padraig away and seek refuge at the workhouse in Shroid. This sent a chill down Sugrue's spine.

'I have to act in the best interests of the child,' she explained.

Sugrue had sleepless nights after that, imagining his grandson with the mark on his shoulder. The dreaded XL – X for workhouse and L for the Longford union. When they brand you on arrival, they brand you for life. To Sugrue, that branding would underline how he had failed Padraig – and Ella May, for that matter. It would stand as a permanent, never-to-be-erased, symbol of how he had put his pride before the needs of his family. It really was going to be the end of the road as far as Sugrue was concerned.

Just then, the door was flung open. Ella May and Padraig stood before him on the clay floor. As soon as she saw him, his daughter-in-law began to cry. She rested her head on Sugrue's shoulder and bawled her eyes out. She didn't speak, just held out a piece of paper for him to look at. Sugrue couldn't believe it. He was afraid to touch the letter, focusing instead on the stripy envelope. The postmark looked strange and wonderful.

'Take it,' she sobbed. 'It's from America, from Padge. He's alive – alive and well. And he has sent for us, Sugrue.'

He had to read it several times before it sank in. The address was from Albany, New York – a long address. The letter was dated September 2, 1845 – almost nine weeks earlier. The first thing Padge wrote was an apology for failing to get in touch for so long. He had a good job in a mill, where he was after climbing the ladder to assistant foreman. He hoped they were well and that they weren't too badly affected by the potato blight – which he heard about from new Irish settlers. He had arranged everything once Ella May and

Padraig got off the *Freedom Bound*, the ship that would sail them to America. A carriage would be waiting to take them to their new home in Albany. He asked Ella May to make sure to bring this letter, and show it on the ship, if necessary, and when they reached New York harbour. The last lines were for Sugrue himself.

'Tell my father to keep up the good fight. While she has sons like him to fight for her, Kathleen Ni Houlihan will one day be free.'

This was something Sugrue used to say to Padge when he was growing up. He hadn't forgotten his old man's words. He hadn't forgotten to carry Ireland – the Kathleen Ni Houlihan of his youth – in his heart. And he hadn't forgotten or abandoned his family.

Sugrue had to sit down. A bittersweet feeling was passing through him. He was finding it hard to hold back the tears. He never wanted anyone, especially Ella May and Padraig, to see him crying. He felt amazing pride in his son. He felt amazing shame too. For Sugrue had begun to believe that Padge had forsaken his family, that he had run off with another woman – an American woman – and left them at the mercy of the potato blight and the British.

'I knew he'd come through for us,' said Ella May.

She hugged Sugrue tightly.

'How did you know?'

'Because he's a son of Paddy Sugrue, that's how.'

Sugrue could hold back no longer. The tears streamed down his cheeks. Padraig came over. He was sad and confused to see his grandad crying. The three of them hugged for several minutes. Then Ella May showed him the money.

'Twenty-five pounds,' she said, holding out the banknote.

Sugrue stared at the note, before suddenly returning to Ella May.

'The handloom?'

'Don't worry, it's not missing,' she said softly. 'I gave it to Mairead and Jim for safekeeping. It belongs here in Ireland, not in America. And the Gorman household is the best place I could think of. It will be something to remember us by. I didn't tell them the good news though, I thought with Shay and everything....'

Sugrue nodded. He understood what Ella May was trying to say.

'We'll tell them together,' she said.

Sugrue smiled with delight, kissed his grandson's cheek and called him his auld son of Eireann.

'We sure will, pet. We sure will.'

Nell Reilly's handloom is still in our house. It's painted and polished, and looking as good as new. It's on the mantel, under the picture of the Sacred Heart. It's the first thing all who enter our humble abode will see – a reminder of those who may be far away in distance, but who are also very near in our hearts.

Twenty – The Crop Failure and Measures (Part 1)

Lord Harold Teale liked to sit at the back of the hall, away from the glare of the top table. Those in attendance didn't call him Lord Harold Teale, but Lord Lacken – his official name for the purposes of these gatherings. He never liked Poor Law meetings. He thought them nothing but a waste of time. They were a talking shop. The Longford Poor Law meetings took place monthly. Lord Teale had considered boycotting this one on account of Shay Gorman and the false evidence Walter Pollach had given in a police interview. He knew Pollach would be present. He knew Pollach would try to make everyone laugh with his bad jokes. The sight of him made Lord Teale angry. But there was a greater good to be considered, especially in light of all that had happened lately. Without a representative of their own, Lord Teale felt it was his duty to look after the tenants' interests. He had already sought to have them represented formally. On that occasion, the committee had looked at one another anxiously, but no answer was made to his request. Walter Pollach was the only one to say anything on the matter, stating from the floor that Crawford and Blacker would soon be running the show if they let the tenants in.

Pollach was particularly vociferous with the returned Viscount de Bromley – in all his splendour – at his side. The top table couldn't get a word in edgeways with all his wisecracking and bureaucratic meddling. The chairman of the Longford Poor Law Commission was a little, chubby, round-faced man with spectacles. He spoke with a half-English and half-Irish accent. He seemed too small for the chair he was occupying. Nevertheless, he took the opportunity – more than once – to warn Pollach about his constant interrupting.

The causes of the blight were being discussed. There was a stalemate in the argument. Most observers agreed that it was the excessive wet weather conditions that had worsened, if not brought on, the disease in the first place.

'Well, I have just returned from Britain and I did not hear anything about this blight business over there,' said the viscount.

'Here, here,' shouted Pollach, obviously showing off to his master. 'Minister Trevelyan may be right in the end. Perhaps it's a sign from God, punishing the natives for their overbreeding and their inherent laziness. After all, He did send a plague of locusts to the land of Egypt.'

Lord Teale had heard just about enough of this nonsense. He could keep his silence no longer.

'Charles Trevelyan would be better served to keep his mind on the business of Her Majesty's treasury,' he said, his voice shaking with annoyance.

'My lord, this is Lord Lacken of Mostrim, or should I say Edgeworthstown,' said Pollach, out loud to the viscount.

Lord Teale ignored them both.

'The business of this meeting is not to speculate on God's providence or whom it shall favour, but to find solutions to a famine that affects us all.'

'Dinna fash, Lord Lacken, and please calm down,' advised Pollach. 'I don't see you dying from malnutrition.'

Once again, ignoring Pollach's attempts at humour, Lord Teale addressed the chairman.

'If a scarcity of food affects one of my tenants, then it affects me,' he continued. 'We need to make Westminster aware of the severity of the blight situation. We need access to a government-appointed

Inspector of Potatoes right away. We need more relief schemes for able-bodied men. And we need these things now.'

'Relief schemes cost money, Lord Lacken,' said Viscount de Bromley, 'and we already have a roadbuilding and a drainage project in progress within this county. How do you suggest we raise subscriptions for further schemes?'

'*We* will have to foot the bill,' said Lord Teale. 'There's no other way out. People are already beginning to suffer badly. Another rotten harvest will create havoc. It's a matter of life and death now.'

He looked around the room as he spoke, engaging faces here and there. He tried to catch Lord Colehill's eye. But his lordship was busy examining his fingernails.

'We, as landowners, can do a lot more. Furrows cost one guinea per acre to plough by horse. Spade cultivation costs a fraction of this – and it's a more thorough system that produces higher yields. It's a win-win situation. One obtains cheaper, higher-quality, labour while stemming the flow of poverty and unemployment.'

Lord Teale's comments caused uproar in the hall. The chairman called vehemently for order and, when he didn't get his wish, threatened to adjourn the meeting and walk out. Walter Pollach could be heard shouting above the noise that horses don't queue up looking for five joeys on a Friday evening.

When he eventually restored peace, the chairman agreed with Lord Teale's suggestion that the Inspector of Potatoes should be applied to for immediate attention within the county of Longford. However, further relief schemes were at the mercy of the British government. Hopes could not be overly raised as there had already been a lot of money allocated to railway, roadbuilding, and drainage schemes over the previous few years. On a positive note, it was pointed out that the provision of £100,000 had been made available from Sir Robert Peel's government for more Indian meal to be sent over and housed in depots, from where it would be distributed – for a nominal fee – to those most in need. The chairman also referred to the Corn Laws, which were removed in the previous months – abolishing tariffs on grain exported from Ireland to Britain. A commission had also been set up to co-ordinate provision of labour and make sure local traders would not capitalise on food shortages by raising their prices.

'Why, pray tell, are we exporting grain to Britain when we are in dire need of it here,' asked Lord Teale, but his question fell on deaf ears.

As the meeting was being adjourned, Pollach turned to the viscount and said aloud: 'Lord Lacken's charity knows no bounds. I believe he has even taken to housing those who were thrown out of other estates for bad behaviour'.

'With all due respect, Mister Pollach,' answered Lord Teale, 'I find it more agreeable to bring families together, rather than tearing them apart.'

The families of the clachan waited by the stone-wall enclosure that separated the outfield from our personal plots. The Inspector of Potatoes was due to arrive. It was seldom we all came together like this. Jabber chewed a piece of hay and looked thoughtfully into the bog.

'Pity the blight doesn't affect the peat instead of the ridges,' he said, deep in contemplation. 'In the heel of the hunt, you can't eat a sod of turf. It would suit me just fine to leave those boyos rotting away on the bank.'

'Too right,' I agreed. 'I'd sooner die of the cold than die of the hunger. Let's hope the blight is on the way out. Maybe this inspector fella will have a bit of good cheer for us.'

The inspector arrived in a carriage with its own driver. He had a suitcase with him. He was a tall, straight, bald man in a fine suit and a cloak, which he discarded and placed neatly into the carriage while the driver went off to get a handful of hay and a drink for the horse. *People* – that was the word he used to address us collectively.

'People, the first thing I will say to you is do not, under any circumstances, eat your own seeds. I know this might sound funny or stupid, but there was a guy in County Meath who ate his seeds instead of planting them.'

The inspector's suitcase was full of pamphlets and other information. He took one out and started to recite his off-by-heart speech concerning the potato crop.

'In regard to fertilizing potatoes,' he stated, 'there is the most typical fertilizer over yonder, provided naturally by our animals.'

The inspector was pointing at a dung heap beside Mooney's back door.

'Out on the coastal counties they use seaweed, although such information is not much good to you people in Midlands, Ireland. Another very good source of fertilizer is guano. This is a mixture of bird droppings and it is imported from Peru.'

'From where,' quipped Jabber. 'Merciful hour! Where's Peru?'

'It is a country beside Brazil and Argentina in South America,' answered the inspector.

'We can't afford to feed the pig to produce a decent dung heap and you're on about importing bird shite from Peru,' Jabber pointed out.

The inspector just looked with indifference at Jabber before returning to his prepared speech.

'The fertilizer with the best long-term benefits to potatoes is lime. The limestone is burned on open fires or in specially constructed lime kilns.'

Anthony Davern, a next-door neighbour to Micheal Mooney, didn't agree with the inspector's advice.

'You're wrong,' he insisted. 'Lime is what caused the blight in the first place.'

'I assure you, young man,' explained the inspector, 'that is incorrect. There is no scientific proof to back up such a view.'

The inspector took some pamphlets out of his suitcase and handed one of them to Anthony Davern.

'It's a waste of time giving me that,' said Anthony, 'I can't read.'

The inspector was unsympathetic to Anthony's plight. He simply handed the pamphlets, titled: *Origins, Causes and Treatments*, to those who were closest and continued with his lesson.

'Starch can be extracted from diseased potatoes. Potatoes should be dried in pits with ventilation funnels or in ovens. This is vital to the survival of the potato in this country.'

Sugrue could take no more of this college boy's bullshite.

'If the potato can survive the armies of Cromwell and King William, it will surely survive a touch of blight,' he pointed out.

Once again, the inspector was in no mood for intuitive discussion. He was simply there to cite the facts and get out of Lacken as fast as his horse and carriage could take him.

'The six-week period before harvest is going to be hard on you people,' continued the inspector. 'So, listen up, you will have to supplement your diets with other foodstuffs. On my travels I have instructed persons who have added oatmeal, eggs, herring, and lard to sustain them during this tough time.'

It was now obvious to most of the clachan that this man was far removed from the ordeal we were facing.

'We don't have the money or the opportunity to get those things,' I tried to explain.

'Well then,' said the inspector, 'I suggest you go back to basics. Nature will guide you through this pre-harvest period. There is an abundance of nutrition available from our hedgerows and fields – nettles, frogs, hedgehogs and snails are among the foodstuffs available there.'

The inspector was coming to the end of his talk. As he restocked his suitcase, he turned to Jabber again.

'You there, give me an example of supplementary nutrition to your potato diet.'

Jabber was put on the spot as the clachan looked on and awaited his response.

'Well, I'd have an odd cup of cow's blood every now and then,' he answered.

'You see, people, there you go. A delicious cup of cow's blood. Perfect. Now you are beginning to get a grasp of what I am trying to teach you.'

'You can join me so,' continued Jabber. 'We'd never dream of letting a guest leave the clachan on an empty stomach. I know where there's a cow nearby that we can bleed.'

The inspector's face went white as Jabber pretended to look for a bucket. The next thing he was bent over, getting sick across the stone-wall enclosure. Jabber went across and slapped a big hand onto the middle of his back.

'That's it, Inspector, get it all up. You won't know yourself after a delicious cup of cow's blood. It'll replace your breakfast nicely, and shorten the journey home.'

Twenty-one – The Workhouse and Other Stories

It was time for Ella May and Padraig to go to America. There was the usual sorrow in leaving. The whole of the clachan came out to watch as their carriage rolled in to collect them. Ella May said a last goodbye with a twirling wave as everyone cheered loudly. She had wanted Sugrue to come with them. She had pleaded with him – pointing out that the twenty-five-pound banknote was more than sufficient to cover his fare on the ship too. But Sugrue was having none of it. He hugged her and wiped her tears, retelling her that his place was here in Ireland.

'You can't teach an auld dog new tricks, and that's the way of the world,' he explained. 'America would be too different for a fella my age. Besides, who's going to keep an eye on the British if I run off to New York. This is Mostrim. This is Sugrue country.'

Being so young, the significance of the move was lost on Padraig. Until he saw his mother's tears, he had been looking forward to America – as long as he could return to his grandad for supper that evening.

The significance of the move was certainly not lost on Jabber Farrell. Sugrue had confided in him just how close Ella May and Padraig had been to the workhouse. As he looked at Sugrue's grandson boarding Bianconi's omnibus for Dublin, Jabber pondered on how the boy would never know just how lucky he was to have avoided such a place. He thanked God for delivering the child and his mother to the safety of Padge. But Sugrue's happy tale had also transported Jabber back to a dark time in his mind, back to children and families who were not so lucky.

Jabber's association with the workhouse began at its very inception. Almost a full eight years earlier, in 1838, the Poor Law Act was conferred on Ireland under the control of George Nicholls. The country was divided up into unions, of which there were then one hundred and thirty throughout the land. In 1839, the Board of Guardians – consisting mainly of the Anglo-Irish gentry class – drew up plans for a workhouse to be built in the Longford union. Jabber believed he had the dishonour of cementing the very first brick in the Longford union workhouse. If he could have foreseen what was about to take place there, he would never have helped build it in the first place. Work started on the monstrosity in May 1839 and took two full years to complete. When this huge red-bricked building was finished and looming large in the Shroid countryside – a townland halfway between the parishes of Mostrim and Longford – Jabber took up work on its inside, as one of the orderlies.

From the beginning, opinion was divided on the workhouse. Many of the Anglo-Irish landowners saw it as a huge inconvenience, a place that milked them financially. There was a belief that now private as well as public money was being squandered on a bestial and violent class of people, who showed no sign or desire to help themselves. Others, including Jabber and many of his neighbours in the clachan, had pity on those helpless souls – dazed by destitution – who were forced to seek shelter and charity in the workhouse.

Jabber was struck by the punitive discipline of the house. Upon entry, families were split up. The girls and women entered one part of the building, while the men and boys were sheltered in another. They weren't allowed mingle. They weren't allowed any contact with family members of the opposite gender. Jabber remembered a five-year-old boy and his younger brother, crying because their mother had been led away some days earlier. Despite their close proximity, these young boys were forbidden to have any dealings – however fleeting – with their mam. This moved Jabber greatly and he spent whatever time he could scurrying over and back between the male and female sections of the house, keeping contact alive between the boys and their mother.

Discipline was not confined to the house. While females engaged mostly in the laundry and preservation of the interior, most able-bodied men and adolescents were put on work schemes and made earn their keep by road and railway construction, drainage and forestry projects. These were usually set up under the responsibility of the Grand Juries. Jabber's heart would break on winter mornings, when barefooted boys as young as twelve would be forced out into the snow, with little more than a cut of white bread and a cup of warm water for breakfast. Some of the Shroid workforce was responsible for maintaining the pipes on the part of the Royal Canal passing through the south Longford village of Killashee – a nine-mile trek before the working day even started. Despite the physical nature and long hours of this scheme, the workers did not receive anything extra from the Inland Navigation. Workhouse males received no monetary payment of any kind, just a bed of straw and enough food for them and their families to survive on.

Within a couple of days of opening its doors, the house was full. After a week it was – and would remain – chronically overcrowded. It wouldn't have mattered if Shroid workhouse had been double in size, it was always going to suffer from overcrowding. Despite the healthy state of the potato crop in the early 1840s, dire poverty was still prevalent. Upon entry, inmates could look forward to a meagre diet – and branding.

Branding was something that really got Jabber Farrell's dander raised – so much so that he refused to have any part in it. However, he was soon warned that if he didn't help out with the *labelling* of new inmates, he would be sacked. Therefore, he was forced to play a role in what Jabber regarded as the most inhumane of procedures. An inmate would be sent to the branding shed, usually within a few hours of admittance. This was at the back of the workhouse, where the males went to do their business. The stench of urine and excrement was overpowering, but was the very least of their worries. Once inside the branding shed, the inmate would be held face-down while a raging-hot, poker-like, instrument was burned into their skin. In Shroid workhouse, the branding iron bore an XL. This was pressed into the area just below the right shoulder blade. Females usually got away without being branded. That was, unless they were caught running away or had tried to enter another workhouse outside their union. In those cases, they suffered the same fate as their male counterparts. Jabber carried a piece of plastic on his person. When the job called for his presence in the branding shed, he would slip the inmates the plastic to place between their teeth. Jabber would then instruct them to bite down hard. He couldn't stand to hear their screams as the glowing metal smouldered on their skin. As time went on, Jabber tried to get the job of brander. His plan was to brand quickly and not too deeply. But his superiors soon reminded him that he was an orderly within the house and only required as muscle in the branding shed. They obviously had more than enough sadists to do the branding.

The fever hospital at the Shroid workhouse was another horrible place. For many who were transferred there, it was the last stop before the pearly gates of Heaven. Here, death was in the air – one could almost reach out and touch it. On arrival at a workhouse, an inmate had a one in eight chance of dying with disease. The nearer one got to the fever hospital, the more those odds increased. Few inmates entered the fever hospital and lived to describe it. Many infections called this place home – typhus, dysentery, consumption, pneumonia. It was quite probable to enter this room with one disease and die of another.

There was another room, just off the fever hospital, at the back of the massive house. It was the place Jabber had dreaded most of all. He never went in without first placing a handkerchief firmly across his nose and mouth. It was known to all as the black room, and it was where the seriously ill were sent to die. The hopelessness of this place could be felt in its eerie silence. Leaning away from the large window of the black room were two thick planks of wood, some two feet apart. These planks were grounded at the mouth of a large open trench. The trench acted as a body-storage area. When a person died in the black room, their body was slid down the planks and toppled into the trench, where they were covered in lime before being shovelled to one side for burial. The gable end of the house, which supported the planks of wood, was charred from all the dead bodies. With time it became known as the black gable and a large fence was erected to keep prying eyes away from this part of the workhouse.

In all the years he worked there, Jabber knew of only one case where a body had passed through the black room, out the window of the black gable, down the planks, into the open trench, and – instead of ending up in a limey unmarked grave – lived to tell the tale. At least Jabber hoped he was alive to tell it. It was the case of Jeremiah Figg – and Jabber had played a leading role in the story too. He smiled as the fair-haired little ten-year-old came back to his memory.

Jeremiah had entered the workhouse with his father, mother, brother, and two sisters. One by one, they all died in the black room and were pushed down the planks and buried. When Jeremiah learned that he was the sole survivor of the family, he ran away. He was caught, returned and rebranded. But every time a chance arose, Jeremiah ran away again. The police would put the word out, and Jeremiah would be caught hiding in some haybarn or outhouse and handed back to the custody of the workhouse all over again. He suffered terrible punishments upon his recaptures, but no amount of beatings could reform him. Eventually, he was chained up in the male common room while the guardians awaited official notice of what to do with him. He sat there, day after day, pondering his fate. One sunny afternoon, Jabber Farrell happened to stumble upon him. Naturally, when he saw the chains, Jabber thought him a young brigand who had been arrested for committing a robbery or some such misdemeanour. Jeremiah looked at him with hangdog eyes and tried to raise his restrained hands.

'Please mister,' Jeremiah begged.

Jabber ignored the plea and continued with his chores, declining to even look in Jeremiah's direction again. But he couldn't get the sad, hopeless, face out of his mind. He enquired about the boy. One of the inmates from the male side of the house said Jeremiah was being shackled because he was inclined to run away. Now that his parents were dead, he was the responsibility of the state. A young nurse from the fever hospital corroborated this news and added that the boy would be sent to a juvenile detention centre, once officially authorised by the government – a sentence that had already been rubber-stamped by the Board of Guardians.

Jabber decided to act. He had been taught – while training for the priesthood – that in certain circumstances, failing to do the right thing was the same as doing wrong. Jabber felt that this was one of those circumstances. He had to give the boy a chance to live – the chance to live that state intervention would only deprive him of.

Jabber crushed some grass into a bowl and prepared a green paste. Then he went in to where Jeremiah was being restrained and slipped him the bowl. He hastily instructed the boy to apply the paste, leave it on overnight, then gently wipe it away with a dry rag.

The next morning there was uproar in the common room when staff saw the state of Jeremiah Figg. He had yellow blotches on his face and hands. Jabber rushed in and caused an even bigger stir by shouting that no one was to go near the boy.

'I've seen this before in the fever hospital,' he exclaimed at the top of his voice. 'Merciful hour, this little bugger is jaundiced. He's highly contagious.'

The other staff backed off instantly, as Jabber placed his trusted handkerchief across his mouth and muttered that it was his duty to take the boy into quarantine immediately.

'Where's the key,' he shouted in pretend panic. 'Go and fetch the key at once, before this runt infects the whole house.'

The key was produced in a hurry and Jeremiah was whisked away to the fever hospital. The doctor was called. Jabber, who knew the doctor's schedule off-by-heart, was safe in the knowledge that Jeremiah would remain unexamined that day.

Later, in the black room – surrounded by the groaning of those about to die – Jabber gave Jeremiah instructions to lie low until nightfall, then make his escape down the planks and get as far away as he could under the cover of darkness. He was to stay off the roads in daylight. Food was smuggled from the lunchroom – energy for the escape. Then, Jabber produced a compass belonging to his dead father. It was hard for him to part with it. But he knew what had to be done. Jabber took one last look at the compass before handing it over.

'Keep east,' he told the boy. 'Get as far as Dublin and you'll be alright. Blend with the city folk and don't come back into the countryside again.'

Jeremiah gripped Jabber's arm as he was about to leave.

'Thank you,' he said, 'and God bless you. I will never forget your kindness.'

'Slide down the planks, then run for your life. Good luck to you, boy.'

That was the last Jabber Farrell had seen or heard of Jeremiah Figg. For weeks he waited anxiously, fearing the worst, but the boy was never returned to the Longford workhouse. If he was dead, then at least he was at peace. If he was alive, then Jabber hoped Jeremiah was enjoying some semblance of happiness – a happiness that could never be his in a juvenile detention centre or Her Majesty's union workhouse.

Twenty-two – The de Bromley Financial Crisis (Part 1)

Viscount de Bromley sat slumped in his study, his ledgers all around him. He dredged through the figures again. He couldn't believe his eyes. Eighty per cent of the occupants listed were behind on their rents. Some were months behind. He chose to call them *occupants* instead of *tenants*, because *tenants* paid rent. What use was owed money. Owed money wasn't going to get him out of his present pickle. The viscount needed hard currency – and he needed it fast. But how could he raise the kind of money he needed in a hurry.

'Labour is the way to go,' he said in a low voice.

The viscount had a habit of talking to himself when deep in concentration. He also had a habit of referring to himself as another person.

'It's Ireland you're in now, de Bromley, so think Irish. Economic productivity relies on cheap labour – how can I farm this estate on the cheap?'

He remembered what his friend, Lord Colehill, had told him at the dinner party a few nights earlier. Sixty-five per cent of the workforce were labourers – very high in comparison to the six per cent that could be relied upon to farm the estates of England. And Lord Colehill had quickly added that because of this, Irish labourers could only reasonably expect half the wages their English counterparts were asking for.

'I say, Bromley old bean, give them five pence per day. If they don't like it, tell them there are plenty of other fellows out there who *will* like it instead,' Lord Colehill had advised. 'I run a tight ship in Abbeyshrule. I wouldn't dream of paying one haypenny more than five pence a day without food.'

That settled it for the viscount. He would lean heavily towards spade cultivation and manpower. This would free up his horses, which could then be rented out for a tidy sum.

The viscount's cost-cutting measures had started the previous Christmas, shortly after his return. Instead of observing the tradition of giving parcels of meat to all his tenants, he drew up a list of persons excluded from receiving meat on the grounds that they were behind on their rents. Back then, he had been certain that providing incentives and rewarding prompt payment of monies owed would do the trick. But as yet, the viscount hadn't seen much improvement in his rent collections. Secretly, he blamed his first lieutenant for this situation. Despite giving Walter Pollach licence to collect rents by whatever means possible, the viscount was still suspicious of his right-hand man – and this wasn't simply a case of all landlords being suspicious of their middlemen. He had always suspected that while he was away on his Essex estate or in Kent, Pollach was sub-letting for personal profit. The viscount was sorry he hadn't taken Lord Granard's advice and chosen a number of head tenants in the townland of Cranley – instead of the manager of his estate – and allocated them rent-collecting incentives within their own communities.

The idea of an incompetent Pollach, unable to enforce the collection of a meagre three shillings a week, had the viscount thinking about all the leeches who were sucking him dry. Lord Lacken and the Edgeworths were beginning to really annoy him. They were badgering him for a considerable contribution to the construction of a new fever hospital in Mostrim – or Edgeworthstown, as his wife and family had become accustomed to calling it.

'Seeing as the village is now named after them, maybe the Edgeworths have a right to meet the expense that goes with it,' he said to an empty space.

Lord Lacken had been quick to highlight that the outdoor relief for the building of this fever hospital would ease the unemployment of the area. Viscount de Bromley couldn't have been more against the idea. Providing lists for this project would be the equivalent of abandoning the workhouse test for eligibility. And besides, there was already a fever hospital attached to the workhouse in Shroid, just a few miles outside of Edgeworthstown. The bottom line was that the expense of a fever hospital was something the viscount did not want to contribute to.

He leaned back in his chair, took off his spectacles, and rubbed his eyes. It was time to call in his puppet. That's what Walter Pollach was to him. The viscount was the puppeteer, with Pollach suspended on his strings. Pollach came in and bowed in front of his master.

'Alas, Mister Pollach, what do you propose we do with regard to this new Public Works Act?'

Pollach looked puzzled by the question. The viscount jumped out of his chair and clicked his fingers.

'Come on, Mister Pollach, have your wits about you. The governor of Public Works is looking for a list. What shall I do?'

'My lord, I think you should provide it.'

'Are you suggesting I fly in the face of the workhouse test on eligibility, Mister Pollach?'

'With all due respect, my lord, what we need is more of these wretched creatures earning Doyle's dollar; it makes sense that they should work for their keep when it's landlords such as your good self who are paying the rates to keep them.'

This suggestion had the viscount deep in thought again.

'The Public Works Act is going ahead, my lord, whether you contribute a list or not. The government is determined to modernise the system of agriculture within the country and this legislation is designed to prioritise agricultural works such as drainage and sub-soiling at the expense of other projects.'

'Other projects? Like what?'

'Like roadbuilding, my lord. Use the law for your own benefit. Milk the system for what you can get out of it. My idea is to draw up a list for the governor consisting of all your tenants in arrears. Then, when the project starts and the Public Works Board sends you their finances, simply refuse to pay out. When the fever hospital workers on your list come for their wages, tell them you're deducting the rent they owe you at source.'

A smile appeared on the viscount's worried features.

'What a good idea. I think it could actually work. Mister Pollach, you surprise me. Indeed, you can be a clever little blighter when you take the notion.'

Pollach felt such pride when the viscount said this. It was so good to part of his decision-making team.

'Thank you, my lord. It's a simple matter of getting the Public Works Board to pay your tenants' arrears.'

'You're dismissed, Mister Pollach.'

Pollach bowed yet again.

'Glad to be of service, my lord.'

Alone again in his study, the viscount began to contemplate the real reason for this urgent need of money. His son had finished his second level studies and was now off to Cambridge University on his first tentative steps towards the Bar Council of Great Britain. Too much gaming had left the viscount in a situation that he had never known before. Lack of funds was a new and terrible concept to a man who had never given a moment's thought in his life to

- 141 -

money. But the viscount was determined to fix things. He would neither be embarrassed publicly nor privately. After all, he was a man of Kent, was he not. His wife knew nothing about his wild booze-fuelled poker games with the Marquis of Salisbury at the Tunbridge mansion. She didn't know about the many mistresses he kept in fox furs and fine satins. And that's the way it would remain – what the viscountess didn't know surely wouldn't worry her.

The viscount hurriedly arranged for his footman to prepare his carriage. Then, calling Pollach to ride with him, he set out for the Joint Stock Bank in Longford Town. On the way, the horses were blocked on the main street. There was a protest in operation. A march had taken place from Pound Street, and was held up on the hill. The police were in the middle of the village, trying to clear the people and their banners. One of the slogans read: *This is Mostrim, not Edgeworthstown*. It was crudely written with red paint – and ran down the placard like blood – on a white background. The viscount opened the window and urged his driver to get a move on. A man took up a position opposite their carriage.

'Let's take back what's ours,' the man roared, 'this is Mostrim, not Edgeworthstown.'

Just then, the viscount spotted the real reason for the holdup. Two men were guarding a ten-foot banner on Pound Hill. It read: '*Property Rights for Tenants March*'. They stood either side of the road, blocking the whole thoroughfare, holding a banner pole apiece. The viscount almost lost his mind.

'Get out of the way, you scoundrels,' he shouted.

He was forced to close his window when a rock came hurtling through the air and crashed against the carriage door.

Reinforcements arrived from the Ballinalee Road, then the peelers drew their batons and started swinging. When Walter Pollach saw this, he grew in confidence.

'My lord, take cover. I'll deal with these neds. We'll be on our way in no time.'

Pollach produced his whip and stepped audaciously outside the carriage. He lashed at the two men with the ten-foot banner until, in the end, they had no choice but to drop their poles and run for cover. He returned to the carriage and the driver took off down the Longford Road at breakneck speed.

'That's O'Connell for you,' snarled the viscount. 'Him and his monster meetings. Now, every one of these ignorant bowsies will be looking for personal property rights. Soon enough, if we're not careful, I'll be the one owing rent to them.'

'Rest assured, my lord, me and my little friend here will make sure that never happens,' Pollach said, folding his whip. 'By the time we're finished lining their backs, they'll know their place and be glad of it – monster meetings or no monster meetings.'

Twenty-three – Court Case 2: Turk

Shaun Burke liked to ride out in the evenings, away from the bustle of Cranley House. He was alone with his horse and his thoughts. De Bromley's estate was certainly expansive enough for the pleasure, the lush meadows sprawling from its border with Lisanore right into the cemetery wall at Aughafin. On this particular evening, Shaun Burke was in bad need of his de-stressing ride. He had been vexed by a threatening letter, found earlier that day, nailed to the tree on the front lawn of Cranley House. His mind was finally beginning to find some tranquillity, as it followed the sound of the horse's even pace. Burke was thinking about Constance Ryan. In all his time in Kent and Essex, he hadn't met a beauty like her. He made up his mind, on his way back to the big house, that she was going to be his bride. He would lavish gifts on her. No expense would be spared; the finest silks and perfumes would be hers. He would whisk her off her feet. They would take carriages to the most extravagant balls and dinner parties. In social gatherings, he would introduce her as his cousin. She was beneath him, but he didn't care. He would keep their romance a secret, then marry her at Tunbridge House. It was the perfect plan. In England, no one – except the viscount – would know her station. With the help of finishing school, she'd fit right in with the rest of the ladies on de Bromley's English estates.

Turk O'Nuallain was making his merry way home from yet another secret liaison with Clarissa Lyndsay. His heart was light as he ran his tongue along his lips, imagining he could taste her kisses still. Suddenly, remembering the curfew, Turk pulled his scarf over his nose. He was confident in his sheltered surroundings, but it was always better to exercise a degree of caution in any event.

As he approached the trees on the Granard side of Cranley House, Burke thought he heard a rustling sound. Drawing closer, the noise became louder and then it stopped. He got off his horse and tied her to a branch. He crouched down and crept along the dirt path to get a better look.

Turk got a start. He could sense someone approaching. He thought he heard twigs breaking and a stomping noise. But he couldn't be sure. His breath was hot under the scarf. He took cover in the trees. He pulled the scarf down and inhaled the cool evening air, before replacing it again. It was almost nightfall. A harvest moon was out already, even though it was not yet dark. If only the harvest was as reliable as the harvest moon, thought young Turk, as he prepared to leave the trees and bolt for the open fields.

Shaun Burke was a skilful hunter. He appeared out of nowhere and dazed Turk with a blow of his riding crop. Then, while Turk was attempting to steady himself, Burke delivered his coup-de-grace – lassoing him at the waist with a deft flick of his wrist and a deadly delivery. The lasso was perfect – the more Turk struggled, the tighter the rope became. He leant back, but to no avail. Burke already had the rope secured to the saddle and was turning his horse for the big house. Turk tried to catch his breath as he got shunted forward. Then he fell and was pulled along with the horse's laboured steps.

'Wait, wait. You don't understand,' Turk panted from behind his disguise. 'I can explain.'

Burke stopped his horse and looked back.

'You can walk or be dragged, the choice is yours,' is all he had to say, before continuing on his way to Cranley House.

Viscount the Bromley was in foul humour as he appeared at the front entrance with a lantern. He had been summoned by a servant at Master Burke's insistence. The viscount was having an informal supper with his friend, Lord Colehill, while discussing ways to raise more capital through the management of his lands.

'Sir, I beg your pardon but this is a matter of some urgency. I found this trespasser on your land only a few minutes ago. Obviously, he has something to do with that message hanging on the tree over yonder.'

Shaun Burke spoke to the viscount with more confidence than Walter Pollach ever could. It was as if he was his equal. And the viscount addressed him casually, more like a friend than his boss.

He went to the tree that Burke had pointed out, held up the lantern, and plucked the paper notice from its trunk. The viscount had been away on business all day, and this was the last thing he needed.

'Indeed, it's a message from the Ribbonmen of Mostrim. Could you not have used the postal system, like decent folk do,' the viscount said to the masked Turk, who was still wheezing from the exertions of being pulled behind the horse.

'This is your only warning. Treat your tenants with respect. Give them a fair rent and fixed tenure. Any more evictions will result in retaliations.'

When the viscount was finished reading, he handed the notice to Shaun Burke to read again.

'And who is our shy guest this evening,' continued the viscount, as he took hold of Turk's scarf and pulled it down.

He shone the lantern to get a better look.

'I know this face,' exclaimed the viscount. 'I've seen this blighter before somewhere. Quick Shaun, fetch Mister Pollach. He may be able to enlighten us as to the name of this young upstart.'

News of Turk O'Nuallain's capture spread like wildfire through the parish of Mostrim – or Edgeworthstown, as it was now known. He was arrested and detained at Cranley House – locked in the basement. The police barracks was being renovated and, therefore, out of service. It was all the same. The basement was like a real prison cell, with iron bars in the windows. Turk could see the people's feet as they passed outside. The police had a guard assigned to the door of the basement for the duration of Turk's stay. At one stage, during those long hours of detention, a young lady's pretty pink boots appeared at the bars. She looked around nervously as she stooped to peer in.

'Who goes there? Wahu, Clarissa, is that you?'

'Turk, I'm not here to make small-talk. I just want to know what you were playing at, threatening my uncle and putting the fear of God into everyone in the house.'

'Ara, I'm fine too, thank you for your concern, Clarissa. As you can see, I'm in a spot of bother here.'

'Yes, and it serves you right. The folks around here were good to you. Are you forgetting my uncle has given you work for the past twelve months? Papa says you're like a bad mongrel dog – you bite the hand that feeds you.'

'The Public Works Board employs me, the work just happens to be at your uncle's place,' Turk pointed out. 'I did nothing wrong. I was coming from seeing you when I was struck and bound by Burke. It was for no reason at all.'

Clarissa was surprised by this. She had overheard her papa referring to Turk as a terrorist and a would-be assassin. She had never questioned or doubted her father in her whole life. But she knew Turk was innocent. She said nothing for some time, only looked through the bars with big watery eyes. Turk had seen this sad look before. It reminded him of the dance at the Edgeworth's manor.

'Why did you ignore me on the evening of the foxhunters' ball?'

Clarissa seemed offended by the question.

'I had no choice. What would papa say if he saw us together. It would cause an outrage.'

Turk was getting offended too.

'An outrage! Get over yourself, Clarissa.'

'You have to see it from my point of view, Turk. I stand to lose a lot more than you. Papa would cut me off financially if he found out. Then, I'd never get to be a baroness.'

Turk knew he was getting nowhere with this conversation.

'Listen, Clarissa. I'm going to be tried tomorrow at the courthouse in Longford Town. I need you to do the right thing. I need you to go to court and tell the truth. Tell them you were with me the same morning the Ribbonmen put up the roadblock, stopping the tithe proctor from getting to Lacken. You remember, the morning I called on you early and we had breakfast in the forest. And tell them I was coming from seeing you, not on my way home from hammering some threatening notice into a tree, when I was captured by Burke. You're my only hope because, if these fellas get their way, I'll be sent to Australia the same way Jim Gorman's son was.'

When he had said all that, Clarissa looked even sadder. Turk tried to make eye contact with her through the bars. She turned her head sideways so she wouldn't have to look at him directly.

'Help me. Go to the court. Do the right thing. Clarissa. Look at me, Clarissa. I'm appealing to you here. For goodness sake, do the decent thing.'

She walked away without as much as a goodbye.

'Follow your heart, Clarissa,' Turk shouted up through the bars after her. 'Look into your heart and do the right thing.'

The next day myself, Sugrue and Jabber made the journey once more to the courthouse in Longford Town. We travelled by horse and carriage. Lord Teale provided the transport. This time they wouldn't let us in. An armed officer at the door of the courthouse stopped us, searched us, and asked who we were and what was our business with the court. Then he said that no unauthorised persons were allowed in as this was an Offences Against the State case.

'All matters concerning the Crown against terrorists are strictly private now,' said the officer.

'We're friends of the accused,' stated Sugrue.

'I don't care, old man, if you're Daniel O'Connell himself. My orders are no paddies in the gallery. You heard what happened down in Thurles last week.'

Myself and Jabber hadn't a clue what he was on about, but Sugrue knew. It was a case concerning a member of a Tipperary secret agrarian society, who was now on the run because four members of his gang stormed the court, held up the judge with a firearm, and busted the accused out of the courtroom. Therefore, we could do no more than sit and wait outside the court, watching well-to-do gentlemen and their aides pass by the armed officer at their leisure, and praying that Turk would be returned to us a free man.

'Fair play to the stone throwers,' said Jabber, 'at least down in the Premier they'll take no shite from anyone.'

Despite being refused entry to the courtroom, Sugrue was upbeat and he told us why. Normally, the Longford Town corporation would appoint the same magistrate for the quarter sessions as they had appointed for the assizes, but this was deemed a different – and a special – case. The Lord Lieutenant had deemed Edgeworthstown a disturbed area for the purposes set out in the 1814 Act. It was, after all, listed as an *Act of Terrorism* trial. Also, the bad press that Shay's case had attracted, especially in *The Freeman's Journal*, had put added pressure on the appointment of the arbitrator. A stipendiary magistrate was now deemed suitable as a contentious trial was foreseeable – a man free of the prejudices that were alleged to belong to the local judiciary.

'Wow, Sugrue. what a mouthful,' I said. 'And I thought Jabber was bad. At least he has a priest's education to thank for all his big words.'

Shaun Burke was first to the stand in the matter of the *Crown verses Turk O'Nuallain*. The magistrate could not get his tongue around the name O'Nuallain, and called for assistance from one of his Irish court clerks. Burke rehashed his story of the evening in question, but added that – as far as he was concerned – Turk might very well have been armed and dangerous, and on his way to take out Viscount de Bromley.

A letter, written by the viscount, was then passed by the prosecution for the Crown to the magistrate and read out in the courtroom. The viscount wrote that, in his opinion, Turk O'Nuallain was a member of a secret agrarian society and a danger to the landowner class of Edgeworthstown. He referred to the incident where Turk had used cunning to pretend to Mister Pollach that he did not speak or understand the English language. The viscount contended that this was deliberately devised in order to deflect all questioning and avoid detection. The magistrate looked at odds as he concluded the viscount's letter. He had been hoping to go easy on the boy and thus claw back some goodwill from the local working-class communities.

When the prosecution had wrapped up, Father Murtagh stomped his way into the witness box in defence of the accused. The first thing the curate pointed out was that this young man stood indicted on a list of charges, one of which was trespassing on private property.

'Well then,' shouted Father Murtagh up at the magistrate, 'what about the inviolability of personal rights that you Victorians pride yourselves so much on – like the human right to enjoy the pastoral effects of nature. This case is a contradiction in terms.'

The magistrate then looked puzzled as well as at odds.

'There's no proof beyond doubt here,' continued Father Murtagh. 'No real proof at all. The circumstantial evidence spoken of is really only one person's opinion. And opinion can be open to debate. The truth of it is, Your Honour, a hand-written letter is no proof at all – whether it be written by a vagabond, a viscount, or Victoria herself.'

Father Murtagh put up a good show. He managed to sow the necessary seeds of reasonable doubt. But Clarissa Lyndsay's testimony would surely win the boy his freedom. Turk looked around the courtroom. There was no Clarissa. She hadn't come to save him after all. The magistrate was in a bind. Father Murtagh's words had given him scope to be lenient. The last thing the legal profession needed was to transport another boy from the Edgeworthstown area so recently after my son.

As soon as a recess was granted, counsel for the prosecution made his way directly to the magistrate's bench and reminded him gently of the terms of the Grand Jury Act 1836, and exactly who paid his wages.

'The rate payers, that's who,' whispered the counsellor, 'rate payers such as Viscount de Bromley.'

This comment had the magistrate at odds again and, when the case resumed, he wasn't long adjourning proceedings so he could take advice from his colleagues on a point of law in camera.

'This court will reconvene at ten o'clock on the morrow,' he concluded, as he clouted his gavel off the bench. 'As the Longford lock-up is fully occupied, and the barracks in Edgeworthstown under reconstruction, I entrust the defendant into the care of the local constabulary at Cranley House, from whence he came.'

Then the magistrate fled the scene.

The prosecuting counsel was fuming. They'd seen it all before. They were certain now that the magistrate was going to find for the defendant. Turk was relieved. Despite having to return to de Bromley's awful basement for the night, it afforded him another chance of meeting Clarissa and persuading her to vouch for him.

Cranley House was crawling with policemen when Father Murtagh arrived. A member of staff stood inside the gate, turning away employees for the day. Horses and carts were lined up on the forecourt. The doctor was there. A policeman had been keeping guard at the great red doors since the small hours of the morning.

Father Murtagh didn't know the full details. A knock had come to his door and the message was that he was needed urgently at Cranley House. He walked in only to find a group of men, including Viscount de Bromley, standing in the great hall. They were drinking brandy and talking in whispers. The sight of the viscount brought back the court letter to the priest's mind. What a vile thing to do – trying to influence a judge's decision based on a hunch.

One of the housekeepers led Father Murtagh out through the kitchens and down into the basement. He couldn't believe what he had just been told. His head was swimming with thoughts. He felt like getting sick or lying down, but he needed to see the body before he would allow himself to believe it. And sure enough, there it was, lying on a cold slab. There were two policemen in the basement. The rope was still around Turk's slender neck. The blood rushed to the young curate's brain. He felt faint, so he sat down.

'Can I take him,' was all he said, to nobody in particular.

'Not yet, Father,' said one of the policemen. 'We're nearly finished. You go on into the house and drink a cup of tea. I'll give you a shout.'

It felt like time had stopped. Father Murtagh went up and waited in the great hall, where the men were talking. Walter Pollach came in and got one of the servants to fetch him a brandy, before making his way over to where Father Murtagh was standing.

'Who'd have thought it, Your Reverence. A bonny wee laddie in the prime of his life. What a waste.'

Pollach shook his head slowly as he spoke. Father Murtagh didn't say a word, just stared into open space. It was a stare that made Pollach uneasy, so he shut up and moved off to join the viscount.

Later that day, Father Murtagh transferred Turk's remains to Milly Farrell's house in Lacken. Milly would embalm the body and get it ready for burial. My wife, Mairead, and a nun from Saint Elizabeth's Convent gave her a helping hand. Myself and Jabber were there too, standing around awkwardly. Sugrue didn't come into the house. He couldn't bring himself to see Turk. He was too overcome with grief and anger.

'Look, he's as beautiful in death as he was in life,' remarked Milly, and she touched his cheek softly with the back of her hand.

And he was – only for the burn marks on his neck. When those were covered up, it was as if he was sleeping. He had a peaceful look on his handsome young face. As they washed the body, Jabber noticed a familiar sight below Turk's right shoulder blade. It was a branded *XG*. Suddenly it became clear to him why Turk had been so much in love with life.

Father Murtagh celebrated Turk's funeral in a field belonging to Lord Teale. Canon Reidy had prohibited the boy from being buried in consecrated ground on account of the doctor's finding of death by suicide. Mairead picked out a spot next to a stream. She said Turk's spirit would forever be soothed by the lapping sound of running water. Lord and Lady Teale read Scripture. Micheal

Mooney donated his coffin – he didn't want Turk to be released through the trap door. He wouldn't be looking for it back.

'It's a coffin fit for a king,' said Mairead, with a lump in her throat. 'I haven't seen the like of it ever.'

'He was a king – a king to us who were lucky enough to have known him,' added Jabber. 'Thank you, Micheal. Because of you, we can now carry Turk, shoulder high, to his eternal reward.'

'My grace is sufficient for you, for My power is made perfect in weakness,' said Father Murtagh, as he sprayed the coffin with holy water and sprinkled a handful of clay on the lid.

His voice was barely audible – croaky whispers escaping from his throat.

Sugrue waited around after we had all gone our separate ways. He just stood there in silence, staring at the grave, as the rain fell softly on his grey hair and the breeze blew the tears from his eyes.

You're responsible for him. You're responsible for him. You're responsible for him.

The voice of Walter Pollach echoed in his brain, and there was nothing Sugrue could do to make it go away.

Twenty-four – A Priest on the Run

Canon Reidy couldn't believe his eyes. It just made no sense. A second, third, and fourth check made no difference. His chalice was gone. There was a brown clay chalice, plain and simple, in its place. He took it out again and checked behind it. He withdrew the big silver chalice he used at Easter time. He removed two pyx boxes. He placed everything on the table beside the altar. He went back and checked again, but all that remained was the smooth white cloth that lined the inside of the tabernacle. There was no two ways about it – his chalice was missing.

'Milly,' he said to himself, and his panic subsided.

But Milly Farrell hadn't touched it.

'Yes, I know the chalice you are talking about, Canon, the gold one with the silver doves and all the sparkle. But I don't even have access to the tabernacle. You and Father Murtagh have the only keys.'

This did not sit well with the canon. Father Murtagh had never borrowed his chalice before. How dare he touch it without asking. The curate knew how much the canon thought of that chalice. It was his pride and joy. Canon Reidy waited an hour. He could wait no longer. He rushed over to his understudy's house, but there was no one home. The next day, and the day after that, there was still no one home. Sunday came around without a peep from the curate. He didn't show up to say mass and that's when Canon Reidy got the police involved. They broke down his front door and searched the house. There was no sign of Father Murtagh. Just like the chalice, he had vanished into thin air.

Father Murtagh found the darkest corner of the Dublin tavern. He sat there, alone with his thoughts and his jar of stout. He had his reasons for leaving. He couldn't put up with his boss any longer. Although, it wasn't really the canon's fault at all. All he had done was tailor his homilies to suit the well-to-do in the front pews, those enriching the collection basket. The canon was only a mouthpiece for the bishop, whose arrogance was unbearable to the young curate. Absolute rule can be a bad thing, he pondered, if managed incorrectly.

Then there was Turk and the circumstances surrounding his funeral – the canon's refusal to allow the burial because of what Viscount de Bromley's doctor had to say. Everybody knew that Turk's death was no suicide. It was plain and simple murder. But knowing it and proving it were two different matters. After the way the Catholic Church had failed young Turk, Father Murtagh could no longer have anything to do with it. He was washing his hands of it all – not in a Pontius Pilate way, but washing his hands nonetheless. It was the end of the line.

There was such a thing as natural justice. Father Murtagh believed in this. It wasn't a concept from Catholic theology. The natural justice that the curate believed in had its roots in the Buddhist religion. It transcended the conventional idea of right and wrong – natural justice was more subjective than that. It was a type of karma. Father Murtagh believed – really believed – in karma. Karma was on its way for whoever was responsible for the murder of Turk O'Nuallain. And it wasn't the type of karma anybody wanted. It was bad, and it would bring destruction wherever it went.

So far, Father Murtagh had done no wrong. That was going to change. He walked out of the tavern and turned into a laneway off Sackville Street. He was about to become a fugitive of the law. Bells jingled as he walked through an old brown door. On the far side of a chipboard counter stood a small man with long hair. The small man looked dirty and tired. His beady eyes fixed their attention on the curate.

'Good day, sir,' he said in a city accent.

'Good afternoon,' replied Father Murtagh, as he took the chalice from its bag, unwrapped its newspaper covering, and placed it on the counter.

'Well, what do you think of that?'

The small man remained poker-faced as the light from the windows twinkled on the chalice.

'Not bad,' he shrugged.

'*Not bad*,' repeated Father Murtagh, 'what you're looking at there is the best – and most expensive – chalice in Ireland.'

'If you say so,' said the small man, and he lifted it up to inspect it.

'There's nothing tacky about that little beauty. Those emeralds are real – and the diamonds and rubies. All authentic stuff.'

The small man replaced the chalice on the counter and fetched his microscope. It came in the shape of an eyepiece. He held it by hand as he used it, instead of placing it in his eye socket.

'Mmm,' was all he would say.

'It's worth a hundred pounds easily,' said Father Murtagh.

The small man stopped his inspection and looked up into the young priest's face.

'Is it really! And why do you bring it to me? These days, I drink my tea out of cups with handles.'

'Come on, there's no need to be cute with me,' quipped Father Murtagh.

'*Cute?* I'm not being cute. You're the one that said it's worth a hundred pounds.'

'Well then, do we have a bargain?'

'You must be joking,' said the small man. 'Where would I get a hundred pounds in the middle of a famine?'

'How much then,' asked Father Murtagh.

'I'll give you a score.'

'*Twenty pounds!* Are you mad in the head? It's worth ten times that. I'm giving it to you at half price.'

'Well then,' continued the small man, 'you're obviously in the wrong shop. I suggest you bring it elsewhere, preferably to the pawnbroker who will give you one hundred pounds for it.'

'Feel the weight of it – that's the weight of real gold. Give me fifty then.'

The small man lifted the chalice a second time. It *was* heavy. He took a coin and tried to scratch it. He hoped the curate would not see him doing this. Then he assumed his poker face once more.

'You see,' said Father Murtagh, 'the coin won't mark it – solid gold.'

'Solid gold, my arse. Nothing's solid gold anymore.'

Despite saying this, the small man knew there was a lot of truth to what Father Murtagh was saying. It was an expensive item and one worth having.

'How did you come by this chalice,' he asked.

'Ah now,' replied Father Murtagh, 'I didn't ask you your business, so please refrain from asking me mine.'

'*Refrain?* What sort of a word is that? You're not, by any chance, a priest?'

'If I was a priest do you not think *I'd* be trying to buy the chalice from *you*?'

The small man thought about that and then nodded his head in agreement.

'Thirty pounds then,' said Father Murtagh, 'and I'm absolutely fleecing myself. Make it up in change. You're a hard man to deal with.'

The small man settled on thirty pounds, adding that he hoped the peelers weren't going to come in looking for the chalice later on.

Father Murtagh scooped up the money, put it in a small bag, tied the bag with string, and hid it away. It was official now. He was, in the conventional sense, a runaway, a thief, and a fugitive – and boy did it feel good. Because from that moment, when Canon Reidy's prized chalice changed hands for thirty silver pound coins, Father Murtagh no longer belonged to the conventional. The young curate had often proclaimed: God *does not close one door without opening another.* This was also an opening, a beginning of sorts – the beginning of Father Murtagh's new ministry. From that day on he would walk the streets of Dublin, lifting the sick and the weary. He would help out in the soup kitchens, feeding the hungry. He would be down at the docklands, praying with those about to leave Ireland forever. And the sweet, ironic, bonus was that Father Murtagh would kickstart this new ministry with the money Canon Reidy's prized chalice had brought in – natural justice in its purest form.

Lord Teale was angered by the column in the *Times*. It referred to Father Murtagh as a liar, a thief, and a probable member of an Irish secret society.

'Is everything alright, dear,' said Lady Jane Teale, 'your toilet looks troubled.'

Lord Teale's *toilet* was fine, but his mind was troubled.

'Old habits die hard,' he said in frustration.

'What's that, dear,' asked her ladyship.

'Oh, the British media,' answered Lord Teale. 'They persist with this tactic of trying O'Connell's repealers, the Young Ireland Movement, and members of the Catholic clergy by media. I'll subscribe to the *Freeman's Journal* yet, I swear to God I will.'

'Please don't swear, Harold, it doesn't become you.'

Lady Jane Teale peered over her husband's shoulder at the front page.

'Now there's a fallen hero,' she remarked, looking at the artist's sketch of Father Murtagh.

'Indeed,' replied Lord Teale solemnly, 'but a hero nonetheless.'

Twenty-five – Assisted Passage Denied

One of the tenants on de Bromley's estate was Val Reagan. His kinfolk had been part of the Cranley cluster for generations. A conscientious and practical man by nature, Val could never have been accused of doing anything but his best for his family. But that was not the case when summoned to the big house for a meeting with the viscount.

'Failing to provide,' were his landlord's exact words. 'Failing to provide and now expecting me to make up the shortfall.'

Val was stunned by the viscount's response. If he thought he was hard-done-by, then he was in for a shock – for worse was about to come.

The whole Val Reagan episode began on a fine September, rent-day, morning in 1846. A second harvest failure had left the cluster in a state of panic. Hope was ebbing away with each passing day and Val knew it. So, he waited for Walter Pollach and the rent-collecting party outside his little cabin. Pollach was in bad form long before he reached Val's place. There was very little money in the estate and the viscount had made it quite clear that he wasn't interested in payments-in-kind.

'I don't want any sad stories, Reagan, just the rent,' shouted Pollach, anticipating the worst from the look on Val's face.

'Please, sir, I would like to talk to Viscount de Bromley.'

'And what do you want to talk to him about, Reagan – repealing the Corn Laws? Or maybe you'd like him to honour you with his presence to discuss the fluctuating price of coal and steel? Will I tell him to have the brandy and cigars ready, ya cheeky wee cunt?'

The men behind Pollach sniggered at this.

'Just the rent if you will, Reagan.'

'I don't have the rent but I *do* think Viscount de Bromley will be interested in what I have to say. It could save him a lot of money in the long run.'

'Hold on a minute. Are you telling me that you haven't the rent? This is the fourth week in a row now, Reagan.'

'Not anover one, guv,' said one of Pollach's rent-collecting bodyguards, in a mock English accent.

Pollach turned and addressed the men behind him.

'Listen to this, fellas. This cheeky bastard cannay pay his rent on time but he wants to meet de Bromley to advise him on his financial affairs. Only in Ireland, I tell you, only in Ireland. What's your message and I'll pass it on.'

'No,' replied Val. 'I want to speak to Viscount de Bromley and nobody else on the matter.'

In the end, Pollach set up the meeting – more out of self-preservation than anything else. It was something of a diversion from the paltry amount of rent money Pollach had collected in the cluster that morning.

That very same September day, Viscount de Bromley sent for Val Reagan. The haste at which the meeting had been arranged was a surprise. Val waited outside the office door for over an hour, until he was called upon to put forward his cost-saving idea. He didn't know how to address the viscount. He was sure there was no such word as viscountness, so he decided he'd call him *your excellence*.

Val was looking for assisted passage on a passenger ship. He didn't care where it was going – New York, Boston, Quebec. It was all the same to Val. The second potato harvest failure had beaten him into submission. It was now clear to Val that if he, his wife, and their two boys and two girls didn't get away from Mostrim soon, they would surely end up in the workhouse. He pointed this out to the viscount.

'Edgeworthstown, Reagan.'

Val looked with confusion at the viscount.

'If you and your wife and your two boys and two girls don't get away from Edgeworthstown – it's not called Mostrim anymore. They renamed it, remember?'

Personally, Val didn't care what it was called.

'It all makes very good sense, Your Excellence,' he continued.

'Good sense for whom?'

'For all of us, Your Excellence. It costs three pounds, fourteen shillings per head for a place on the ship. But it costs five pounds per head for a year in the workhouse. And that's only *one year*. It costs another five pounds for the year after that.'

Val began to feel quite confident. The fear he had entered the room with was quickly subsiding. He was putting up a good case and he knew it.

'You have your homework done, Reagan, I'll give you that.'

'Thank you, Your Excellence. If I may say so, it would benefit all concerned.'

'What doesn't benefit me, Reagan, is how you have the sheer audacity to march in here and ask me to assist you and five others to emigrate. In other words, if my sums are correct, you are asking me to fork out twenty-two pounds and four shillings to help you escape a property that you already owe one month's rent on. Do you realise what you are asking me to do? And when the other slackers see me doing this for you, no doubt they'll want to avail of their *soft touch* landlord too.'

'Your Excellence, I promise you once I am settled with a new job in America or Canada or wherever, I will send you every penny I owe in rent and, of course, the price of the passage as well. I give you my word on this, as God is my judge.'

Val Reagan's promise made Viscount de Bromley laugh out loud.

'What do you take me for, Reagan? Do you think I'm an idiot?'

'Your Excellence, I admire and respect you.'

'Well then, why do you insult me so gravely? You've done nothing but insult my intelligence since you walked through that door. Get out of my sight quickly. Get out, before I have you thrown out.'

It wasn't long before Val Reagan *was* thrown out – thrown out of his home. He couldn't raise a weekly rent. He offered a shilling whenever he could, but was struggling to feed four hungry children with diseased potatoes and Peel's stale brimstone. In the end, he met the same fate as Aidan Skelton. His family watched as their thatch went up in flames. Their few belongings lay on the dirt track outside, the cabin desecrated and ready for flattening. This would send out the sort of message the viscount wanted his tenants to heed – the only sort they understood.

But the viscount hadn't bargained on the backlash to the Reagan eviction that then took place. A rent strike was called on the Cranley estate. As they were entering the cluster, Pollach and his rent-collecting party encountered a group of strange men who identified themselves as members of the Longford Tenant Right Movement. The strangers outnumbered Pollach's party. Some of them were armed with long knives, which they flaunted in their belts.

'A combination has been called on this estate,' said one of the strangers – the spokesman of the group.

'Mind your business,' snapped Pollach, 'and get off this land. You're trespassing on private property.'

'This is *our* business,' replied the stranger, 'and we're going nowhere while your landlord continues to abuse the tenants of this estate.'

There was a rush from some of Pollach's men and the members of the Longford Tenant Right Movement drew their weapons.

Deep down, Pollach's heart was racing. He was afraid of being caught in the middle of a vicious row. These land-agitation men had a reputation for brutality and, once blood was flowing, for stopping at nothing until they – or others – were dead. Pollach looked around instead, hoping to disarm the situation with a smile.

'Gentlemen, please. There is no need at all for violence. This wee spat can be resolved amicably, I'm sure of it. We will do the sensible thing and retreat, to allow everyone to calm down. Safety has always been my primary concern.'

'Was Val Reagan's safety your primary concern,' asked one of the knife-wielding strangers.

Pollach made no comment to this.

'We will remain here for these tenants as long as we are needed,' stated the spokesman of the Tenant Right Movement.

'Then there is no more to be said until the blood has cooled,' Pollach retorted, before retreating to the big house.

Viscount de Bromley was willing to play the long game. He knew the passing of each day would hurt the families more and more. He was tabling his offer and then it was up to the tenants.

So, the day after the standoff, a letter was delivered to the spokesman. He was asked to read it out to the nineteen surviving families of the cluster. The viscount wrote that until the combination ceased, no Indian meal would be available for purchase on the estate. However, if prompt cessation of the rent strike occurred, the viscount promised to return all those affected to their Public Works Board and private employments without penalties or loss of earnings. No mention was made of returning Val Reagan and his family to their home and therefore, encouraged by the presence of the Tenant Movement men, the Cranley cluster was determined to hold out until this situation was put right.

However, the viscount had delivered his terms and nothing more was heard from him. Slowly, as the days wore on, the tenants' resistance began to crumble. Before the week was out, their resolute stand in defiance of Val Reagan's eviction had cracked and the Tenant Movement men were asked to leave.

Walter Pollach smiled as he looked at the clearing where the Longford Tenant Right Movement had been housed for the previous five days.

'I knew you'd win in the end, my lord. So much for Val Reagan. Out of sight really does mean out of mind with that caboosh of wasters,' he said.

'Eleven families gone, nineteen to go,' replied the viscount. 'I hope you fellows are ready for what's coming.'

'You should have charged them rent for the nights they spent in that clearing,' quipped Pollach, and his rent-collecting party guffawed in unison.

The viscount waited until all the laughter had dissipated.

'What would be the point of that, Mister Pollach? You can't even collect from a few old biddies, so what makes me think you'd have the stomach to get money out of strong, fearless, young men.'

Twenty-six – The Crop Failure and Measures (Part 2)

The autumn of 1846 was another bleak one. The parish had now two names but still no harvest. The potato crop had turned bad again. Only – this time – it was worse than before.

Blight-ridden potatoes were sliced in two and resown – with hope, longing, and a gnawing hunger. Seeds were reset too. But hope and longing were beginning to turn into fear and desperation. Panic set in as some people realised that they wouldn't survive another crop cycle, diseased or not.

Lacken was hard hit. Myself and Mairead tried to rally around the neighbours. It was important to identify the most vulnerable and stick with them. Jabber and Sugrue joined us in the relief effort. It really was all hands to the pump. But things never got too bad because Lord and Lady Teale made a huge contribution, relieving the suffering of their worst-off tenants.

In the village, Maria Edgeworth had returned from her country estate in Black Bourton, and she too made a big effort to alleviate the pains of the townspeople.

Cranley was a different matter. Here, things were really beginning to get out of hand. The push for rent money was as relentless as ever. Five more evictions had reduced the number of families living in the cluster to fourteen – less than half the number that had lived in the tenant estate a mere two years previously. Lawlessness and petty theft were becoming commonplace, with malnourished residents often raiding their neighbours' near-rotten potato reserves when opportunity arose. The Indian meal on Cranley estate was also in danger, and the viscount was forced to keep two armed men guarding the storage bunker at all times. Tenants were still turning up to work on their master's estate each day, but they were getting weaker-looking all the time.

The autumn of 1846 was also a bleak one for Sir Robert Peel and his Conservative party. Not because they were facing the prospect of starvation, but because they were beaten by the Liberals in the general election. John Russell became the new Prime Minister of Great Britain and Ireland, and Charles Wood took over from Tory Secretary at the Treasury, Charles Trevelyan. This was a cause of optimism for the majority of the Irish public, who felt that the Conservatives did not quite grasp the enormity of our food-shortage crisis.

The Liberal Whigs got to work immediately on the problem of Ireland. They were determined to introduce a new laissez-faire approach. But first and foremost, law and order had to be restored. Vigilantes for Economy was set up. This consisted of an army corps, under the direction of Randolph Routh, whose responsibility it was to watch and protect the activities of the relief committees.

Public works were also reorganised and revitalised under the new government. However, this did not benefit the ordinary worker. Delays were still long, wages often not paid in full or at all, and the numbers now looking to get a place on the work schemes increasing all the time.

Russell and his new government also set up direct outdoor relief. A new Poor Law Amendment Act was introduced and only needed to be ratified. This gave the Board of Guardians more scope and the power to grant relief outside the workhouse. They also concentrated on extending the number of fever hospitals in Ireland, as there were over twenty-thousand patients in dire need. Jabber's mother, Milly, worked in the fever hospital in the parish. It was based at Aughafin. The in-house joke had long since worn thin that the fever hospital was in an ideal location – right across the road from the graveyard – so those entering through its doors wouldn't have far to travel when going back out them again. Milly was a good person as well as a good nurse and, when she could do no more for a dying patient, she would often be heard saying an Act of Contrition into their ear. You could say that all those years working in the church had rubbed off on her.

New charities and benevolent organisations were springing up as the situation continued to worsen. The Society of Friends was set up. The British Relief Foundation was busier than ever. Soup kitchens became commonplace in most towns and villages. There were two soup kitchens in the parish of Mostrim. Sugrue helped out in one of these. He said it lessened the boredom since his sacking at Cranley estate and the departure of Ella May and Padraig. But I knew otherwise; working in the soup kitchen gave Sugrue a huge sense of wellbeing and satisfaction.

'It's the one in Pound Street, the one that doesn't bully the poor people into changing their religion by dangling a mug of hot broth under their noses,' was his eloquent explanation to myself and Jabber.

Sugrue could be as subtle as a battering ram when he wanted.

Every morning at eight o'clock, myself and Jabber were given a reminder of the growing crisis. The work schemes at Cranley estate were overcrowded with poor souls who were, quite simply, unfit for purpose.

'God bless us but some of them are like death warmed up,' I remember saying, as we watched workers staggering up the great avenue to their various jobs.

'Walking skeletons, Jim, regular walking skeletons – so many of them.'

'You know what it is, Jabber, cottiers and landless labourers are mad for public work now. They want money for their employment, and who could blame them – you can't eat rent-in-lieu. The landowners are complaining though.'

'What's new about that,' asked Jabber. 'That shower is always bloody complaining.'

'They're claiming the land is being neglected, and they're blaming this new outside relief approach the Board of Works is taking.'

'It's *their* land, let *them* work it if it's being neglected so much. They've lorded it over the common man for long enough, giving out about how lazy we are and how all we're interested in is what we can get out of our landowner bosses. They'll know all about it when they've nobody to slave over their big precious farms for them.'

'Most of the top boys are blaming Russell. They're saying he hasn't a clue, that they'll have no estates left by the time the Whigs are finished with them. They say O'Connell is in for a field day. Him and his young fella are on the pig's back now. What do you think of Peel and the Conservatives getting the boot?'

Jabber shrugged his shoulders indifferently.

'In the heel of the hunt, it doesn't matter to me who's in power.'

'Course it matters. After all, the Prime Minister of England is the Prime Minister of Ireland as well.'

'That's a load of bullshite, Jim, if you'll excuse my language. As far as their treatment of Ireland is concerned, they're all the same to me. When it comes down to it, the Whigs will be every bit as good to us as the Tories were – and we named the Tories well, robbers and bandits the lot of them.'

I could see that Jabber was getting hot about it, so I decided to say no more. Despite his good education from Maynooth seminary and his obvious interest in dead Irish patriots, he wouldn't have been as informed on present-day politics as myself. I always kept up-to-date with what was going on. Constance knew I had a keen interest in current affairs and would keep whatever newspapers were stacked and ready for the Cranley House rubbish tip. She would slip them to me on a Friday after work. They were mostly English papers, but beggars can't be choosers. They kept me in the know and gave me a different slant on things. They also gave me the ammunition to wind up Jabber.

'Shame about Charles Trevelyan though. Not a bad fella, behind it all. *The Times* reckon there'll never be another treasurer like him,' I said, shaking my head in utter disappointment.

I knew how much Charles Trevelyan was disliked by the man in the street. Jabber had a particular hatred of him. He would scan the *Nation* for anything derogatory he could find on the former Secretary at the British Treasury, and would blow his top when he heard me praising old Charles. But on this occasion, he didn't take the bait.

'Yeah, an awful shame altogether,' he said with a smile, as the two of us headed into the shed to collect our tools.

Twenty-seven – Climbing the Ladder

Growing up, Sugrue was best friends with Tom McAndrew. They were the same age. They had also soldiered together for many years, on the battlefield and off it. It all started in 1798. They were spritely sixteen-year-olds, with revolution on their minds and freedom in their hearts. They had seen first-hand what the spirit of enlightenment had done for the French and wanted to sample it for themselves. Kilcock was their first call to arms – then Ballinamuck. They spent months on the run after that. They slept and ate together. They shared everything and watched out for each other. The next big campaign was the Emancipation rallies. They marched shoulder to shoulder in the parades and demonstrations. They kept guard for the speakers of the monster meetings. The battles with the police were legendary. They didn't mind offering their backs to soften the blow of a baton intended for one of their comrades. Emancipation whetted their appetites. They wanted more. As members of the Mostrim Ribbonmen, they immersed themselves in the tithe and tenant-rights' struggles. Their actions were of the secret kind. One relied on all. The chain was only as strong as its weakest link. As the 1840s drew near, and the two men approached their late fifties, Tom and Paddy could look back with satisfaction. Steady progress had been made. There were many victories achieved, even if the ultimate goal was still out there.

Then it all stopped. Tom McAndrew had had enough. Just when Sugrue was ready to step up their challenge for the promised land, now that their families were fully reared, Tom reckoned he had taken it as far as he could. There was no great announcement or farewell. He simply stopped going to the secret meetings of the Ribbonmen. When they bumped into other in the village, Sugrue noticed a change in his old pal. When he brought up the struggle or produced a page of the *Nation* for discussion, it no longer sparked something in Tom. It was like he had become a different person overnight. Sugrue just couldn't understand how this could be. Finally, he confronted his erstwhile pal over his sudden lack of interest in something they had devoted their whole lives to.

'You're not sick or anything like that,' Sugrue asked bluntly. 'The family is okay, I hope?'

'No, thank God, nothing like that, Patrick. The struggle is over. My struggle is over, at any rate. Emancipation was all they were willing to give us. And we were lucky to get it. There's no point in flogging a dead horse.'

Sugrue couldn't believe his ears. He was stunned by what he was hearing, and it was some time before he could process this. One of his dearest comrades – a dear friend who had lain side-by-side with Sugrue for hours in rat-infested drains while the British hovered overhead – was actually saying he wanted to quit. Until that actual moment in time, Sugrue didn't know there was such a thing as quitting. He wasn't aware that you could just stop one day and say it was over. Some of the things Tom had said swirled around in his brain for weeks. When he was alone, Sugrue would sometimes repeat them in a low voice.

'I just want peace. I've never known peace in my lifetime – and I'm almost fifty-six years of age. Nobody need worry, I will forever remain loyal to the secrecy that surrounds the organisation.'

At first, Sugrue was waiting for Tom to laugh his head off. He was waiting for his lips to stop moving and a great big smile to take over his mouth. But that didn't happen. Sugrue couldn't believe that one of the true-blue fighting men of Mostrim – a man he would have trusted with his life – could say such things. What peace was Tom on about. The British hadn't gone away. And until the British were gone, what peace could there be – what peace did he expect. Why did Tom feel the need to make reassurances of his loyalty to the secret oath. This played on Sugrue's nerves. Staying loyal to the oath went *without* saying. There was no need to reassure anyone on the matter. The secret oath of the Ribbonmen was a secret oath for life, and the penalty for breaking this oath was death.

Very little of Tom McAndrew was seen after that. He kept a low profile. Then, one day in the summer of 1839, there was great activity in and around his cabin in Lacken. The clachan people all gathered for a look. Tom was nowhere to be seen, but a carriage had arrived and some of his possessions were being towed away. News filtered through that the family were moving – lock, stock and barrel. They had purchased a brand-new Bengali-style bungalow in Whitehill, in the parish of Ballinalee. The rest of us in the clachan were puzzled. It was different for his kids, but why was Tom moving at this stage of his life. Where did he get the money for such a swanky house. Shortly after the move, Sheila McAndrew, Tom's eldest daughter, secured a job at Cranley House. This would not have been unusual, except that she wasn't starting as a junior cook, or a chambermaid, or any other job at the foot of the stairs. Sheila leapfrogged straight into a senior position – in charge of domestics, and then, less than six months later, the cooking staff.

The following year, in 1840, the Municipal Act was passed in Ireland. It was treated as both a blessing and a curse by the peasantry. New civil service rules meant that Catholics could now, in theory, climb the social ladder and represent their people to some degree. However, this Act also brought new court legislation and practices – a new toughness against secret societies and faction fighting. The police and soldiers became reorganised under the provisions of the new Act. Eyebrows were raised in the clachan of Lacken as the news broke that Tom McAndrew was embarking on a new career, and had just secured a senior civil service position for the east Longford area. What the clachan people didn't know was that one of the responsibilities on the desktop of the new civil servant was the collecting of Edgeworthstown parish tithes. McAndrew understood, from years of fighting on the opposite side, the precise course of action to adopt. He raised the salaries and bonuses of the Ardagh and Legan tithe proctors, sacked the present tithe proctor in the Edgeworthstown area and appointed Roger Giles to the position instead. He needed a man of unshakable character in charge of this troublesome area, not the bungling fools that he had opposed for years on end. But every appointment he made was carried out in secret. The last thing Tom McAndrew wanted was Sugrue and the rest of his former comrades knowing anything about his present duties or weakening his position.

The general election of 1841 turned out to be a blessing in disguise for McAndrew and other high-ranking Catholic members of the local council. At first, things were looking grim when the Whigs were defeated and the Tory's returned to power. The Whig-O'Connell alliance was over. In fact, O'Connell was decimated at the polls, with only 18 Repealers elected to Westminster. O'Connell even lost his Dublin seat. Secretly, Tom McAndrew didn't give a toss about O'Connell and the Repealers. But what if his religion caused Tom to be ousted from the position of comfort he now enjoyed. There was no need for him to worry, as both Viscount de Bromley and Lord Colehill gave him a public vote of confidence at their next council meeting. The viscount had particular praise for McAndrew in his new role, emphasising how, since he had taken charge, the collection of tithe payments had never run as smoothly.

And so, after years of hiding in ditches and sleeping in haybarns, life was finally coming together nicely for Tom McAndrew. His children were doing well – particularly Sheila, who was now in the most senior managerial position at Cranley House and did the hiring and firing and calling of shots in relation to staff duties. Tom did not regard his hefty civil service salary as a betrayal of his former colleagues, but as severance pay for a lifetime of putting his body on the line, fighting an unwinnable war, and not getting a scrap of recognition for his efforts. After decades of scrimping and scraping, Tom McAndrew had eventually come to experience what it was like to make an actual difference to other people's lives. There was a warmth in being important. It was good to sample the finer things of life. Finally, it was nice to be on the inside – looking out.

Twenty-eight – Franno Wilks

One cool December morning in 1846, a strange nervousness took hold in the clachan. Older members of the settlement threw furtive glances out half-doors and windows. Youngsters stopped their play and stared at a gaudily-dressed man, a woman, and a crew of pimply teenagers. They strutted down the lane in silence, the gaudily-dressed man grinning broadly as he met the children's inquiring eyes. They marvelled at his stylish, colourful clothes – his sky-blue britches and his neat-fitting matching waistcoat. The gold chain of his pocket-watch sparkled in the sunshine. White, knee-high, stockings protruded from his silver-buckled boots. His tailcoat was royal blue. He capped off his impressive ensemble with a yellow linen shirt and a green and white polka-dot cravat – accentuated by a strategically-placed diamond pin. He had a walking cane that he didn't use. It was made from mahogany and had a golden handle. He carried it everywhere. But it was only for show, and – occasionally – bashing skulls.

When the gaudy man stopped, the woman and teens stopped too. When he walked on again, they did the same. They weren't as garishly dressed as their leader. They had no overcoats. But they did wear waistcoats, knee britches, and good shoes. The woman wore an ample cloak, dainty bodice, and a midi skirt over a shift that was visible. Her hair was wild but clean. In her grey cloak and strappy sandals, she was a throwback to Queen Maeve – the pirate queen. She remained as expressionless as the teens as they followed along.

The gaudy man's name was Franno Wilks, and he had good reason to be grinning broadly. He was in the process of becoming a millionaire. Business was booming. Recently, he had been making a fortune. Money-lending was always profitable, but lately, food was the big cash cow. Since the potatoes went to muck in the ground, Franno had been having a great time on the black market. He would buy up large quantities of foodstuffs, store them until the time was right, and then sell them on to the highest bidder. The British government played their part too in making Franno a wealthy man. Long delays in the importation of supplies during the summer of 1846 suited local monopolists and money-lenders down to the ground. Lack of price control and the hoarding of certain essential foods meant Franno was an expensive man to do business with. His exorbitant prices were worsened by the generous interest rates he awarded himself.

On this particular day, Franno and his little party were going on house calls. Terry Morley's cabin, the one nearest the outfield, was to be their first stop. Terry had once lived on the largest tenant farm in Lacken. He and his wife tended a full four acres in the old days, when they were newly married. But it had been Terry's life ambition to be rate-free to the Poor Law Commission. To achieve this, one's farm had to be one-quarter acre or under. And so, he set about his task with great diligence. Over the next fifteen years, Terry – or to be more exact, Terry's wife – had sixteen children. When the time came, he settled each child in a cabin with a quarter acre and his blessing. After the last of his children got married, he placed her in the family home. It was a three-roomed cabin – far too luxurious for an elderly couple – so Terry decided that himself and his missus should take up residence on the Teale estate. Therefore, he had finally realised his ambition – keeping himself and the rest of his family below the requirements of the quarter acre rule and out of the way of the Poor Law rates.

Wilks hammered on the door with his walking cane. The suddenness of the attack excited Franno as he waited for an answer. He had done right in leaving the horses and their rather cumbersome carriage at the entrance to Lacken Lane. But he was beginning to think it was all for nothing now. Not for the first time, Terry seemed to have given him the slip.

'Mister Morley,' said Franno, and rapped hard again, deliberately making a fuss at the front door – in full view of the neighbours.

The door remained closed, but then Terry's little head peeped out from the side of the cabin.

'Look, he's out the back,' shouted one of the teens.

Terry had been spotted, but he didn't mind. This time he had no intention of running and hiding. Franno's eyes danced with delight as Terry ambled around from the back of the house, where he had been shaping a pot with a hammer that was still in his grip.

'My dear Terence, how delightful. You are one very hard man to get a hold of. Put away the hammer please. You won't be needing it – hopefully – and besides, there's a lady present.'

'Hello Franno,' said Terry, aware of the sarcasm in his creditor's voice.

'I decided to call in for a visit, with the wife and a few young fellas from my neighbourhood. They've never been to Lacken before and they're always nagging at me to bring them along to see a bit of the countryside, you know how it is.'

Terry didn't need any of Franno's smartness. He knew why he had really come. And he also knew that those hardy-looking young fellows weren't on a sightseeing tour. They were Franno's henchmen and their reputations preceded them. They were tough and hungry and ruthless. They would kill a man if Franno told them too.

'I've got your four pence inside,' said Terry.

'You see boys, I told you this old stager was straight to the point. No messing around with Terence Morley, he's all business,' said Franno, joking with his entourage. 'I knew he'd come up trumps in the end.'

Terry tried to go into the house to fetch the money. But as he attempted to pass, Franno stuck out an arm to block the front door.

'The problem is you're three weeks late. Time is money. You owe eight pence now, my good man, not four.'

'That wasn't in our agreement,' said Terry. 'There was no mention of a penalty of any kind.'

'It's standard procedure in my line of business. Late payment has accrued extra charges and interest. That'll be two joeys please.'

'You'll get four pence like we agreed,' snapped Terry.

Without arguing any further, Franno nodded and two of the teens sprang forward. One grabbed Terry and twisted his arm behind his back. The other gripped him by the throat.

'As I said, Terence, two joeys after charges and interest. You're not going to embarrass me now in front of my wife and the boys, are you?'

Terry was searching for breath as the grip tightened around his windpipe.

Franno moved ominously close to his face.

'I think we understand each other, am I right, Morley?'

Then a stone came flying in their direction. Franno and his woman looked hurriedly around.

'Hey, you pups get your hands off that man.'

It was the voice of Sugrue, and he threw another stone for good measure. Franno was startled, but soon regained his self-assurance.

'My oh my, if it's not the one and only Paddy Sugrue. I thought the Brits would have done us all a favour by now.'

'Let go of him.'

'This is none of your business, Sugrue, so piss off.'

'Yeah, well, maybe. But I'm making it my business. I won't stand aside while two young curs beat up an old man. You always were a piece of scum, Wilks.'

'*Me, scum*? That's a rich one coming from you, Sugrue. Here's the scum that won't pay his debts.'

'What debts,' asked Sugrue.

'He owes me for four large bags of potato seeds at a penny a bag.'

By then the teens were unsure of what they should have been doing, so they released Terry and awaited further instructions.

'Now, I'll tell you again, Sugrue, piss off and mind your own business. Or I'll take the price of it out on *you* instead. It makes no difference to me.'

As soon as Franno Wilks issued that threat, I stepped out from behind Shay's cabin – hurley in hand.

'Anyone for a game of sprocking,' I said, 'it's a grand day for a right old dust up.'

Then, Jabber Farrell walked slowly out the back door of his mother's house. He was primed for action, his shirt sleeves already rolled up in anticipation. I could tell that Jabber was really looking forward to a good, hard, bout of fisticuffs. The confidence drained from the teens' faces as they watched him approach.

'Great to see these little buggers in the clachan. I haven't been in a decent punch-up for years,' said Jabber, and he smiled at the thought of it.

We walked over and flanked Sugrue.

Franno no longer appeared so sure of himself. His behaviour became less menacing.

'Do you owe this man for four bags of seed,' Sugrue asked Terry.

'Yes, I do. I owe him four pence, but he's now looking for double.'

'And was there anything about eight pence in your original agreement?'

'Absolutely not,' replied Terry. 'He added that bit on himself, because I'm behind in my payment.'

Sugrue nodded and asked if there was any more to the story. He told Terry to go into the house, get the four pence, and pay his debt. When he had done this, Sugrue warned Franno Wilks about ever pulling a stunt like that in the clachan again.

'It's enough that we have to put up with the landlords, them and their rack-rents, without having to suffer the same from our own,' said Sugrue. 'Now you take your flashy clothes, your spotty thugs, and that thing you call a wife and get out of here. Don't let me see you again, Wilks, or there will be trouble. Do I make myself clear?'

Franno nodded his head reluctantly, before he and his entourage slipped out of Lacken – their tails firmly between their legs.

'You're an awful man,' I said to Sugrue, 'embarrassing the poor chap in front of his woman like that.'

'Four big bags of seed,' said Jabber, licking his lips. 'So where are they, Terry, these lovely potatoes? Sharing is caring, you know.'

Our bellies rumbled at the thought of some nice floury spuds.

'They're in my quarter acre,' answered Terry, 'and the quarter acres of every one of my children – and it's there they'll be staying. They're full of the blight.'

Terry thanked us for our backing.

'That's the way it is from now on,' replied Sugrue, 'we stand up for one another, and we stand up together. Nobody is going to blagguard us around here anymore.'

Terry allowed himself a smile when he heard this. He said that, as far as he was concerned, Sugrue was always a great man to lead from the front – like Daniel O'Connell or the old high kings of Ireland.

'He's the High King of Edgeworthstown,' quipped Jabber, winking at me.

'I told you before,' snapped Sugrue, 'and I won't say it again. Enough with your Edgeworthstown – this is Mostrim.'

Twenty-nine - Constance

Constance Ryan was disgusted by the sight of the dress. It was laid out on the bed, all brand new. She went over and took it by the shoulder straps, measuring it against her body.

'I'm not wearing this,' she said to Sheila McAndrew, forgetting her fear in the moment.

'You *will* wear it girl, I guarantee you that,' fumed her boss. 'You'll wear it with a smile. And you'll wear those shoes with it. You promised the master – and over my dead body are you going back on that promise.'

'There was no mention of *this*,' replied Constance, holding the dress aloft. 'I would never agree to wearing this.'

Sheila McAndrew made for the door. She wasn't going to discuss it further. After all, she had more important things to be dealing with. In her new role as senior manageress, she had more to be worried about than a dress.

'Put it on and let that be an end to it – or else, face the treatment. The choice is yours,' she said calmly and left the room.

Constance sat on the end of the bed. She couldn't stop the tears from flowing. She fidgeted absentmindedly with her Saint Anthony's medal. Wearing this dress would be so embarrassing. It was way too short. It was far too low cut. She would freeze in it – her arms completely exposed, and most of her legs. She thought about her grandmother. What would Missus Ryan say if she knew Constance was parading around in such a thing. What would Shay think if he could see her. And then there was the crowd of men who played cards with Viscount de Bromley – the men she would be serving. It sickened her to her stomach to even think about how they would be looking at her and what they would be imagining as they looked.

What choice had Sheila McAndrew left her; it was either the dress or the treatment. Constance had had the treatment before, not long after her arrival at Cranley House. She certainly didn't want it again. The treatment involved Sheila grabbing a hapless subordinate by the hair and forcing her head into a basin of water. When the subordinate was struggling sufficiently for breath, Sheila would pull her face up out of the water again. This went on repeatedly until the subordinate agreed to whatever Sheila was demanding of her. Constance remembered just how scared she had been under the water, not knowing when McAndrew would allow her up. She wasn't alone. The other chambermaids lived in fear of the treatment too, so much so, that all McAndrew had to do was mention the treatment to have her own way.

It was ironic how Constance's current misery had sprung from her happiest spell at Cranley House. She loved nursing Viscount de Bromley's niece and nephew. And the children – Herbert and Hilda – adored their time with Constance. They were two balls of energy, getting up to all sorts. But they were never bold with Constance, the way they were when in the sickly company of their mother. Lady Ivens preferred it when she could neither see nor hear the children. Constance fed the youngsters, bathed them, and put them to bed. She filled their night-time wonder with folklore. She told them all about Fionn and the Fianna, about Oisin taking Niamh away to Tir na nOg – and how he had aged three hundred years once his saddle broke and he touched the soil again. The children couldn't get enough of Constance's fairy stories. One evening, Lady Ivens overheard her telling them about the slua si – and what they did to those who disrespected their forts and fairy rings. Lady Ivens had been going to her parlour to powder her nose, a drink in one hand and a long cigarette in the other. She wasn't happy about these fairy stories. She didn't want Constance fuelling her little darlings' imaginations with tales of the little people. She claimed there were enough superstitions in Ireland without Constance adding to them. But the real reason Lady Ivens wasn't happy was because of the curse that the locals claimed still existed over whoever owned Cranley House and its English equivalent. Viscount de Bromley and Lady Ivens' father and grandfather had both died in suspicious circumstances and, although she never acknowledged this curse as anything but the idle fantasies of the great unwashed, Lady Ivens secretly feared such supernatural notions. But Constance was keeping the children quiet and out of her sight, so Lady Ivens' protestations were short-lived.

One evening, just as Setanta was striking a sliotar into the mouth of the ferocious hound of Culann, the door to the children's room opened. Sheila McAndrew stood there with an oil lamp burning, a girl from the kitchens by her side.

'The master wants to see you,' Sheila declared.

'Shish,' went Constance, putting her finger to her lips.

This only encouraged Sheila to talk even louder.

'The master wants to see you *now*. Annie will take over here.'

Annie was new to the house. She was a standout country hick in a houseful of country hicks. She spoke with a Cavan accent, but it could have been north Longford. That was, of course, when she spoke – which was not very often. She clung to her boss's arm like a baby. Annie was a scrawny, awkward, adolescent who fidgeted nervously. Her eyes weren't big enough for the splendour all around her. She looked dazed as Sheila escorted her into the children's room.

'Don't you ever shish me girl,' Sheila warned, squeezing Constance's arm while marching her down the long, cold, corridor to the viscount's office.

The viscount was counting coins, so they stood for a while – unsure of what to do. Eventually, Sheila McAndrew announced their arrival and took off again. The viscount didn't look up. Instead, he collected a stack of gold sovereigns and moved them in a hop – like a chess piece – to one side of the table. When he did look up, he smiled and apologised to Constance for his preoccupation.

'You girls caught me in the middle of my sums,' he explained, and got up to pour himself a large one.

He then showed the decanter of whiskey to Constance.

'Would you like a little drink?'

'No, thank you,' said Constance, feeling uneasy at the question.

'Alas, how silly of me, Constance. It is *Constance*, is it not?'

She nodded and he sat down again, nursing his glass in both hands.

'You...,' he was searching for the right word, 'you *ladies* would hardly be used to such destructive substances. Here, this is more like it.'

He got another glass and filled it with water from a jug on his table.

'It's out of Saint Barry's well, across from the clover field. The Edgeworths own the clover field if, and do pardon the pun, my *sources* are correct.'

Constance nodded again and took the glass of water. She was growing more apprehensive all the time. The viscount had not brought her here, when she should have been turning into bed in the servants' quarters, to talk about the Edgeworths and the clover field.

'I bet you're wondering why I asked Miss McAndrew to summon you at such an hour – and I wouldn't blame you for wondering. I'll cut to the chase, as my hunting pals would say. I'm told you are very good with my nephew and niece, Master Herbert and little Hilda. That is, indeed, great to hear and I commend you. Hearing a servant, nay, an employee, is competent fills me with a warm feeling, for I know I can trust that employee. I know I can rely on them in times of trouble. And I like to reward competent and trustworthy employees by giving them the opportunities to earn more than your run-of-the-mill worker, who, for all their endeavour, will always remain average and ordinary. How would you like to be *extraordinary*, Constance?'

Constance sat looking at the viscount, not knowing what to say. She didn't really know what *he* was saying either.

'Minding children is important, I grant you, but it's ordinary. I feel it my duty to guide you in a more suitable path for a girl of your extraordinary abilities. I've a role in mind for you – a more important role than just wiping children's arses and putting them to bed. A more lucrative role, may I add.'

If that *wiping arses* jest was the viscount's attempt to break the ice between them, Constance didn't see the funny side of it.

'Pardon me, my lord, but I really like minding Herbert and Hilda. They're adorable little children.'

At hearing this, the viscount broke into a gentle laugh and took a generous mouthful of whiskey.

'No doubt you do, Constance. I'm told your nursing abilities are second to none. This is why I have singled you out for a special role, a role that requires someone with your obvious skills in hospitality. You would be taking me out of a situation. More than that, you would be doing me a personal favour. And I never forget those who help me out with personal favours. Without further ado, I'm promoting you to the position of head waitress of the smoking room. What do you think about that?'

Constance didn't have to think about it. She didn't want to be head waitress of any room. She was good – excellent even – at minding the children, and she enjoyed it. But she was afraid to say no.

'Pardon once again, my lord, but can't one of the other girls be a head waitress? Lady Ivens says that she can't do without me.'

'Alas, you just leave my big sister to me and don't worry your pretty little head about a thing,' chirped the viscount. 'Miss McAndrew has installed that new girl in your stead. She can be their nanny from now on. Ann, is that her name? Something like that. Anyway, can I rely on you to do this one thing for me, Constance? You would really be helping me out.'

He leaned in close, as if to tell her a big secret.

'Between you and me and the chandeliers, a lot of money changes hands during my card games. I can't have just any old girl as my head waitress.'

He sat back and winked at her.

'I need to know I can trust my waitress to keep the secrets of the smoking room. And I know I can trust you, Constance.'

He took a gold sovereign and pressed it into the palm of her hand. She didn't want it. She wouldn't close her fingers around it, so he closed them for her.

'As I said, I like to reward those who help me.'

It was a done deal. Constance became the head waitress to a group of men who were drinking, gambling, and horse-playing around. Despite the job-title implication that she was head over something or someone, there was no other smoking-room staff. Constance was on her own. And she didn't like the idea of it. But what could Constance do. She couldn't say no. She knew these people well by now. She knew their mannerisms and their moods. She knew that saying no to Viscount de Bromley would mean big trouble – not only from him, but also from Sheila McAndrew. Constance wasn't any more than a servant to him, despite all his talk about extraordinary abilities and obvious skills. She was his property – one of his fixed assets, no more and no less than any one of the other girls who worked at Cranley House. But Constance also knew what she was inside. She was a decent, hard-working, country girl, who couldn't be bought by a sovereign or the promise of more money. She had her good name and a loving grandmother in the clachan of Lacken and, please God she prayed, some day she would have her fiancé back from Australia and their own little boys and girls to have and to hold, to love and to cherish, for ever and always.

Constance limped around the whole evening like a turkey in stubble. If the dress wasn't bad enough, the new shoes were killing her. They were brown clogs, and they kept slipping off her feet. She would be walking around with the tray of drinks and then one or other of her feet would lose its shoe and the tray would be ready to topple. In the end she just shuffled along, like the China woman who worked in Bianconi's taxi-carriage office in the village, lifting her legs as little as possible.

The dress was brown too – brown with white trim. It left little to the imagination and made Constance feel insecure. Everything was on show, or so it seemed to her. Her arms were bare and her legs were bare. She had asked Sheila McAndrew could she wear a pair of stockings and was told that if the master wanted her to wear stockings, he would have supplied them. Constance felt that the top half of her bosom needed covering.

'Be thankful you have breasts, and not the two fried eggs that Annie has,' said Sheila, 'besides, it has always been fashionable for Victorian ladies to wear their dresses like that.'

'Not the Victorian ladies I know,' Constance replied, under her breath.

To finish the ensemble off in style, Constance's hair was gathered into a bun and placed neatly in a white headscarf. The viscount himself highlighted the importance of the headpiece. It gave a Continental flavour to the uniform. It was in Paris where the viscount had first encountered this little number – in a café just off the Champs-Elysees. He underlined the practicalities of Constance's new uniform, pointing out the *obvious* advantages it bestowed on its wearer – there was no danger of tripping on a hem or of dunking one's sleeve in a glass of sherry.

Whatever about their differing opinions regarding the new uniform, there was no denying that when Constance entered the smoking room an almost reverential silence took hold. There were five men, alongside the viscount, in top hats and tails and the rest of their finery. The sight of Constance killed the hum of conversation instantly. They were mesmerised by the angel who had just come into their midst. She was like a magnet, drawing their eyes wherever she went.

The indoor life had taken effect on Constance's appearance. Almost two years previously, she had trudged into Cranley House with a bronzed complexion. Back then, Sheila McAndrew referred to her tanned skin as *a sure sign of the peasant*, because it was a well-known by-product of long, hard, days of manual work carried out in bogs and hayfields – when there is a deadline to meet, our womenfolk toil just as hard as our men. But twenty-two months of indoor employment had faded Constance's golden tan. Her skin had taken on a healthy white sheen instead. As his gaming friends retreated to the comfort of their brandies, Viscount de Bromley beamed with delight. He prided himself on having the best of everything – including the prettiest serving girl that any of his guests, even those who had been around for a very long time, had ever set their gaze on.

Lord Duxbury was first to break his silence.

'Bromley, my dear boy, are you trying to give us old farts a heart attack? For fifty years I've been all over this empire and I believed I had seen it all.'

'I'll fetch you a chair, Lord Duxbury. It would hardly be fair to leave a gentleman of your maturity standing for long,' replied the viscount. 'You might get too stiff.'

Two younger guests were sitting at the poker table, their cards faced down and drinks in their hands.

'Wow,' said one, before taking a gulp from his glass.

'Wow indeed,' replied the other. 'It's just a pity she's off limits.'

'Off limits! Whatever do you mean, old chap?'

'A peasant girl, that's what I mean. She's nice to look at, but I wouldn't touch her in a million years, old boy.'

Shaun Burke was standing on his own by the marble fireplace. He was sipping chilled water. A surge of excitement raced through his muscles as he set eyes on Constance. He watched as she waited on each man in turn, replenishing their drinks. While she was finishing her rounds, he made his move. As she approached, he collected up some empty glasses. Reaching for a tray, he stacked the glasses and carried them out of the room.

'Sir, you don't need to do that,' said Constance, following him into the corridor.

'Don't be silly, this tray is heavy,' he insisted, 'and please, less of the sir. You know my name is Shaun?'

'Yes,' admitted Constance, 'you live in the family quarters on the second floor.'

'Correct,' he said, chuffed with her observation.

'I'm sorry, sir, but I've been instructed to address all residents of the family quarters in a formal manner,' explained Constance.

'Indeed,' replied Shaun, forgetting his smile for a moment. 'Well, you can be as informal as you like with me. May I say how beautiful you look tonight, Constance. It is Constance, right?'

'Thank you,' she said, and then she blushed.

'That's not to say you don't look beautiful all the time. It's just that we don't get to see enough of you in those long aprons and baggy cardigans the domestics wear.'

'Good night, sir,' she said abruptly, taking the tray from his sweaty hands.

As she attempted to turn into the kitchen corridor, Shaun Burke grew bolder and took her right arm – stopping Constance in her tracks. Her skin was smooth and cool to the touch.

'I know this is rather forward of me, but would you escort me tomorrow night? I am attending a dinner party at a friend's house in Granard.'

'I thank you, sir, but I will respectfully decline.'

'Well, what about going for a ride in my carriage early on the morrow? We could have a private picnic in the peace and solitude of the countryside, away from the industry of this place,' he again suggested.

Constance met Shaun's hopeful eyes.

'Sir, I thank you but I must decline. I'm engaged to be married.'

'Yes, I've heard,' Shaun replied, with none of the charm he had been using up to then, 'to a criminal who terrorised this very house before being sent packing for Australia.'

Constance was shocked by the sudden change in his manner. He grabbed her by the arm again, this time much rougher.

'Sir, the tray,' said Constance.

'I'll be kind and give you a morsel of good advice. Forget about your man in Australia. He's dead already – dead to us at any rate. You'll never see him again, so get him out of your head. I'm prepared to do you a favour and help you move on.'

Constance wrenched her arm free, knocking glasses from the tray. She charged down the hallway and into one of the kitchens. As Shaun turned to go back to the party, he noticed the stocky, smiling, figure of Viscount de Bromley standing at the window of the smoking room.

'What are you so happy about,' asked Burke, as he skulked across to his master.

'There's nothing wrong with your eyesight, I'll give you that. Alas, never mind old chap, there's plenty more fish in the sea,' replied the viscount.

Shaun Burke's embarrassment turned to seething anger as he realised the master had witnessed his failure.

'How much,' he growled under his breath.

'How much indeed? How long is a piece of string? She's a spirited one, that lassie. It could take a while to break her – especially when she's not for sale.'

'No bitch servant turns me down,' hissed Shaun Burke. 'Now, how much?'

'Oh, jolly well,' said the viscount. 'Come into my office. We may just be able to strike up a bargain.'

Thirty – Death by Starvation

It was shock and horror in the parish of Mostrim. Maisie Rourke had been found dead in her cabin in Lisnageeragh Lane. Her daughter was found with her, lifeless in her arms. The rent collector, an agent for O'Farrell of Lizzard, made the dreadful discovery. Maisie was found sitting upright on a straw mattress, her back to the wall. At first, O'Farrell's man hadn't noticed the daughter, a seven-year-old little girl, because Maisie's hair was long and covered the child's face. Their deaths stung the community and drove home, in the worst way imaginable, the seriousness of the failed harvests of the previous years. Up until that point, Mostrim had been impoverished but coping – looking after its citizens enough to get them through. But that had all changed now.

Inquests were being bandied around, thick and fast. Everyone had their own take on it. In the clachan, where the only topic of conversation was the goings-on in Lisnageeragh, Soyer's soup was apportioned the biggest slice of the blame. It was castigated for its lack of any real nutritional value. According to a woman who knew the doctor in Ardagh, one large bowl of Soyer's soup provided just ten per cent of the necessary daily intake of calories. This was viewed by those around her as useless to a hard-working, fully-grown, woman who, in the good times, had been accustomed to consuming three good-sized meals just to maintain the energy to farm. Another theory exonerated the lack of nutrients, claiming that the harsh effects of Soyer's soup had killed Maisie Rourke. She was known to have suffered from dysentery, and doctors had recently warned the public that the soup was actually harmful to anyone suffering with the disease.

Myself, Jabber and Sugrue sat on the stone wall, staring into the outfield while listening to the post-mortems.

'God be good to them, the poor unfortunates,' I said eventually, and blessed myself.

This shook Jabber from his trance, and he spat out the blade of grass he was chewing.

'*Poor unfortunates?* At least they're dead and out of their pain. Look around you. Who are the poor unfortunates now, I ask you?'

Lisnageeragh went harder on some people.

'I knew the family well,' said Sugrue, 'many a day I ploughed with them. I'm talking about a time long before Emancipation. They were well off compared to most people back then – thick cuts of bacon with gravy while the rest of us were on nettle soup and griddle cakes. And decent to a fault – chronically decent. You wouldn't stoop for an hour after the dinner auld man Rourke would put up. Thank God he's not around to witness this latest scene.'

'And what happened them to end up starving,' I asked.

'When auld man Rourke died, his young fella – Maisie's husband – drank the place out of it. There wasn't a bullock in the field by the time he was finished. It's a sad day for all concerned. And I'm including us when I say that. In all the food shortages I've known during my sixty-four years in this parish, it has never got to this stage before. Maisie Rourke's death is a shame on all of us. It's a shame on the British establishment, which is supposed to be governing our people. It's a shame on the Catholic Church, who's supposed to watch over its flock. And it's a shame on us too – the people of Mostrim – who have always, up until today, made sure that nobody ever died from starvation in our parish.'

The Lacken branch of the Young Irelanders was gathering at the other end of the stone wall. Jabber was quietly taken with them. He admired their bold revolutionary style from afar, but considered himself too old to join them outright. I didn't join them either. I was too much of an O'Connellite all my life to go against the counsellor now. But Micheal Mooney supported them openly. He was in the thick of them, talking excitedly with a tall man who eventually got up on the stone wall and began to speak.

'Friends and fellow Irishmen and Irishwomen of Lacken, the Young Ireland Movement welcomes you here today,' said the tall man, a stranger to my eyes.

Sugrue plucked another blade of grass and leaned across the stone wall, as if there was something of great interest in the outfield.

'By now, I'm sure you have all heard the heartbreaking news from Lisnageeragh. Tragic, indeed, and terrifying it truly is. But it is not too early for the question to be asked – could this have been avoided? The answer, my friends, is surely yes. While I would never side with the warped mind of Charles Trevelyan, whose assumption in the *Freeman's Journal* – that the potato blight and the resulting starvation is down to God punishing us for Catholic Emancipation – is shameful nonsense, I do think that other assumptions and bad political decisions could be at work here. Daniel O'Connell's decision to separate from us and join the side of the Whigs, and his support for the Whigs and the Tories in repealing the Corn Laws, has indirectly led to this day's disaster in Lisnageeragh.'

The crowd was beginning to grow around the tall man. He was now only visible from the waist up.

'Daniel O'Connell and his supporters know the seriousness of our present situation, yet they've done nothing but give the nod of approval to a shabby, incompetent, and insufficient charity structure that has been sent over here to appease us. Where was the Society of Friends – the Quakers – when Maisie Rourke needed its help? The British government tells us its raised two hundred thousand pounds for food, clothing, and crop seed. Its ministers boast about how they're encouraging industry and improving agricultural practises, developing fishing stations and redeeming fishing gear. It's all a pack of lies, my friends. The British government has hung us out to dry. They don't want to help because they haven't bothered to find out what they're supposed to be helping.'

'And what are you going to do,' shouted a voice from the crowd.

'I'm glad you asked,' continued the tall man, even more vehemently than before. 'I will do what the tenants of Cloonahee did on the twenty-second of August last year. I will send a petition to Doctor O'Higgins, the bishop of Ardagh and Clonmacnoise, on behalf of the people of Mostrim. It will not be a nice petition. It will comprise of some harsh realities. In it, I will tell of the outrages that we have suffered. I will forewarn that the peace of the countryside will be much disturbed if relief is not more extensively given to the peasantry. We would never condone or assist in anything illegal or contrary to the laws of God. But I will make it clear that, if faced with the gravest situation resulting from hunger, we will not be held accountable for whatever shall result. We don't want Peel's rotten brimstone. We can't eat it. We don't want Soyer's soup, which has left Maisie Rourke and her little one in an early grave. We want real food – food we can eat and survive on.'

There was sporadic applause then, but some of the crowd were already walking away. They had heard it all before. Myself, Jabber and Sugrue went back to examining the outfield. We had heard it all before too.

'What a fool,' said Jabber, *'petition the bishop.* What does the bishop know, above in that palace of his, about the suffering of ordinary people? He might as well be living beyond in Westminster with the rest of them.'

'It wasn't the soup that killed Maisie Rourke, but the lack of it,' I said.

Sugrue's face lit up when he heard this.

'What has you in such good humour all of a sudden,' asked Jabber.

'Good man, Jim Gorman, you're a genius. For the day that's in it, why don't *we* feed the locals?'

'Are you stone mad,' I said.

'I'm with Jim on this one,' added Jabber, 'how do you propose we do that – only Jesus Christ could perform the miracle with the loaves and fishes.'

'We'll create our own miracle,' gushed Sugrue. 'There has been an awful lot of talk around here today, but very little action – lots of giving out about charities and bad food and different things. How much money have you fellas got? Turn out your pockets.'

I had a shilling and a few pennies. Jabber had two fourpenny bits. Sugrue had almost the equivalent of two shillings – not bad going for a man who hadn't been working for monetary gain in quite a while.

'What are the ingredients of Soyer's soup,' asked Sugrue.

'Well, there's beef,' answered Jabber, 'drippings, onions – or whatever vegetable is handy – a little flour, pearl barley, a bit of salt and a bit of sugar.'

'Excellent. Take this money and head into the village. Bring Jim with you. I'll get a couple of buckets and go to the well. See you back here in two hours. There's almost five shillings there. See how much ye can buy with that. I'll stock up and boil the water.'

'We should be able to get enough for ten gallons of soup with this much,' said Jabber, warming to the idea.

'Right, my auld sons of Eireann, that's settled so,' Sugrue concluded, as he set out with his buckets. 'Tonight, we're going to feed the people of Mostrim in honour of Maisie Rourke and her little girl. We'll feed them our own version of Soyer's soup, until it's coming out of their ears. You'll never hear another complaint about it ever again.'

Thirty-one – Secrets of a Country Manor

Sheila McAndrew *was* spot on; the first time was the worst for Constance. After that, she put a distance, psychologically, between herself and the men in the smoking room. She steeled herself against their lusty stares. She kept telling herself it was only a job. What choice had she anyway – Viscount de Bromley had asked her to do it. And that was the same as saying Viscount de Bromley had told her to do it. Nobody, especially an employee, refused the viscount on his own estate.

But no matter how much distance she put between her new uniform and the men in the smoking room, Constance still felt a deep sense of shame gnawing away inside her. Thoughts of her grandmother filled her with guilt. Those same questions resounded over and over in her brain – what would the old lady say if she could see her beloved granddaughter parading around like this in a roomful of men. Was her new job a breach of her promise to Shay.

The management became nicer to Constance after her first night in the smoking room. Sheila extended an invite to her own private quarters, which she had converted into a dressing room. She made sure Constance had full use of her beauty parlour. She began to slip Constance's clothes in and out of her own large oak wardrobe. A dressing table was positioned in the corner of Sheila's room – complete with handy drawers for hair and face products, and a large mirror that could swivel in all directions. An armchair with cushions was also provided. Sheila began to bring presents to Constance. She said they were from the viscount, to show his appreciation for Constance's application to the new job. He sent word that she was doing marvellous – a joy to everyone in the smoking room. Sheila brought rouge for her cheeks and gloss for her lips. She placed them on the dressing table, telling Constance it would please the master greatly if she would apply them. She brought bottles of clear liquid, the like of which Constance had never seen before.

'What's in those,' she asked.

'Liquid for your skin,' explained Sheila. 'It's moisturiser – another present from the master. You're one lucky girl, Connie, the master has really taken to you.'

Constance hated the name Connie. Lately, it had been following her around. Not only Sheila, but most of the other staff had settled on this shortened version of her name.

'Rub it on. It puts a beautiful shine on your skin. Here, let me help you,' said Sheila, unscrewing one of the bottles and pouring a copious amount of the clear liquid into her outstretched palm.

She took Constance's hand without warning and started to massage, working her way up towards the shoulder.

'Look at that,' exclaimed Sheila, showing Constance her new arm, which was all shiny and wet, 'you're positively glowing.'

Then Sheila did her other arm. She boldly slipped off *Connie's* clogs, before moisturising her feet and legs too. Constance wasn't sure about the moisturiser – she felt slippery and uncomfortably. She was hoping Sheila would be finished soon.

'That's quite enough, Sheila.'

'Nearly there,' said Sheila, 'almost done. I'll just finish off now.'

Instead of finishing off, Sheila started on her shoulders. Constance could feel the hot breath on the back of her neck. Sheila's hands moved down and around her ribs. Constance felt tickly and weird. Sheila asked if she was relaxed, before her hands inched their way around to the part of Constance's chest exposed by her dress. Sheila began to search for breath in short, sharp, pants.

Constance began to feel disturbed. She noticed Sheila's flushed face in the mirror, as her fingertips tap-danced their way down Constance's breasts and between her bosom.

'You've a really beautiful body,' whispered Sheila, as her hands parted and her fingers began to circle Constance's nipples. 'Very strong and firm.'

Constance felt light-headed. Instinctively, she took hold of Sheila's wrists, lifting her hands out of the dress. Sheila just smiled at Constance, before kissing her tenderly on the lips. She winked seductively as she walked away, leaving Constance looking at her wide-eyed reflection in the mirror.

Constance began to work the smoking room with more confidence. She perfected her fake smile, her pearly white teeth complementing her large, glossy, lips. The card players secretly pined for her presence. Whether they won or lost, Constance became the highlight of their night. And she had a word for them all. Each man's spirit soared at the sight of her, at her smell, and at the sound of her voice. Each man, that is, with the exception of Shaun Burke. The odd time he appeared, he ignored her – despite her efforts to put him at ease. She brought him his chilled water with a smile, letting him know there was no bad feeling on her part. But Shaun's pride had been dented. A girl of the house should have been flattered, nay honoured, by his romantic advances – especially a servant girl. Did she fail to comprehend that it was he who was lowering himself to her level, and not the other way around. Despite this, he just couldn't help but steal a glance at her when nobody, least of all Constance herself, was looking. Her smooth sculpted legs in those platformed shoes, her toned arms, her firm breasts pressing against that tight brown dress – it was enough to create a nervousness in the pit of his stomach and a tingling in his loins.

Constance felt awkward about using Sheila's dressing room after the kiss. Just the thoughts of going in there felt strange. But there was never any more about it. Sheila didn't try to kiss her again, or explain why she had kissed her in the first place. Constance was okay with this. She didn't give Sheila the cold shoulder or anything like that. It was a weird situation for Constance because, while she didn't want a repeat performance of the kiss, she also didn't want to embarrass Sheila – risking a backlash from her dirty temper or the treatment. Once she didn't try it on again, everything was fine as far as Constance was concerned.

One week after the kiss, Constance walked tentatively into Sheila's room to get ready for work. The viscount had arranged an after-dinner poker game and, with ten gentlemen expected to attend, it was going to be a busy evening for Constance as the lone hostess. Sheila – in a bad mood – told her to get a move on. The master was having trouble locating a rare champagne he had set aside some days earlier.

'Come down to the cellar and give me a hand.'

'What's the name of the bottle,' asked Constance, 'I have all the different brands in order and stacked in their groups.'

'Oh, it's some French name, I can't get my tongue around it,' snapped Sheila.

She waited impatiently while Constance dressed. They lit their lamps and headed down the cold, lonely, corridors that led to the cellar. The viscount had had his wine cellar specially built. He insisted on his fine wines and cognacs having a room to themselves – so they could breathe properly without the stench of porter in the air. All beers and other ales had been relegated to the basement. They were stacked beside sugars and teas and all types of goods in brown wooden boxes, sent over time from the four corners of the empire. Every single year, without fail, the viscount received a large chest of tea from the Gambia in Africa – a present from the Marquis of Salisbury, whom the viscount had long become personal with from their legendary card games in Kent.

When they neared the cellar door, they could hear the sound of voices from within. There was a conversation taking place, Constance was sure of it. But when they entered, the viscount was standing all alone, a lantern burning by his side. Constance felt that something wasn't right. She had often helped Sheila sort out the drinks, but had never seen the viscount in the cellar before. It must have been a very special champagne indeed – to required his personal attention. Constance's suspicions were heightened by the nervous expression on the viscount's face, as Sheila led her over to him.

'Good evening, my dear, may I say you're looking as radiant as ever.'

Constance whispered a thank you to her master.

'I fear we're having a smidgeon of trouble down here, I trust Miss McAndrew has filled you in. We're finding it difficult to locate a certain label. I was hoping to pamper our guests tonight.'

The light of her lantern showed the anxiety in Constance's face.

'My lord, I assure you I did not take anything from your cellar. I would never do such a thing.'

The viscount flashed a disarming smile and assured Constance that he was in no way accusing her of stealing.

'On the contrary, you're doing such a splendid job as our hostess that I'm going to give you a pay increase.'

The viscount told Constance not to look so worried, that a pay increase was a good thing. Then he said he had a confession to make.

'The real reason I requested your presence in the cellar this evening has nothing to do with a bottle of champagne.'

Constance looked around at Sheila, who was gesturing towards a stack of barrels in a corner of the room. Suddenly, a shadow moved from behind the stack and grew in the light of the viscount's lantern. It was the tall figure of Shaun Burke.

'You know Shaun, don't you, Constance?'

'I do, my lord.'

Constance's heart was beating wildly and she felt a dryness in her mouth.

'Shaun tells me he's very fond of you,' continued the viscount. 'Are you fond of Shaun?'

'Yes, my lord. I'm as fond of him as I am of all your family and friends in the house.'

'Well, that's not exactly what I mean, Constance. Shaun is, let us say, so fond of you that he's in love with you. Putting it plainly, he would like to marry you. What do you say to this, Constance?'

Constance didn't want to say anything at all to this.

'I can't hear you, my dear. What do you think of Shaun's affection for you?'

'I really don't want to think about it at all, my lord. I have told Mister Burke already that I am engaged to be married to another.'

'Yes, indeed, the scoundrel who ransacked my home and who's now enjoying his just deserts at the pleasure of Her Majesty's confines.'

Shaun Burke passed Constance by. He stood behind her, next to the door and Sheila McAndrew. This made Constance even more nervous – she didn't like him standing in her blind spot. But what could she do. She couldn't turn away from the viscount, who was addressing her directly. Constance wouldn't show such blatant disrespect to her boss – the lord of Cranley House.

'Alas, there's no need to be alarmed,' the viscount assured her, trying to ease her worried face. 'Nobody here will hurt you – only help you. I'm always ready to help my staff as if they were my own family. You and Shaun shall be married and will live a happy life together. Shaun assures me that you will want for nothing as his wife. He has kindly agreed to take care of all your family's needs as well. And believe me, Constance, Shaun is a man of considerable means – despite his tender years. He has worked for me for nigh on twenty years – starting when he was no more than seven or eight – and let me tell you, a harder worker I have yet to meet in all my travels through this great empire of ours. So, my dear girl, you've really struck it lucky. I'm elated for you both.'

Eventually, Constance turned and looked at the pair standing behind her. Sheila McAndrew was expressionless in the light of the lantern. Shaun Burke was giving his best smile to the only girl who had ever forced him to break his golden rule.

When starting out as a stable lad on the plantations in England, Shaun Burke made a vow to the viscount which he labelled his *golden rule* – despite his rough hands and shabby clothes, Shaun would one day marry a high-born maiden, a girl of considerable means and social status. This vow had been the driving force behind all Burke's actions. He had invested every penny he ever earned. He had never even tasted alcohol. He had been single-mindedly determined to eradicate the bitter memory of that snotty-nosed kid of seven, half-starved and barefoot, who had staggered into Cranley estate all those years ago. And he was also determined to never again feel the desperation that had led him there from a shack in Lisanore, and a consumptive teenage mother awaiting her turn to die.

The viscount still remembered the look in Shaun Burke's eyes the first time they met. He never saw such want in another human, such raw desire to do whatever it took to survive. Burke built up his worth steadily until he became a young man of modest wealth. He made Viscount de Bromley a considerably richer man in the process. He was ruthless, and whether it was terrorising rents out of tenants or intimidating gentlemen into business deals with the viscount, it didn't really matter to Shaun. His cruelty crossed all sectarian and social divides. To him, it was just another day's work.

And now there was Constance, the girl with the face and the figure that compelled him to alter his golden rule. From the moment he set eyes on her, Shaun Burke couldn't get her out of his mind. After a decade of social networking at illustrious parties – with all their ladies of glamour and grandeur – Burke had yet to see a girl as striking as Constance Ryan. He had to have her, despite her lowly station, and that was the end of it.

Constance turned back to the viscount. Now came the moment that she had been dreading.

'My lord, I'm sorry but I can't marry Mister Burke. I won't.'

This stung the viscount, who wasn't used to a servant refusing him – and, to make matters worse, in front of others.

'Oh, but you will, my dear. It has all been arranged. You shall be married on Saturday next. I don't want to hear another word.'

'I'm already engaged, my lord, to Shay Gorman. I love him and he loves me. We have agreed to be married on his return.'

The viscount could hold his happy face no longer, but there was no point in arguing or shouting. What he had decreed was not up for discussion.

'Is this your final word on the matter,' he asked, his voice trembling as he threw a look over her shoulder and nodded.

'It is, my lord.'

Constance had barely the words out when Shaun Burke produced the handkerchief. He gripped her by the hair, jerking her head backwards and pressing it forcefully against her mouth and nose. She shrieked and struggled, frantically at first, but with every breathe thereafter felt the strength draining from her limbs. The handkerchief was overpowering her. She pulled weakly at Burke's arm, but her head was getting lighter all the time. Everything went black and her arms fell limply by her sides.

'That'll teach the bitch her place,' said Burke.

'Put her down gently,' ordered the viscount. 'Quick, hide her in those sheets, the carriage is waiting. Fetch her legs, Shaun.'

The viscount opened the trapdoor to the secret passageway. It was in the far corner of the cellar, beside the wine barrels where Shaun had been hiding.

'Grab her arms, you nincompoop,' snapped the viscount, as Sheila stood with her mouth open like a dummy.

'Make haste, both of you, out of here. Once you're through the gates, she's your problem,' he said, gripping Shaun Burke by the collar of his cloak. 'If you're caught, I'll deny all knowledge.'

When they were clear, the viscount slammed the trapdoor shut. He replaced the rug across it and shone his lantern around the cellar. Everything was in order. He hurried up the corridor towards the family lodgings.

'She could have made things so much easier on herself,' he muttered as he scurried along.

But, then again, when he thought about it, what did he expect – they rarely made things easy on themselves. There was a savagery in the native Irish mind that defied cultured, British, comprehension. They had to make it difficult – even when their masters were only trying to look out for them. He was heading for his private quarters when he remembered – there was no one there. The viscountess was away at her sewing circle. It was time for the smoking room instead, and all the alibis the viscount could ever wish for.

Thirty-two – The de Bromley Financial Crisis (Part 2)

Walter Pollach was staring into his master's face.

'What,' said the viscount.

He couldn't even say the word *what* without returning to a fit of laughter. As the carriage rolled along, on its way home from Longford courthouse, Viscount de Bromley was in danger of bursting with giddiness.

Pollach wondered what it was all about. Only a few days earlier the viscount had looked under pressure. He had been in a black mood, barking out instructions at anyone he came across. Had he gone completely mad, especially in light of what Pollach had just perceived in the courtroom. While the viscount was stepping out of the witness box, the sheriff was happy to inform him that he had secured further capital to increase the workforce at de Bromley's drainage scheme on Cranley estate. The viscount shook the sheriff's hand and belly-laughed back to the gallery.

'Don't fret about it, Arthur,' Pollach heard the viscount say, 'keep those monies and use them elsewhere. Things have changed with regard to the scheme.'

'But under the terms of this new Public Works Act...'

The viscount stopped the sheriff in mid-sentence.

'Poppycock, my dear man. I know all about the new Public Works Act. I had a fellow from the board out at the house. He told me how they are now prioritising agricultural works over road and rail building. The blighter wanted to send me a sub-soiling expert, but I told him that he was only wasting his time.'

Arthur the sheriff was shocked. Did he hear the viscount correctly, telling him to keep the Public Works' grant money. Pollach was shocked as well. The viscount didn't even ask for the return of his backhander cash.

'May I be so bold as to ask why you are in such high spirits this afternoon, my lord,' said Pollach, as they rolled on in the rocky carriage.

'What's the point in going around with a long face, Mister Pollach? Life will pass us by if we don't enjoy ourselves, that's what I say.'

'Pass us by, my lord?'

Pollach wasn't happy with this answer. His master was being deliberately vague. But he felt he had to ask. He was getting anxious about his own position. What was de Bromley planning to do, now that he was giving away the grant money. The viscount sat up on his cushion and put Walter's mind at ease.

'Actually, I'm glad you asked, Mister Pollach. You deserve to know what's going on, especially as you're the main man in my future plans. You stand to make a lot of money – if you meet our targets.'

Pollach was delighted with what he was hearing so far.

'Things have changed rapidly at Cranley. As you already know, the long-term plan was to clear all existing tenants from my estate. And as you no doubt heard, there have been a number of suggestions for this long-term clearance – a recolonization with Protestant tenants and a changing in the way farming land is being utilised are just two examples. But earlier this week, I received a substantial offer – subject to certain conditions – from one of my English counterparts. And that's where you come in. You're now the vital cog in all of this. I need you to make this offer a reality for me, Mister Pollach. Rid my Cranley estate of all my tenants by the end of this calendar year and I'll make you a very wealthy man.'

'But this is set to cause anarchy, my lord. We have already had mince trouble from the Tenant Rights Movement. An attempted clearance in such a short timeframe will cause mayhem. Some of your tenants are looking to *buy* their holdings. Crawford and Blacker have their heads gone astray. Take the Kiernans, for example - now that a few dollars have arrived from across the water, they've got notions above their station and are mad to buy out.'

'Mister Pollach, use your brain, man. I said clear the lands, not start a war.'

'With all due respect, my lord, mass evictions are certain to start a war.'

'I'm not talking about *evictions*, Mister Pollach. I'm talking about *incentives* for dispossessing tenants – incentives so lucrative they won't be able to resist.'

'Incentives for dispossessing?'

'Yes,' explained the viscount, 'incentives – like cash, wavering of arrears, the right to keep their crops or other goods, the right to keep thatch and timbers so as to construct other shelters and, in limited cases, the right to occupy the land they have given up as caretakers for a proposed time. And here's the best part, Pollach. We get to clear the estate and nobody can say one bad word to us for doing so. The Tenant Rights group won't have a leg to stand on. We're not evicting anyone. We're giving the tenants a choice. We're providing them with a goodwill gesture – however limited or unlimited that goodwill may be construed. At the same time, we're taking them out of the system – they're no longer a burden under the terms of the Poor Law Act. As for Kiernan, I'll put forward an alternative for him and others in his situation. He can keep his American money, and I'll provide him and his family with assisted passage to wherever – that way the Tenant Movement cannot accuse me of throwing him out on the side of the road. My English counterpart has plans for the land that Kiernan's trying to buy, and he does not figure in those plans.'

All morning long Pollach had been dreading that his master was going mad, but now he was fully sure de Bromley had completely lost his marbles.

'*Assisted passage, wavering of arrears, cash incentives* – do you realise what you're saying? My lord, all of these remedies are sure to run into thousands of pounds.'

The viscount took into another belly-laugh as Pollach looked on in dismay.

'Yes, they will. The more money, the better.'

'Are you feeling alright, my lord? I fear you're not yourself.'

'Oh, I feel splendid and make no mistake, Mister Pollach. The lands will be cleared whatever the cost. Because – and here's the best part – I'm not paying for it. My English counterpart, and future lord of Cranley House, has left instructions to clear the lands regardless – with all costs accruing to be met by him personally.'

Walter Pollach sank into his cushioned bench as the carriage made its way into Edgeworthstown. He felt important at long last. His master needed him to complete his masterpiece. What an opportunity now presented itself. He would get the chance to cleanse de Bromley's land of the native riff-raff – perhaps even in favour of *British* settlers should the future owner of Cranley House decree it – making himself a wealthy man in the process.

The thoughts of discarding his Poor Law contributions made Viscount de Bromley fizz with excitement. He had always hated being responsible for spongers. That was his pet name for those tenants who fell into arrears – *spongers*. Now he had the opportunity to cut those spongers loose and rid himself of them for good. The viscount hadn't felt such relief in a long time. It was positively liberating. The deal couldn't have come at a better time – just as the viscount was in danger of being financially exposed.

Now his money troubles would never come to light. He would be able to send his son to Cambridge University, keep his wife – and mistresses – in the style and luxury they had become accustomed to, considerably reduce his rate-paying obligations, and ultimately facilitate his return to his estates in England. The deal would take a few weeks to finalise. Until then, the viscount had the money from Shaun Burke – the thousand pounds he had received for the provision of a wife – to cover his personal expenses.

'Shaun Burke didn't leave a handkerchief up at the house for me, by any chance. I told him to give it to you or the viscountess for safekeeping, my lord, when he was finished with it,' said Pollach.

'*A handkerchief?* Like a napkin? Is that all you can think about after the news I've just bestowed on you, Pollach?'

'No, my lord. But it was a beautiful white handkerchief with a red and green design. He borrowed it from me last Tuesday morning.'

'Shut up about it. It's only a napkin. What triviality.'

'Och, yes, well… it's just that it was an expensive item with sentimental value, my lord.'

'Sentimental value! Such foolishness. You'll be able to afford cashmere handkerchiefs with golden-thread designs by the time we're through with our land-clearing project. That much, Mister Pollach, I can guarantee.'

The viscount put his lips close to the carriage window and breathed on the glass until it fogged up. Then, he drew a face with a big smiley mouth in the steam. Walter Pollach looked across and laughed, before giving a big thumbs-up. He took a hipflask from his overcoat, uncorked it, and passed it across to his master.

'Tan a wee dram of brandy, to toast your good fortune.'

'Oh, do speak proper, Mister Pollach. It's high time you spoke correct English, and not that Highland mumbo-jumbo.'

Thirty-three – Sugrue and the Raid

Sugrue didn't call a meeting. He didn't like them. Even the old meetings of the Ribbonmen –which were watertight – were viewed with a degree of suspicion by Sugrue. Instead, he chose his men and went around on them individually. It was his favourite way of dealing with secrecy. It was also the best way of knowing if his chosen few were up for the fight. Sugrue always began his one-on-one with the most shocking or difficult detail of the subject in question. That way, he could judge from body language and facial expression whether or not he could trust his man in the heat of battle.

The evening of the Maisie Rourke debacle had reminded Sugrue of the important things in life, and how good it felt to help others. Watching people enjoy the soup he had helped buy and prepare had given Sugrue a lift. There were no strings attached to the meal either and that was important to him – he wasn't lining them up, allowing them to smell the broth, and then keeping it from them until they signed over their faith or their allegiance.

'We'll have to do this more often,' Sugrue told us with a big smile.

'Ah now, they'll canonise you a saint before the blight leaves us,' joked Jabber.

'He will be accused of many things before he croaks it but being a saint isn't going be one of them,' I added hastily – and honestly.

Some people in the parish just couldn't get access to food and this, in particular, made Sugrue mad. Basic staples were now the subjects of constant bidding wars. It reminded him of Cornwallis's old tactic of starving out whole towns at a time. Only now it was Westminster that was doing the starving out. Ironically, governmental price control of rent – which was designed to help Irish tenants – was another separator of the people from the food. Although members of parliament gave themselves a big pat on the back for their perceived fixing of the problem, they had no idea of just how bad the situation had become in Ireland. And up until the dreadful discovery in Lisnageeragh two weeks earlier, neither had Sugrue nor the rest of us for that matter.

The demise of Maisie Rourke and her daughter reminded Sugrue of something else – their deaths were as much a shame on us in Lacken as they were on those in Lisnageeragh. If Sugrue was going to try to help people get access to food, he was going to try to do it for the whole parish. It wasn't about helping the people of Lacken or the people of Cranley, it was about helping the entire people of Mostrim.

Sugrue did the rounds and everyone had their orders. On the following Friday evening – the penultimate day of July, 1847 – at the stroke of six o'clock, Jabber Farrell and Pius Mooney would cause a disturbance at the food sub-depot in Longford Town.

'Can we wait until after six,' asked Pius.

'What do you mean,' said Sugrue.

'Can we wait until a minute past six? That way we'll have a chance to answer the Angelus bell.'

Sugrue thought this was a joke, until he realised Pius was deeply in earnest.

'Okay, grand. One minute past six,' agreed Sugrue, 'but no later. And say a prayer for the rest of us while you're at it.'

The plan was to stage a decoy attack on the sub-depot. When news was cabled through that the sub-depot was under siege, the police were sure to send reinforcements from the neighbouring parishes – one of which is Mostrim. That would leave de Bromley's basement in Cranley House a relative sitting duck for Sugrue, Peter Hogan, and myself.

It was a smart move on the part of Sugrue. Everyone knew, since January of the previous year, that the government had been stocking the sub-depot to the rafters with Peel's brimstone. The main depots – set in the large urban areas of Leinster, Munster, and Connaught – couldn't cope with the £100,000 worth of Indian meal originally imported, so they were forced to filter some of it through sub-depots. Longford was heavily guarded, as this was by no means to be the first attack of its kind. Only a couple of weeks earlier, a large crowd of starving Longfordians gathered at its gates and demanded food be handed out. When their wishes were not respected, desperation took hold and they tried to storm the building. The militia held out until the police arrived and began their counter-offensive. Altogether, five people were killed and a large number injured. Sugrue learned a lot from that attack and, this time around, had something different set up for the relief commissioners and their guards.

Sugrue had done his homework on some of the other attacks as well. On October 7, 1845, the cavalry and infantry had to be called in to prevent a mob – angry, impatient and starving – from breaking into the food depot at Roscommon Town. Sugrue had read all about it in the *Freeman's Journal*, his mind going into overdrive as he dissected every detail of the report.

Now the planning was over. It was time for Sugrue to mastermind the feeding of his people – the Mostrim people. The food was there, it was just a matter of getting his hands on it. Turk had told him all about it, how sacks of porridge oats hung in the basement of de Bromley's house. Enough porridge to feed a small army, that was the way Turk had put it. Tea and sugar and all sorts of other edible goods were down there too. Sugrue would have to bring sacks with him, as most of the goods were stored in wooden boxes too heavy and awkward to transport by hand. Turk had told Sugrue everything, and even drew him a map – complete with a system of tunnels and corridors to and from the basement. A tinge of sadness crept into Sugrue's mind as he revised the map.

'This one's for you, my auld son of Eireann,' he heard himself whisper.

So, on the Friday, Jabber and Pius lay low until they heard the bells of Saint Mel's Cathedral ring out the Angelus across Longford Town. They moved swiftly to the gates of the sub-depot, pulled their scarves across their faces, and opened a bulky turf bag. Pius lit the camphine-soaked sods and Jabber fired them onto the roof of the building. They disappeared into the background and waited. A whistle went off. The guards were soon at the gates. They were pointing their guns all around. Jabber immediately recognised the guard with the grey beard in the militia uniform. Not only was he at the eviction of Aidan Skelton, but also protected the tithe proctor at the roadblock in Lacken. Jabber had forgotten his name. A young guard came out with a bucket. He looked up at the spreading fire. People were gathering outside on the street. Jabber and Pius had a supply of rocks and started throwing them at the guards inside the gates. The crowd on the street picked up stones and started firing too.

'That's a bonus,' said Pius.

'Keep pegging,' replied Jabber, aiming for the militia man with the grey beard.

The guards couldn't retreat to the burning building, so they waited in an outhouse for reinforcements. A shot was fired over the heads of the stone-throwers.

'Next time I'll plug one of you animals,' shouted the militia man with the grey beard.

After a while the police arrived. The rocks and stones were still flying. The crowd backed off as the police drew their batons. A long wooden table was brought from the outhouse and placed against the gates as a barricade. More police carts ground to a halt. The rocks and stones became fewer as the crowd was beaten back. Jabber and Pius had done their part well and now it was down to us lads in Mostrim.

Peter Hogan supplied the transport for the evening. His elderly uncle in Granard owned a horse and carriage. It had been arrested many times for having the wrong signature. In the old days, when the peelers had pulled his uncle over, it was always *O Hogain* on his nameplate. He was warned a few times about this. He was ordered to replace his nameplate with the English equivalent. Then the old man was handed several two-day jail terms to help refresh his memory. But it didn't matter. He was as passionate about the Irish language and as patriotic as his beloved nephew. And as far as Peter's uncle was concerned, no invader was going to come into his country and tell him what to do. Peter would have to ditch the nameplate for the raid. Sugrue had told him to make sure to leave it at his uncle's house. But with all the plotting and planning, Peter had forgotten to do this. He was on the road when he thought of it, so he threw the nameplate in the back of the carriage. What Sugrue didn't know wouldn't bother him.

I had suggested that Lord Teale would provide me with a horse and carriage. All I had to do was ask. But Sugrue didn't want Lord Teale's help in this case. It wasn't that he was an Anglo-Irish landlord or anything like that – those feelings belonged to the past. Sugrue had watched Lord Teale help out with the soup kitchens, even setting up his own feeding station in Lacken since the second harvest failure. He respected and appreciated what Lord Teale was doing for his tenants and the other needy people of the parish. Sugrue just didn't want to incriminate Lord Teale, or risk getting him into trouble of any kind. When Peter Hogan said he could provide a horse and carriage, everything was sorted.

The three of us were sitting in the hollow tree in the parson's field, keeping an eye on the brand-new police station. We waited and waited. Finally, a peeler rushed out – a telegraph message still in his hand – and untied the horses. Another policeman followed hot on his heels, bolted the station door in a hurry, and they both rode off in the direction of the Longford Road.

'The coast is clear,' said Sugrue. 'It's time to go to Cranley. We'll wait for the twilight there.'

'We won't be vilified for this, will we,' asked Peter Hogan nervously.

'Vilified! You wouldn't hear the Edgeworths coming out with a word like that,' said Sugrue.

'It depends on the view taken,' I replied. 'If we get caught, the locals will see it as an act of kindness. The authorities will see us as thieving scumbags. The *Times* will have a field day at our trial. The *Freeman's Journal* will campaign for leniency and have someone compose a poem in our honour. One way or the other, at least you won't have to worry about your job, Peter. You're not about to be hired as a teacher around these parts again. Canon Reidy has already put paid to that.'

'Will you whisht. They won't catch us – to call us anything. Besides, we're *not* thieving scumbags,' Sugrue pointed out. 'Think of it more along the lines of us being three little Santy Clauses – only we come bearing gifts for the people in July, when they're alive, instead of next December, when they'll be dead from the hunger.'

Peter pulled the carriage into a boreen across from Cranley House and tied the horse in the bushes. He seemed the most nervous of the three of us, even though my stomach was in knots as well. I understood his position – teaching children had always been his forte, not burglarising country manors. Sugrue asked him one last time if he was sure he could go through with this. Then it was away with us down the boreen and into the forest behind the big house.

Sugrue knew exactly where he was going, even when we had extinguished our lanterns. While myself and Peter were still feeling our way in the darkness, Sugrue had the grass covering off and the double doors open in jig time. We were in, through the corridor, and past the point of no return. We walked quietly and quickly behind Sugrue, unsure but steady. I could hear Peter Hogan's quick breaths. Sugrue took a right, then a sharp left. We were in the basement.

'Hurry now, the porridge first,' whispered Sugrue, producing the large cloth sacks. 'I'll fill the tea and sugar.'

We set about our task with great efficiency, lugging bags of meal and porridge out to the carriage in the boreen. Then it was the tea and sugar. After that, God knows what was waiting for us. Every time we returned, Sugrue had our next load bagged and ready. He hopped them up diligently on our shoulders and we were away again. The three steps at the basement entrance were partly lit by a full moon. Thank God for small mercies. Myself and Peter took the greatest of care on these steps, ensuring we didn't trip or make any more noise than we had too. We were getting tired, but Sugrue told us that we were nearly finished. Despite his advancing years, you could tell he was used to hard work and had no difficulty loading and lifting the heavy sacks.

'That's the last of it,' said Sugrue, as we emerged from yet another trip to the carriage.

We were very glad to hear it. We took the last three bags and made for the doors. But there was no moonlight to show us the steps. There was no light of any kind. The double doors had been fastened against us. Peter began to whimper with panic, but Sugrue put his finger to his lips and crept towards the steps. There were voices on the other side of the double doors.

'I found them like that, my lord.'

It was the Scottish twang of Walter Pollach. He was on the other side with Viscount de Bromley.

'I jammed them shut with that iron bar.'

'You did rightly, Mister Pollach. Are the other men alerted?'

'Yes, my lord. I roused them from their rooms. Here they come now.'

There were more voices then.

'Are we ready? Splendid. You fellows stay here and guard these doors. Mister Pollach, Shaun, and I shall go in through the front. If there's a scoundrel still in there, we'll flush him out through the corridors. Wait on our signal. When you hear the call, open the doors and come on through.'

Sugrue retreated from the steps.

'We're trapped,' gasped Peter.

'We'll have to storm the doors,' I remember saying. 'We've no other choice but to overpower them.'

'No,' said Sugrue, maintaining his cool. 'We don't know how many men we're dealing with, or what's on the other side of those doors. They may be armed for all we know. I've another idea, let's get to the cellar as quick as we can.'

'The cellar! Are you mad, Sugrue? We need to get out, not trap ourselves in further.'

'I've no time to explain, Jim. Trust me, I know what I'm doing. The cellar, now.'

Sugrue led myself and Peter through a maze of dark tunnels. As before, he seemed to know exactly where he was going. We reached the cellar door just as the light of three lanterns came rushing in our direction.

'There they are,' shouted Walter Pollach. 'The cellar. Quickly, they're away to the cellar.'

Sugrue closed the cellar door, holding his shoulder to it while myself and Peter fumbled around for something sturdy.

'Give me a hand with this barrel,' said Peter.

I groped around for the rim of the barrel but, instead, felt something else in my hand. It was a small cloth of some sort. I stuffed it in my pocket and helped Peter roll the barrel up against the door. We could hear the footsteps getting faster and closer, before the door latch was tried – and then voices.

'Go signal the men outside,' instructed the viscount, 'and tell them to fetch an axe on their way.'

'We've got them now,' said Pollach.

Shaun Burke hurried off down the corridor to get the rest of the men. Walter Pollach stayed alongside the viscount – a lantern in one hand and a musket in the other. While they waited for the others to arrive, Pollach decided to reason with us.

'There's no point resisting. You're trapped and hopeless. I've got a firearm and I'm only waiting to use it. Come out and surrender now, and it won't go so hard on you.'

He waited for a response – some call for leniency – but all there was from our side of the cellar door was silence.

'You're only making things worse on yourselves,' Pollach continued.

Sugrue asked if anyone had a light. Peter had a box of matches, but he left it in the carriage when he was returning the lanterns.

'I didn't think we'd need any more matches,' he lamented.

'Okay,' whispered Sugrue, 'it's not your fault. It was me that said no lights, that they would only draw attention.'

It was pitch dark, so Sugrue told us to get down on our hands and knees and feel the floor for a rug. I found a rug in the corner of the room. Sugrue wasted no time in removing it, then began feeling the floorboards again.

'What are you doing, Sugrue,' I asked.

'There's a handle here somewhere,' he replied.

When he felt it, he twisted the handle and, as if by magic, something popped.

'What's that noise,' said Peter.

'A trapdoor,' answered Sugrue. 'All's not lost just yet.'

Right then, we heard an almighty thumping at the door. It was the axe. The voices outside were getting louder. There was a chink of light in the door as the axe came crashing into it a second time.

'Quick fellas, through here. Don't forget your bags.'

Peter went first and I was next. I hoisted myself down. I was feeling for firm ground beneath me. There was none. I dropped into another tunnel – a secret passageway. Sugrue went back to get something – which, from the clinking sound above my head, sounded like bottles. We could hear the barrel rolling and the force of the axe. Then Sugrue was in the tunnel, beside myself and Peter, and the trapdoor was slammed shut above him.

'Run,' shouted Sugrue, 'we've got very little time on them.'

The tunnel led back into the forest. Peter was first out. I was at his heels. We waited anxiously. Sugrue, who had twisted his ankle in the drop from the trapdoor to the secret passageway, finally showed through the scrub.

When the door was broken in, Walter Pollach entered the cellar cautiously with his musket, ready to blast the first thing that moved. Shaun Burke came through, shielding the viscount. Another man – the one who had chopped through the door – entered as well, shining a lantern all around as he searched. There wasn't as much as a mouse-squeak to be heard. They looked behind the barrels, and in every nook and cranny, but there was nothing. More men poured into the cellar as shadows danced and criss-crossed on the walls. But there wasn't a sign of the men they were seeking.

'Where did they go,' asked Pollach. 'We saw them come in. They couldn't have just vanished into thin air.'

'Maybe this place is haunted after all,' said the man with the axe.

'I'll give you haunted if you annoy me,' snapped the viscount, lifting the rug from where it was flung and shining his lantern into the corner where the trapdoor lay.

'Quick, open it up,' shouted Shaun Burke, 'let's get after them before they get away.'

'There's not much point,' said the viscount ruefully.

Burke made a lunge at the trapdoor, but the viscount pulled him back.

'I said there's no point. It's not as if they've escaped by accident.'

'We have to do something,' roared Walter Pollach. 'We can't just stand here and let them away scot-free.'

'Take your men and search the forest,' said the viscount to the man with the axe. 'But don't get your hopes up. Whoever these blighters are, they've as much knowledge of Cranley House as any of us.'

Peter Hogan headed for Granard on the orders of Sugrue. It was much too dangerous to go the other way. Mostrim would soon be swarming with the viscount's men, out checking carriages at gunpoint. The police would be back as well, now that the trouble was over at the sub-depot in Longford Town and the fire under control. At Kilcoursey, we parted company. Myself and Sugrue would have to make the long trek back to Lacken through the obscurity of the fields.

'When you get to your uncle's house, don't forget to fit his nameplate back on the carriage. You don't want to attract any sort of suspicion. Stash the food. Hide it away from the house and await further instructions. I'll be in touch in the next few days.'

Sugrue reached out and shook Peter Hogan's hand.

'Oh, and by the way, here's a little something for you and your uncle to enjoy – courtesy of Viscount de Bromley.'

Sugrue produced a bottle.

'Oh lovely, *La Grande Annee*, my favourite,' quipped Peter, reading the label.

'It's far from *La Grande Annee* you were reared,' I said.

Sugrue placed the bottle of champagne on the driver's plank beside Peter, before we headed off into the darkness.

The full moon gave us enough light to pick our steps through the fields. When we got to Goshen Cross – half a mile from home – Sugrue sat down for a rest. He was exhausted and exhilarated at the same time.

'Tonight's events reminded me of the old times, Jim.'

'They must have been fairly nerve-wracking so. Thank God I wasn't around in the old times.'

'It was like ninety-eight all over again. What a bit of fun.'

'Fun is one word that certainly doesn't come to my mind. Tell me something, Sugrue, how did you know there was a trapdoor in the cellar floor?'

'Never mind all that, let's have a drink. We deserve a tipple after what we've been through.'

He took out a second bottle of champagne.

'This one's on the viscount too,' he said, as he stared at the big, bright, button of a moon.

'No, hold on and answer me. How did you know about the trapdoor?'

'Turk,' he whispered, a glint in his eye. 'Turk told me all. That girl he befriended – the viscount's niece – showed him everything. He even drew me a map. Only for Turk, we'd have been in big trouble tonight.'

I could hear it in his voice, Sugrue was choking with emotion. Then he went silent, his mind deep in thought.

'Well, there's only one thing for it so,' I said eventually, passing the bottle back to Sugrue. 'Let's drink to Turk O'Nuallain.'

'To Turk O'Nuallain,' repeated Sugrue, 'only for that poor gossan we'd be on our way to Van Diemen's Land in the morning.'

I knew Sugrue meant nothing by it, but when he mentioned Van Diemen's Land I started to think of Shay. I missed him so much. Sugrue picked up on my heavy mood.

'Don't worry, Jim, you'll see him again. Where there's life, there's hope. Leave it to God.'

I nodded, but said nothing more on the matter. A bead of sweat ran down my brow. Remembering the cloth I had found in de Bromley's cellar, I took it out to wipe my face. It was a handkerchief, all beautifully embroidered in a red and green Celtic design. A shiver went down my back as I took a closer look. It was just like a handkerchief I had seen so many times over the years. It couldn't be, I remember thinking. But it was. It really was my son Shay's Confirmation handkerchief. The sight of it brought tears to my eyes.

'I'll tell you what we'll do,' said Sugrue, passing the champagne back across and putting a hand on my shoulder, 'we'll make a toast to both of them – a little prayerful toast. To Shay Gorman, my auld son of Eireann, come home to us.'

'And to Turk O'Nuallain,' I added, 'who has already gone home, home to Heaven, be with us now and always. Amen.'

Thirty-four – Roger Giles

An old man with a grey beard searched the outskirts of Cranley House. He combed the area, checking and rechecking the grass verges. He prodded with a stick as he walked along. It had been a full three days since the robbery at the big house. He wasn't satisfied with the police verdict. They said it had been such a professional job that it left them no clue whatsoever. As far as Roger Giles was concerned, these new peelers weren't a patch on the proper policemen of his generation. All they wanted were the wages and an easy time. He had no faith in these young lawmen – in their capabilities to find the evidence to solve this case. And that's why, on his day off from collecting tithe payments and his other militia duties, Roger was sunk to his kneecaps in bushes and ditches and drains.

Giles had been putting the events of the previous Friday evening in loose order in his mind. He was sure the arson attack on the Longford sub-depot, which he had been guarding, was connected in some way to the robbery at Cranley House. This had been rubbished when he suggested it to the police. And, if past history was taken into consideration, Giles suspected Paddy Sugrue of being someway connected. It was only a hunch, but Roger felt it was a good enough hunch to merit his voluntary investigations. Giles and Sugrue had a long history of conflict, stretching back to the latter part of the previous century. Over the many intervening years, Giles had come to know how Sugrue and his kind thought and acted.

The police had already been down the boreen – opposite the gates of Cranley House – but Giles decided to check it again. He walked down one side of the verge, prodding the ground where the grass was long. Suddenly the mulching sound from the tip of Roger's stick was replaced by a solid tapping noise. He bent down and fumbled about in the watery undergrowth. He pulled out a carriage nameplate. *O Hogan* was written in crude white lettering. A smile crept across Roger's face as he tucked the nameplate under his arm and headed up the great avenue towards Cranley House.

Roger Giles's career in the governance of County Longford had begun as far back as May 1793. George Forbes, the sixth Earl of Granard, appointed him as one of twenty-two new governors from among the ranks of the gentry and Church of Ireland clergy, in response to the ever-growing number of insurgencies breaking out in the area. Despite all the trouble, the Earl of Granard, together with Sir Thomas Fetherston of Ardagh, drafted long-term plans to harmonise the county by campaigning for the same rights for Catholics as already enjoyed by Protestants. They looked to the future, and who better to pave the way for this harmony than energetic eighteen-year-olds like Roger Giles.

With this in mind, there were high hopes of new beginnings at a meeting of the nobility, gentry, clergy, and freeholders, convened at Longford on August 22, 1794. Instead, by the time this meeting was over, the gulf between the Anglo-Irish Protestant ascendancy and the native Irish Catholic majority had become wider than ever. The purpose of the meeting backfired, as the ruling elite and the protectors of law and order declared to the chairman: *we feel it our duty to assure Your Excellency of our loyalty to the king; of our steady attachment to our excellent constitutions, and of our unalterable determination, by every means in our power, to suppress every appearance of tumult, or attempt to introduce innovations and anarchy, as dangerous to our morals, disgraceful to our long established character, injurious to our industry and rising manufactures, and eventually fatal to the prosperity of Ireland.* Fifty years had gone by and Giles could still recite this declaration by heart.

But it was the two attacks – in 1796 and 1797 – that eventually copper-fastened Roger's decision to defend the status quo and fuelled his determination to keep Irish Catholics firmly down at heel. On January 3, 1796, elected MP for Longford, Caleb Barnes Harman, was murdered. In May of the next year, Alexander Montgomery, vicar of Abbeylara, was viciously attacked. That was it as far as Giles was concerned. It was now his firm commitment, his new mission in life, to ensure that these lawless and barbaric natives would remain under the thumb of the present establishment. He became active in the setting up of four Orange Lodges in Longford county in the late 1790s.

The twenty-one-year-old Giles was in the market square of Longford Town when the court carried out thirteen capital convictions for burglaries and robberies at the Spring Assizes. He looked on contentedly as the convicted mob, which included Pat Sugrue – Paddy's father – was roped up like common thieves, despite their last wishes to be shot as soldiers of Ireland.

1798 was the year Roger Giles came face-to-face with Paddy Sugrue for the first time. Their debut battle was a violent encounter in Mostrim on September 5. Despite the best efforts of pacifists like Lord Oxmantown, the revolution had begun. Three days later, Giles was again on the opposite side to the sixteen-year-old Sugrue, this time at Ballinamuck, where the slaughter was said to be immense. He helped snuff out the rebellion, sending what was left of the French forces scurrying back to Europe.

Afterwards, there were a couple of quiet decades in the Giles-Sugrue war. Not that either of them had taken a backward step in their respective quests. Giles became a member of the Brunswick Clubs – societies which bitterly opposed Catholic Emancipation. Sugrue threw his lot in with the O'Connell effort, organising his political rallies at local level. In 1828, Giles became a member of the local militia – which was part of the 35,000 British soldiers stationed in Ireland – and became notorious among the anti-tithe agitation groups over the next decade. He was assigned to the Irish Yeomanry that same year. These were voluntary guards for emergency situations. They were gentry-raised and trained. Giles's duties as a yeoman quickly earned him further notoriety. He was present at the 1831 massacre in Castlepollard, County Westmeath, when 17 people were murdered. It was here that Giles was slashed in the face, ironically with his own turnpike, henceforth forcing him to wear a beard to hide the terrible scar on his strong jaw. He also courted controversy among the locals in Mostrim, guarding tithe proctors and destroying anything he couldn't collect in lieu of payments. He was present the very first time the proctor called at the Sugrue household to collected one tenth of their wheat harvest. His only disappointment was that old Missus Sugrue, Paddy's mother, paid up in full – denying Giles the chance to teach them a lesson.

That should have been it for Roger's long and distinguished career of law enforcement in the Longford area. But then, in the summer of 1846, when men of Roger Giles's vintage were enjoying their retirement, he was handed another chance at prolonging his mission to preserve natural order and the rightful ruling claims of the Anglo-Protestant class. This time it came from the most unlikely of sources – the Liberal Party. After John Russell came to power, Giles – an out-and-out Tory – was suddenly staring at life on the fringes. Then the Whigs set up their *Vigilantes for Economy*, the army corps at the command of Randolph Routh. It guarded the new food depots and sub-depots that were packed to capacity with Indian meal – the saviour of the starving millions as far as the British were concerned. The Whigs needed as many guards as would sign up, regardless of their political sentiments and allegiances. Then came the call from East Longford's new senior civil servant, Tom

McAndrew. Roger Giles was back in business at the grand old age of sixty-nine.

Giles marched straight into Viscount de Bromley's office unannounced. He threw the nameplate down on the desk without as much as a hello.

'To what do I owe the pleasure, Mister Giles?'

'This,' returned Roger.

'This, what? It's a carriage signature.'

'It's the answer to your robbery the other night,' said Roger.

'Have you taken leave of your senses, Giles. These nameplates are ten-a-penny. How on earth could this possibly have anything to do with last Friday night?'

'Because I found it in the boreen across the road from this house – well down the lane – where a carriage could be easily hidden, yet still be near at hand. Because the name on this plate is *O Hogain* – or Hogan to you and me – and the only Hogan around Edgeworthstown is the former hedge schoolmaster, Peter Hogan. He has no carriage. But his rich old uncle, who lives in Granard, does.'

The viscount's face changed slowly from a confused frown to a smile, as he recognised the potential in what Roger Giles was alleging.

'You never cease to amaze me, Giles. Please take a seat and have a cognac, you deserve one after all your private investigations.'

Roger's discovery led to a search of old Mister Hogan's place in Granard. Peter Hogan almost got away with it. There was nothing in his uncle's farmhouse that could connect Peter to the Cranley robbery. He had carried out Sugrue's instructions in full, stashing the food in a different location. Then, just as the police were about to depart, a bottle of champagne with the brand name *La Grande*

Annee – exclusive to Viscount de Bromley's cellar – was found on a rubbish heap in the farmyard. Peter was arrested and taken to a holding cell in the newly refurbished Edgeworthstown barracks. No matter what the peelers attempted, they couldn't get any information out of him. They tried to plea bargain in the end, offering Peter complete immunity if he would give up the names of his partners in crime. Finally, Peter Hogan cracked. A triumphant English chief constable emerged from the questioning room with a very broad grin of satisfaction.

'Well,' said one of his subordinates, 'did he finally see sense?'

'Did he what,' boasted the chief constable, 'he sang like a bird. As I always say, there's no point sending a constable to do a chief constable's job. The names of the men you will be seeking are a Brian Boru, one Cormac Mac Art, and a ginger-haired swine known as Owen Roe O'Neill.'

Roger Giles looked at the chief constable in disbelief. He didn't correct him – there was no point. He told a policeman to stand guard at the front door of the barracks and let nobody in. Then he sought out a lump hammer and a pliers.

'I'll take the smartness off him,' he said to the confused chief constable.

Giles hesitated at the questioning-room door, holding up the hammer and pliers.

'I'll never comprehend these people, not if I live another lifetime. This is the only thing they understand.'

'What do you mean,' asked the chief constable, slowly losing his smugness.

'Owen Rua O'Neill indeed. I *will* get the truth out of him – but it will have to be the hard way.'

Thirty-five – The Paddy-wagon Crash

Sugrue told everyone to keep a low profile until things settled down after the raid on Cranley House. He travelled to Granard to move and distribute the food. I went to work as usual the following Monday. Jabber said I was mad. But the way I looked at it, missing work would only attract suspicion. Jabber didn't see it like that. He stayed well away from anything to do with Cranley House, sending word to the Public Works Board director that he had pneumonia and wouldn't be available for a couple of weeks. The Monday was grand. I did my work as normal. I came away from Cranley estate without an eyebrow being raised. The Tuesday was a different matter. I was just finishing up when three men swooped. They arrested me as I was putting my tools in the shed and took me into Cranley House, to the viscount's office.

'What is this all about,' I asked, trying to sound as natural as possible.

'Lodge him in the basement,' said the viscount, ignoring my question, 'Mister Pollach has kindly volunteered to watch him until the police cart arrives.'

Milly Farrell received the news from a kid, struggling – from sheer effort – to get the words out. The kid was a runner from the village, who had been dispatched as soon as my workmates knew of my arrest. The boy warned Milly that her son was also in danger of being lifted. Despite the pouring rain she rushed to nearby Goshen, where Jabber was staying with a friend.

'Quick, Joseph, you must do something. Jim Gorman has been arrested at work.'

It was never about self-preservation as far as Milly Farrell was concerned, or the preservation of her family. She just loved helping others. When she returned to her Lacken homestead, two peelers and their horses stood outside.

'You know why we're here, Missus Farrell, so don't waste our time. Where is he,' said one of the policemen.

'I don't know, constable,' replied Milly, the clothes stuck to her from the sleeting rain. 'But if you see him, make sure to tell him his supper is ready.'

After getting the news, Sugrue thought for a moment before seeking out his small shovel. He called at Goshen, collecting Jabber on the way. They took the fields to the village. Time was of the essence.

Walter Pollach didn't speak for some time. He just eyeballed me. I knew what he was at, so I stared back as blankly as I could. Eventually, he realised it wasn't working and adopted a new approach.

'If you confess all, they might let you live,' he said.

I kept a dignified silence, determined that Pollach wouldn't succeed in breaking me down.

'We're going to bring it out as an act of terrorism. You'll get the same treatment as that wee Turk fella; your neck will be stretched over this.'

I smiled. This angered Pollach.

'You won't be smiling by the time we're finished with you,' he continued, before reaching for his whip and cracking it against the wall.

I looked indifferently at the whip. I knew my silence and my calmness was bothering him. I scratched my nose with my two hands, as they were tied together with baling twine. Pollach folded the whip and walked back towards the door. He was deep in thought. Then he turned and darted back to where I was seated.

'I put the rope around your wee friend's neck,' whispered Pollach into my ear. 'It wasn't suicide at all. I knew he was going to get off lightly, so I decided to don the black cap myself.'

This time Pollach smiled, and the calmness left my face. I could feel the anger rising in me. My cheeks became flushed. All I wanted to do was smash Pollach's head off the stone wall behind us.

'Where's your smugness now, Gorman?'

The sweat began on my forehead. Soon, it was stinging my eyes and meandering down my face. I reached into my trouser pocket and pulled out a handkerchief.

'Where did you get *that*,' shrieked Pollach.

He snapped it from my bound hands and studied it closely. It *was* the handkerchief he had given Shaun Burke on the day the chambermaid had been brought away. He checked the red and green embroidery. The design was the same Celtic cross. The sight of the handkerchief had given Pollach a nasty shock.

'You stole this handkerchief, didn't you, from Shaun Burke?'

I didn't know what Pollach was talking about.

'I stole nothing. That's my boy's hanky. And you give it back *now*.'

Pollach laughed when I shouted that.

'You don't get to make demands around here, cunt. You see, I *know* it's your boy's handkerchief. Wasn't it me who planted it in the cellar, the day I framed him and got him transported to Australia. Ha, you see, he gave it to the chambermaid and I took it from her room.'

Pollach had played his trump card. He knew this would really set me mad. There was such delight on his face as he spoke. He really enjoyed letting me in on his secrets – the greater the depravity the better. As far as Pollach was concerned, he was talking to a dead man anyway. In the wake of Peter Hogan's admission – on pain of torture, I may add – the court was sure to sentence me to be hanged for treason to the Crown. I struggled with the knots in the twine, but only succeeded in embedding them deeper in my wrists. I was crazy with temper now, like a wild man, and all I could think about was getting free to avenge the wrongs that Pollach boasted of.

'Stop your wriggling.'

He didn't ask a second time. Taking a step forward, he lashed out with his whip, cutting the side of my face.

It was an education for Jabber to watch Sugrue in action. The old man knew, instinctively, what must be done. He waited patiently for the police cart to go by, on its way to pick me up at Cranley House. Peter Hogan occupied the holding cell in Mostrim, so I was going to be remanded in custody at Longford barracks. Sugrue always referred to the police cart as a paddy wagon, most likely because it was his most frequent mode of transport through the years. He took note of the policemen on board – especially the one carrying a rifle – and the speed of the horses' gallop. He had the palm branches already gathered so, when the police cart had gone, he set to work with the shovel. He dug a trench on the right side of the road. He walked ten paces further on and dug another trench on the opposite side, this time wider and deeper than the first. He covered the trenches with palm, spreading clay on top to make the road look natural. He found a good hiding place, arming himself and Jabber with two good-sized sticks.

'What's with the two trenches, Sugrue? Could you not have put up a roadblock instead?'

'Can't do that,' he answered. 'There's an armed peeler on board. We need to topple the paddy wagon – cause it to crash. This is the way it was done in the old days. The small trench on the right will stagger the wheels. The horses are taking the middle ground – two out front, two behind – so they'll keep their fast pace as the carriage is rocking. The second trench will bring the whole lot tumbling down – I hope.'

Jabber was impressed by Sugrue's knowledge. But the old man in no mood for compliments. Instead, he said he was nervous. Luck would play a big part in it now. All they could do was sit and wait, hoping for the type of crash that would be of benefit – the type of crash that would incapacitate the armed policeman, or at least separate him from his rifle.

The driver brought me out to the police cart. He looked at the blood running onto my shoulder and then looked back at Walter Pollach.

'He was giving trouble,' Pollach explained, before stuffing the handkerchief into his pocket. 'I had to quieten him.'

'You'll have to come with us,' said the armed policeman, as Pollach was turning to go back into the big house. 'There's paperwork to be filled out in Longford barracks. Viscount de Bromley said he will send a carriage for you later.'

Pollach sighed with annoyance. This was going to ruin the whole evening. Now he would have to put his night's drinking on hold.

'So much for volunteering to watch the prisoner,' he said under his breath, as he followed me into the police cart.

'I sit up front,' shouted the policeman with the rifle, 'so you can close the door behind you, Walter.'

Then we rolled down the great avenue and away from Cranley House.

They could hear the horses' hooves before they could see them. Sugrue had chosen their position carefully – right in the middle of Cranley Lane – between de Bromley's mansion and the Granard Road entrance, where the wheels would be at their fastest. The four brown stallions drove on, unaware that behind them the right-sided set of wheels had begun to rock the carriage. Then they hit the second trench. After a snap from the side bars and a yelp from the driver, the front of the carriage hopped up in the air. Then came an almighty bang, as the police cart spilled onto its side and its roof careered into the trunk of a big ash tree.

Jabber was still coming to terms with what was unfolding when Sugrue was up and out of his hiding place. He kicked open the bolt on the police-cart door, then went to check on the armed policeman. He was lying in a gripe, between the road and a field. He moaned as Sugrue lifted the rifle. He tried to say something. Sugrue looked for the other policeman – the driver. He was asleep beside the ash tree, blood flowing from his cheekbone. Sugrue checked his pulse, then went back to the policeman lying in the gripe. His arm was twisted under him.

'Can you hear me,' asked Sugrue.

The policeman nodded.

'I think your arm is broken.'

The policeman nodded again.

'There's no need to worry. Nobody's going to harm you,' Sugrue assured him. 'I have to take your weight off the arm.'

He carefully rolled the policeman's body, so his arm wasn't trapped underneath. He roared for a few seconds, then settled down. Sugrue uncoupled the frightened horses.

Jabber was by the cart door. He looked in. Walter Pollach was lying in a slumber. A bruise on his left temple was showing already. I was only coming too. Jabber shook me until my eyes opened.

'Merciful hour! Are you hurt,' he said, noticing the blood on my shoulder and the cut to my face.

I was stunned. Jabber shook me again.

'Come on, Jim, get your wits about you. We have to move fast.'

'No, that was earlier,' I said, in reference to the blood. 'I'm grand. I'm not injured.'

'Let's go, now,' said Jabber, cutting my hands loose with his knife.

I staggered to my feet and tried to follow him over to Sugrue. Then, I stopped and turned back. All I could think about was the handkerchief. I went back to the police cart, where Pollach was lying, and searched his pockets. There it was. As I was pulling Shay's handkerchief out, Pollach was beginning to stir. He moved onto his side and coughed. The whip fell out of his belt. Without another thought I seized it, wrapped it around Pollach's neck and squeezed as hard as my strength would allow. Pollach looked sideways and made gurgling sounds. His eyes bulged and his face went purple. He moved his hands in a plea for mercy. I could sense the strength leaving his struggling shoulders as I listened to the sound of his choking. Then I heard something else, the sound of Sugrue's voice at the police-cart door.

'Jim, listen to me. Don't do it. He's not worth it.'

I continued to squeeze. I was trying to block out Sugrue.

'Don't stoop to his level. Jim, you're better than this. You're not a murderer.'

I could ignore him no longer.

'Murder – now that's a funny word around here. Was it murder back in ninety-eight when you did it?'

'Jim, look at me. I'm on your side. That was totally different. It was war. This will be murder, and I know you don't want that.'

'He confessed it all – he's to blame for Turk *and* Shay.'

Jabber was stooped next to Sugrue, looking into the police cart.

'Jim, if you strangle that bastard it's all over. Neither Shay nor Turk will ever get the justice they deserve. Our only hope is to keep him alive, if we're going to clear the names of those two boys.'

I tried to relax my grip, but I couldn't let go of the whip. Sugrue crawled in behind me and eased my hands away, as Pollach fell in an exhausted heap.

'Come on,' whispered Sugrue. 'We haven't much time. We'll deal with this scumbag again. Right now, we have to get as far away from this paddy wagon as possible.'

Sugrue brought me for a walk up the road and gave me a drink from his powder flask. Jabber put the policemen into the cart with Pollach and secured the bolt. It was time for us to get going. The roles were now reversed – the hunters had suddenly become the hunted.

Thirty-six – On the Run

The peelers were back in Lacken. Since the assault on their police cart and their officers, they had been watching the place closely. But this time a separate matter had brought them to the clachan. A hopeful Missus Ryan opened the top half of her cabin door. She talked with the policemen, then looked away in disappointment. There was still no news on her granddaughter. As far as Viscount de Bromley was concerned, she had run off with an employee from one of the work schemes. He told the policemen he didn't know the man's name, but that Mister Pollach, his chief recruiting officer, would fill them in further. Missus Ryan's eyes filled up and she slammed the half-door shut. It was all a big cover up, just as Mairead Gorman had told her. There was no man from *one of the work schemes*. Constance had been missing for almost a month. Hopes of finding her were fading with each passing day. Something awful had happened to her granddaughter – Missus Ryan could feel it in her bones.

Milly Farrell waited for the peelers to leave first, before quenching her lamp. As darkness began to take hold of the kitchen, she looked around, aware that it would be the last time she would ever see her picture of the Sacred Heart and her clay statue of the Blessed Virgin. Everything was neat and tidy. She ventured out into the cold air, pulling the headscarf tightly about her ears and making off at her best pace. By the time she reached Camlisk Lane, Milly was in a stagger. Missus Langan, her best friend, got the fright of her life. Milly was crouched at the door, the cloth she held to her mouth thick with blood. Missus Langan lifted Milly and placed her in a warm bed. The coughing continued. It looked like tuberculosis. Milly caught Missus Langan by the sleeve as she was propping up her pillow.

'Send a runner. I need to see Joseph before I die.'

'But he's in hiding,' replied Missus Langan. 'He could be anywhere.'

'I know where he is. Micheal Mooney told me. I need to see him very soon. I haven't long left, Alice.'

At midnight, Missus Langan opened her door to a pre-arranged knock. Jabber stood on the clay step. He entered the house and knelt by the bed where his mother lay. A whole world of emotions raced through his mind. He was close to tears. Missus Langan made herself scarce.

'I'll be in the kitchen, Joseph,' she said. 'Take your time, sonny. There's food out here when you're ready.'

Jabber's stomach had been rumbling on his way through the fields to Missus Langan's house, but the sight of his sick mother took the hunger off him. He held her hand as he spoke.

'Ma, I never said sorry for not becoming a priest.'

'Oh Joseph, you don't have to be sorry, love. I'm the one who should say sorry. I gave you a hard time and there was none of it your fault. I wanted you to become a priest. It was my dream and not yours. I should have encouraged you to be what you wanted. But I am proud of the man you are and I thank God for you.'

Milly's voice was weak.

'Ma, I told you about those fever hospitals and not to be working in them.'

'I had to work there, Joseph. It was my calling from God to care for the poor and the sick. What use is my Bible if I don't practice what it says. You can have no greater love than to lay down your life for the good of others. But it wasn't the fever hospitals that made me ill, Joseph.'

'What was it then?'

'Nothing in particular. It's just my time, that's all.'

'I'll stay with you. I won't leave you alone, Ma.'

'I'm not alone, Joseph. My best friend, Alice, is with me. I'm taking up her bed, for goodness sake. Alice has always been there for me. She will look after me and make sure I die with dignity, not the way so many poor Irish people are dying at the moment. But you cannot stay now, son. Your work is not finished. That line in the Bible, it applies to you too. You can have no greater love than to lay down your life for others. Well, you must keep Jim Gorman safe. I promised Mairead you would protect him and return him to her one day. Promise me, Joseph, and then you must go.'

'I don't want to leave you, Ma.'

Jabber's eyes were dropping tears onto Missus Langan's bed linen. Milly touched his face affectionately.

'Oh, don't worry son. You're not leaving me. You'll never leave me. And I won't ever leave you. But it's time for you to go back to your men.'

Milly took a scapular from under her pillow. She placed it in Jabber's strong hand.

'Wear this, Joseph, it will keep you safe. It's the Holy Family. I called you after Saint Joseph the carpenter. My mother had a great faith in him, she always prayed to Joseph for guidance and protection. Now, you must live up to your namesake. You must guide and protect Jim Gorman and Paddy Sugrue through this terrible time. I know I can rely on you. God bless you and keep you.'

Jabber wanted to say God bless you too Ma. But the words got caught in his throat. He kissed her forehead as his tears wetted her face. Missus Langan waited in the kitchen, but Jabber didn't call. She heard the latch of the door lift and fall instead.

For a big man, Jabber could move with great ease. He entered the haybarn with deathly silence. He crept up behind the stacked bales.

'The O'Ferrall county says hello,' he whispered, just as Sugrue had instructed.

This was the password. Immediately, a bale in the middle of the stack was pushed out, allowing Jabber to climb through the hole. Sugrue had the haybales stacked in formation. They provided excellent fortification. They kept us hidden while we watched the outside world. They were also a means of attack, and could be toppled on intruders in an instant.

Micheal Mooney brought us food and other requirements. He was careful never to create a pattern – arriving, instead, at all hours of the day and night and from all sorts of directions. Sugrue had Micheal briefed on every detail; he knew exactly what to do and what not to do. He was told to travel alone, trust nobody and not to tell a single soul – not even his own wife – where we were hiding.

'The peelers will be watching everyone in the clachan, especially Jim's wife and Jabber's mother. Giving them information puts *everyone* in danger,' said Sugrue.

It was hard on Micheal Mooney. He was good-natured. He had already given in to the desperation of Milly Farrell, fetching Jabber to her bedside. But that was as far as he was willing to bend, despite the pressure from Mairead for a visit. This was something Micheal could not grant, for her own safety as much as mine. Therefore, it really tested Micheal's patience when my wife turned up, yet again, at his door.

'I can't help you, Mairead. You shouldn't even be here. What if the peelers are following you?'

She had a large envelope in her hand.

'Alright, Micheal, take it easy. I'm not going to ask you again. Lady Teale came around this evening. She had this for Jim. I just thought you could deliver it to him when you think it's safe.'

Mairead put the envelope on Micheal's kitchen table and walked away.

Micheal was an old softie. Watching her leave, his heart was sore with pity. He knew all about lost love. When he thought about it, the rules didn't seem so important anymore.

'Mairead, you can deliver it yourself. I'll take you to him, even though Sugrue will skin me alive.'

There were very few policemen left around the parishes of County Longford. One constable was kept back to patrol each barracks. The rest joined forces with the militia and concentrated their efforts on reprimanding the culprits of the paddy-wagon crash. The yeomen were called in. Roger Giles organised their campaign from the front line. Viscount de Bromley put up a reward for information leading to our capture. One hundred pounds was on offer. Every day for the next week they searched for miles in all directions, looking for what the *Irish Times* had described as the *Sugrue Gang*. Each day brought its own frustrations. Not a single clue was unearthed. The yeomen kept a close eye on things in the village. They called daily to the local artisans. The blacksmith was under constant scrutiny. The baker's bread was even examined. It was as if the Sugrue Gang had just vanished from the face of the earth.

Captain Giles didn't believe we had just vanished. He instructed his men to concentrate on the locals – *they* were housing us. According to Roger, this was one of the games the natives were renowned for – hiding their fugitives and making a laugh out of the law and ruling class in the process. He ordered his men to keep a constant watch on certain members of the public. There wasn't much more could be done after that. It was all down to a waiting game now.

Mairead shivered with anticipation in the darkness. Micheal Mooney said they would take the Goshen fields – one of his many routes to and from the haybarn. She secured Lady Teale's envelope in her belt and set off behind him. The haybarn was in Tinnynarr, a good mile and a half from Lacken as the crow flies. Mairead followed Micheal into an empty cow shed, out the back, and over a gripe. Then, after a long time of walking blind through the pitch dark and long wet grass, they came to the Sugrue Gang's lodgings. Mairead noticed some of the lanterns in the distance. They were on the outskirts of the village. Despite its growth in recent years – and the new name of Edgeworthstown – we still called it *the village*. That's how we remember it from when we were small – and old habits die hard. It was typical Sugrue mentality – where better to hide than right under the noses of those who are looking for you.

Entering the barn, Micheal Mooney could hear the sound of our conversation. Sugrue was discussing manoeuvres for the following night – when we would be moving our base out of Mostrim. It would have to be done in the small hours, because if anyone – even someone we thought we could trust – happened to see us, then it could well have been the end for the Sugrue Gang.

'A one-hundred-pound reward can do queer things to a person's head. If history has taught us anything, it's that the Irish are nothing if not consistent at squealing on their own,' warned Sugrue.

'I think it's a downright disgrace,' said Jabber.

'Yeah, informing is a bad business,' agreed Sugrue.

'No, I'm talking about the bounty. The viscount is a pure skinflint. One hundred pounds is not nearly enough for a dangerous criminal like me, never mind you two thrown in as well.'

Just then, the whisper came from the other side of the haybales – *the O'Ferrall county says hello* – and, when the bale was removed, Micheal Mooney popped his head through the hole. Sugrue got a start as a second head followed. I couldn't believe my eyes when I saw Mairead. She began kissing my face and crying. It was a bit embarrassing in front of the lads. Sugrue turned and gave Micheal Mooney a cold stare.

'I had no choice,' Micheal explained.

Sugrue went off to the back of the barn with Jabber and Micheal. There wasn't much he could do about Mairead now, so he let us have some privacy.

'She'll be back again,' said Jabber, 'now that she knows where we are.'

'No, just this once,' Micheal assured them. 'I made it quite clear to her. Only that she has a letter for Jim, she wouldn't have been brought at all.'

'And when did *you* lose the power of your legs and arms,' snapped Sugrue. 'Next time, why not invite the post mistress along?'

Inside the haybales, Mairead was getting all romantic. There's something about an outlaw that sends a woman mad with excitement. But our time together was getting short.

'I almost forgot,' she said, taking out the envelope, 'I have something for you from Lady Teale.'

I opened it right away. A hundred pounds – in five-pound bills – stared back; more money than I ever had in my whole life. A wave of shame washed over me, as I remembered a time when I had considered the Teale's with the utmost suspicion. There was a note from Lady Jane Teale also. It read: *Dear Jim, I am sorry to hear about your present plight. I never got to properly thank you for what your beloved Shay did in saving my dear Henry's life. Please use this money to make a new start in a safe place. Rest assured, we will look after your family and friends in your absence. Also, please find enclosed a letter for America. God bless you, LJT.*

At the bottom of the note, she wrote in a post script: *There's a ship leaving Dun Leary for New York on 1st October, and another four weeks later.*

It took me a few minutes to steady my nerves. Mairead didn't know whether to laugh or cry. This money meant freedom – or at least the means to achieve it. I took the letter for America in my shaking hands and examined it closely. It was folded, with the Teale stamp branded in red wax at the top of the page. It was addressed: *To whom it may concern*, and that *Mister John Brown is hereby attending New York on the business of Lord and Lady Teale of Edgeworthstown in the county of Longford, Ireland.*

'Hello, Mister John Brown,' quipped Mairead, getting all excited again, 'I'm Missus Gorman. I'm very pleased to make your acquaintance.'

The fellas were excited too. Jabber acknowledged the importance of making that sailing on the first of October. Sugrue acknowledged the difficulty in making it.

'What difficulty,' said Micheal Mooney, 'you've got more money than John Jacob Astor. Hire one of Bianconi's carriages the whole way to Dublin docks. Then, simply buy your tickets for America at the terminus.'

'And no doubt Bianconi's driver would relieve Jim of the fare, before carting us off to Dublin Castle and collecting the hundred-pounds reward in Cranley upon his return,' replied Sugrue. 'Whisht and use your brain, man. The peelers will have every carriage driver and omnibus in a thirty-mile radius on the look-out.'

'What will ye do,' asked Micheal.

'We'll have to plan something new,' said Sugrue. 'But we can't afford to wait six weeks for a sailing, that's too long to be hanging around. It's like Jabber said – we need to be in Dublin for the first of October and on that ship.'

Before being dragged away by Micheal Mooney, I eased Mairead's distress by promising that I'd write as soon as I got to America. I asked her to thank Lady Teale for this wonderful and unexpected opportunity. I took the red and green embroidered handkerchief from my pocket. Mairead jumped as soon as she saw it.

'Shay's confirmation,' she gushed.

'Yes. It belongs in Lacken – in our house,' I answered. 'Keep it safe for Shay, darling, until he comes back.'

She left the haybarn clutching the handkerchief and sobbing.

'We'll never see them again, Micheal,' she wailed.

'You'll have to quit your crying,' said Micheal Mooney, as they returned to the gap leading into the fields, 'we need to be as quiet as we can now.'

As Micheal and Mairead once again took refuge in the darkness of the Goshen countryside, the militia man stepped out from behind a hedge and started his walk into Edgeworthstown. A whole week of hiding in thorny Lacken ditches had finally paid off. And soon, this militia man would be one hundred pounds richer. His heart thumped at the thought of it. He was the only one who gave ear to what Roger Giles had told them – Mairead Gorman could hold the key to the mystery. Now, he couldn't get to town fast enough with the news that was about make him a very wealthy young man.

Roger Giles took two men only to the haybarn. He knew stealth was important for a swift arrest. The larger the number of men, the more noise they would make. Besides, two armed guards were more than sufficient to bring in three unarmed and unsuspecting fugitives. An arrest was now a foregone conclusion, but Giles didn't want them running off into the night. Then he'd only have to go looking for them. They stalled the horse and carriage along the road, where the Sugrue Gang could neither see nor hear them. He knew the right thing to do was stay with the carriage until his officers returned, but Roger couldn't resist the thoughts of putting the manacles on

Sugrue personally. So, he tied his horse and went with the militia men.

As he stepped into the barn, Giles could hear us chatting away. He held up his hand to the militia men at his rear. He looked around. All he could see were bales of hay. Where was the noise coming from. Roger stopped in his tracks. There was something not right about this place. The militia men caught him up and Roger placed a firm finger to his lips. The talking was coming from behind the bales stacked in the centre of the barn. Roger pointed to the bales that he wanted the militia men to dislodge. He could feel a bead of sweat on his forehead. He was almost there – almost at the end of a lifetime's ambition to finally bring Paddy Sugrue to justice. The first militia man climbed to the middle bale. As he shuffled along, he signalled his colleague to climb up and join him. Suddenly, there was a scraping sound from under his boots. He stepped off the corrugated-iron sheet as fast as he could. Giles and the militia men froze on the spot. They listened carefully and heard nothing – nothing but the sound of Sugrue's voice. They all took a deep breath of relief. Giles made two more hand signals. He wanted the militia men to split up and approach from either end of the stack.

There was a loud creaking sound. Looking up in exasperation, Roger saw the top bales hurtling towards them. There was no time to get out of the way. The militia men were floored by the collapsing wall of haybales. Giles had his arm trapped in the avalanche. His restrained hand groped for the pistol which was no longer in his possession. One of his colleagues was knocked unconscious, the other pinned under the scattered bales – with his gun lying in the clearing before him.

Myself and Jabber appeared from where the wall of bales used to be. We checked the younger militia men. Sugrue went over and picked up the gun in the clearing. He walked slowly over to where Roger lay on the ground. I was worried that Sugrue might do something stupid. He stood over Giles for what seemed like an age. Then he put his hand in his coat pocket and pulled out his powder flask.

'Are you hurt?'

Giles remained silent.

'I asked are you injured,' said Sugrue again.

Then he offered Giles a *drink*.

'Do you remember this? Such are the spoils of war.'

Giles couldn't hide his surprise as he looked upon his old powder flask for the first time in almost fifty years. He was barely able to speak with the weight of the bale on his chest.

'Like the scar on your forehead,' he panted eventually.

'Correct,' said Sugrue, offering the powder flask once more, 'more of the spoils of war. Unlike the scar you hide with your beard, the one you received by your own weapon during the slaughter of innocents at Castlepollard.'

Giles was furious – you could see it in his eyes – as Sugrue knelt down beside him.

'You see, Roger, I have my sources too.'

'No quarter asked for,' Giles replied, refusing the drink a second time. 'Do your worst. I'm prepared to meet my God.'

Sugrue pointed the pistol at Giles, who closed his eyes and waited. Then he turned it skyward and emptied the bullet into his hand. He checked the barrel to make sure it was clear. Then he flung the weapon back into the clearing.

'Well then,' said Sugrue, 'I'll expect no quarter in return. But what I will expect is some sort of fair play for innocent young women – women like my daughter-in-law. You know what I mean.'

He lifted the bale off Giles and sat him beside the other militia men. Jabber tied them up, while I secured the barn door with an iron rod. When the Sugrue Gang got to the road, a nice surprise was there to greet us.

'We might as well avail of the free ride, gentlemen,' said Sugrue, before untying the horse and settling into the box seat.

Sugrue ditched our transportation before we reached Mullingar. He carefully let the horse loose. He loved animals – the last thing he wanted was for her to sustain an injury from being tied to an empty trailer.

'That's as far as she takes us,' he lamented. 'We can't chance going into Mullingar. Giles and his militia men may already be found. If that's the case, the Mullingar police will be looking out for us.'

It was the end of the comfortable travelling as we took to the fields on foot. Sugrue had an immense talent for surviving in the wilds. Jabber was a good man to catch game with a trap. But Sugrue was something else again. He caught rabbits by hand – then skinned and prepared them for eating. He knew when and where to set a fire. He could travel on the darkest night – a huge advantage to men on the run – taking his direction from the formation of the stars. Myself and Jabber were mightily impressed. When asked about his survival instincts, Sugrue put it down to a misspent youth of fighting the Brits on his wits and an empty stomach.

'I learnt a lot of this stuff back in ninety-eight,' he told us, 'back then it was fairly basic knowledge. Nowadays, young fellas wouldn't know how to wipe their bums in a field of dock leaves.'

It was clear, from the moment we had left the barn, that Sugrue was not travelling aimlessly through the countryside. He was following a careful plan to get us safely to Dun Leary for the first day of October.

Roger Giles was also following a careful plan. Once freed from his binds and the haybarn – thanks to the viscount who, wondering why it was taking so long, sent some men to Tinnynarr to look for Giles – he wasted no time in gathering the best scouts the militia could offer. He armed his company of yeomen, brought in a pack of sniffer dogs, and headed off in the direction of Dublin with a convoy of horses and carriages. He wanted the militia to secure the Dublin exits, guard the harbours and ports, warn the shipping people, and then comb the area back into the city. The yeomen and their dogs would bring up the rear, searching the countryside and provincial towns along the way. Roger's horse had been found wandering close to Mullingar, so that was their starting point.

Viscount de Bromley tried his best to dissuade Walter Pollach from entering the search. His doctors had been treating Pollach for the bruised temple and concussion he had sustained in the dramatic paddy-wagon crash, but there was no keeping him in bed. Once Pollach heard what had happened to Giles and his militia men, he jumped up from his goose-feathered mattress and grabbed his whip. He wasn't going to miss out on the action. His nurses at Cranley House would have had to strap him down in order to stop him. Despite the protestations of the viscount – who could be heard quite vehemently labelling his second-in-command as the *eternal showman* – and his medical team, Walter joined the yeomen and their pack of hounds.

After the third night of flat-out walking, Sugrue decided we should stop and bed down for a few daylight hours of sleep. Then we would proceed to our first port of call.

'Where's that,' I asked, more exhausted than I ever thought I could feel.

'Maynooth.'

'Maynooth! Are you crazy, Sugrue? They'll be swarming all over Maynooth.'

'Whisht. They'll be swarming all over everywhere by now,' he answered.

'What are you planning we do,' asked Jabber, 'buy some black robes and hide among the priests? I tried that before, it didn't really suit me.'

'A fine lump of a farmhouse on the outskirts of Maynooth. That's where we're headed, boys,' said Sugrue. 'If we can make it that far, we stand a decent chance of getting the rest of the way to the boat.'

I laid out some rags for a bed in a patch of dry grass. Just as I settled in, there came the distant barking of dogs. I thought it was a dream. Sugrue was up in a shot, calling Jabber and shaking me out of my slumber.

'Get over the hill and keep an eye out for water,' Sugrue instructed.

The three of us scurried over the top. There was a house, but no water. The barks got louder. Then the dogs could be seen. Jabber looked up at the trees. The dogs were straining on their leashes. They were going wild now, yelping and pulling the yeomen along.

'We'll get high up in the trees,' said Jabber, his heart in his mouth.

'No,' ordered Sugrue, 'stay on the ground.'

'We'll be got on the ground,' exclaimed Jabber.

Sugrue opened the door of the house. The stench hit him like a slap in the face. He instinctively retreated into the fresh air. He placed the sleeve of his shirt across his nose and went back in for a look. He beat the flies away and edged into the bedroom. They were swarming in a settle bed in the corner of the room. Sugrue went across to the bed. His stomach was turning over. He pulled back the sheets and a decomposing body stared back at him. It gave Sugrue a fright. Long wisps of grey hair hung from the pieces of skin still attached to the skull. Sugrue replaced the sheet and made his way back to the open door, his stomach retching and the dogs' howls ringing in his ears. It suddenly occurred to him what he must do. He told myself and Jabber to get inside.

'There's half a chance of getting out of this, but it's not going to be pretty,' Sugrue explained.

He uncovered the corpse again. The smell was horrific, but the fear of getting caught was worse. Then Sugrue took the body and the dirty linen out of the bed.

'Get under the mattress,' he said.

When myself and Jabber had climbed under the bed, Sugrue tore open the mattress and covered us with its straw. He returned the linen to the bed, spread it out neatly, lay the decomposing body on top of it, before climbing under and into the hay with us. It was the worst smell ever. There were maggots everywhere. I quietly emptied the contents of my stomach. It was so hard to lie still. Then the dogs could be heard at the door. They were scratching and barking mad. A man could be heard complaining about the putrid smell. He was shouting back at another man. I could see a little from my hiding place in the straw. We were sitting ducks. The dogs and the man were in the room. He was trying to restrain them as they pulled towards the bed. He was still giving off about the smell. Another man came to the door, the clipping sound of his boots getting louder all the time.

'The wee gadge frightened the life out of me,' he said, as he looked in at the corpse from the doorway.

The voice was instantly recognisable – it was Walter Pollach.

'Teddy, get away from that bed now,' he shouted through a napkin at the man with the dogs. 'Do you want to end up like your man in the bed?'

'We were told to check everything,' said the man who was obviously Teddy.

'I said get out *now*, you and those dogs. Do you want to pollute the lot of us,' continued Pollach. 'Can you not smell it in the air?

Get those dogs away from that body, they can carry it too, you know.'

'Holy shit,' said Teddy, covering his mouth all of a sudden.

He fought his way out as fast as he could, pulling his dogs – who were growling and stripping their teeth at the straw under the bed.

'Well, at least that's another one less,' said Pollach, pulling the door behind him.

It was some time before Sugrue decided it was safe to come out from under the maggoty straw. He had been afraid of a spotter – someone coming up late from behind the main bunch. It was a tactic that Sugrue's column had used in ninety-eight and it was very successful in flushing out the enemy. Jabber was first into the fresh air, where he removed his shirt and turned it inside out.

'Oh, that smell is unbearable, even worse than the black room,' he said.

'Did you notice anything about the voices,' asked Sugrue.

'About the voices?'

'Pollach,' I interjected, 'you couldn't miss that soft Scottish tone.'

Jabber shrugged and admitted he had been too scared to notice. I got sick again and washed my mouth out with water. Sugrue strolled around, puffing his cheeks out with relief. Then he broke the tension with a good laugh.

'It's easy laughing in the heel of the hunt,' said Jabber, 'but how did you know we'd be safe in the straw?'

'I didn't,' replied Sugrue, 'I had to gamble, simple as that.'

'How do you mean, *gamble*,' I asked.

'Gamble that Pollach and his buddy with the dogs wouldn't disturb the body. And gamble on their fear of catching disease. We're not the first to see that poor man's corpse. That's why he's half rotted away by now. There were others before us in that bedroom, afraid to touch him in case they caught their deaths. It's no accident that he hasn't been buried – there are decomposing bodies being found all over the country. Come on, let's do the decent thing.'

'I'm not able,' I confessed, 'I'm after spending all the time I possibly can with that smell. As you'd say yourself, Sugrue, can we not leave him to God?'

'We should give him a respectable burial, Jim,' said Jabber, 'it's only fair. He's the only reason we're not heading south in chains.'

'Or waiting for the hangman's noose,' added Sugrue.

As night-time approached, we found ourselves hiding behind a bush while looking into a fine farmyard. Sugrue fired a stone at a gaggle of geese, sending them waddling into a shed. A sheepdog arose from the doorstep and barked. A light was raised, then disappeared from the window. A grey-haired man appeared, similar in age to Sugrue, holding a lantern and looking around.

'The O'Ferrall county says hello,' said Sugrue.

The old man stopped in his tracks. He turned and looked at the door that he had just left open. Then he heard it again.

'The O'Ferrall county says hello.'

'Sugrue,' cried the old man.

Sugrue stepped out, as bold as brass, from behind the bush.

'Oh my God! Paddy Sugrue,' said the old man, rushing towards him. 'I knew you'd return one day – with your shield or on it.'

'Jeb Turling, my old comrade-in-arms. How very good to see you after all these years,' said Sugrue, as they greeted each other with a salute.

Thirty-seven – Remembering '98

Jeb Turling escorted the Sugrue Gang into his beautiful abode and hung a large pot on the crossbar of the open fire. Within seconds, the warmth was coursing through our weary bones. Sugrue took note of his old friend's dominance of the kitchen.

'Your good wife?'

Jeb shook his head.

'Gone, Paddy, this ten years now. Consumption.'

'I'm sorry to hear it, Jeb. Maureen was a topper. She looked after us when we were at the races from Cornwallis and Lake.'

'Aye. That's the way of it, Paddy.'

There was an awkward silence. Jeb went into another room and returned with three pipes, their bowls filled to the brim with brown tobacco.

'Here ye go lads,' he said, handing the pipes around, 'this will put in the time for ye while we're waiting for the bacon to boil.'

Jabber was used to the odd smoke. But I felt awkward, not knowing whether to take the pipe or leave it. I didn't want to insult Jeb's hospitality.

'That man doesn't smoke,' Sugrue pointed out.

'Ah, I might give it a try,' I said, taking the pipe and handing it to Jabber to light.

If the outlaws I read about in the *Freeman's Journal* Wild West weeklies smoked away to their hearts content, surely I could give it a go.

'And who are these fine men,' Jeb asked.

'Two of Mostrim's best,' answered Sugrue. 'Jeb Turling, I give you Jim Gorman and Jabber Farrell.'

Jeb shook our hands and told us we were very welcome to his house.

'Jabber, that's an interesting name.'

'Well, sir, Joseph is my real name.'

'They call him Jabber because back in the twenties, when he was only a gossan,' explained Sugrue, 'those big paws of his beat fifteen Peep O'Day boys on a single fair day in Ballymahon. He was undisputed champion of Leinster, outside of the Pale.'

'Another Dan Donnelly,' remarked Jeb, 'the steps to strength and fame.'

Jabber reddened, and Jeb could tell that he didn't like the limelight.

'Do you know how this old codger got his name, boys,' said Jeb, turning the attention on Sugrue, 'from all the time he spent *playing* with the Redcoats back in ninety-eight.'

I didn't get the joke and looked blankly at Jabber.

'*Sugrudh* – the Irish word for playing,' he whispered.

A joke was never the same when you had to ask for the punchline.

'But ye have to give him credit, fellas,' continued Jeb, 'he's a prime example of what I consider the bottom line of war – come back with your shield or on it. That was the philosophy of the Spartans in ancient Greece. And those boys were no pushovers. Come back with your shield in victory, or lying dead on it. But don't attempt to return home without it. You see that little beauty.'

Jeb drew attention to Sugrue's scar by running a finger down his own forehead.

'I remember the day he received that wound. It would have got the better of a lot of men.'

'The spoils of war,' said Jabber, 'that's how one person described it. How did he come by it?'

I would have asked if Jabber hadn't, because we'd always wondered about that scar.

'That's for my friend here to tell,' answered Jeb, and I have to say I was disappointed.

After a hearty meal of boiled bacon and cabbage, Jeb agreed with Sugrue that the house wasn't the safest place for us to be. He had a better idea. We followed him through the farmyard and into a big shed, then up a ladder and through a flap in the ceiling. We entered a loft – the most comfortable loft in Ireland. It was a purpose-built safe house. There was a table in the centre and a couple of makeshift beds in the corners.

'I'll get a lock of blankets,' said Jeb, 'I hope ye boys don't mind sharing.'

It was like fugitive-heaven – with sheepskin rugs on the floor and plenty of newspapers. It felt good to be in a place where one could relax without having to watch over one's shoulder.

Jeb returned with more than the blankets. He handed large jars of porter and a jug of whiskey through the flap. Sugrue placed them on the table. On the centre beam, close to the roof, hung a full-page picture of Daniel O'Connell from the *Nation*. Beside O'Connell hung the old flag of Ireland – a golden harp on a green background.

'Ah, the counsellor,' said Jeb, responding to Jabber's curious stare, 'may the Lord have mercy on his brave soul.'

On closer inspection, Jabber noticed the date at the top of the page – Saturday, May 22, 1847 – one week after the passing of the great liberator.

'So, you're a Davis man yourself,' quipped Jabber.

'Because I read the *Nation*? I don't believe in all that guff about being a Davis man or being an O'Connell man. I'm an Irishman. And I fought as a proud Irishman at Ballinamuck and in Kildare. This country is too small to be divided up into Davis men and O'Connell men,' said Jeb. 'I read the *Nation* the same as I read the *Freeman's Journal* – not because I'm politically loyal to one or the other. But, simply because they're the newspapers of the common man and common woman in this country.'

It was clear that Jeb was as insightful in his thinking on Irish politics as Sugrue. They spoke in similar terms. They were passionate, yet still accommodating to other points of view. I could sense that fighting alongside each other, as they did at Ballinamuck, had shaped their views on many of Ireland's political problems. They not only talked the same but, in ways, they looked the same. They were smallish in height, with dark complexions and bony limbs. They wore their hair the same way too – curled in, strangely, at the nape of their necks.

'It's all the style among the senior citizens these days,' I whispered to Jabber.

'Yeah, inspired by Sir Lancelot and the Knights of the Round Table. Those old timers wouldn't know what style was if it bit them on the arse,' he replied.

The four of us sat around on stools, drinking porter and telling yarns. The lantern on the centre of the table threw jumpy shadows on the walls. It was such a comfortable setting – our only comfort in weeks. Sugrue filled Jeb in on what had taken place with Shay and Turk, why we were on the run, where we were headed, and those who were hunting us down. When he mentioned the name Roger Giles, the smile disappeared from Jeb Turling's lips.

'Don't tell me he's still on the go,' he said. 'The old bastard, God forgive me, just doesn't know when enough is enough.'

'Language, please. He's leading the charge right enough, with a nasty piece of work called Walter Pollach heading up the yeomen.

I don't know how those young fellas are ever going to make the sailing on the first day of October, Jeb.'

'You might not know, but I do. I guarantee you, Paddy Sugrue, I'll have them on that ship and sailing for America. Mark my words – have I ever let you down before? I still own a barge and I'm known on the canal. We'll talk more tomorrow.'

After enough porter had been drank, out came the small glasses and the whiskey jar. I respectfully declined, telling Jeb that I wasn't much of a drinker and the porter was after doing a job on me already. The real reason for my abstinence was that I couldn't relax. Despite knowing I was in the safest place possible, I still couldn't blank out the feeling of danger in my brain. Jabber, on the other hand, was having a ball – drinking to his heart's content and enjoying the old veterans' war tales.

'I met this man on the first day of June, eighteen ninety-eight, amid the forty-five hundred rebels who fought with William Aylmer on a muddy battlefield in Kilcock,' Jeb recalled.

'And, even though we lost, we lived to fight another day,' continued Sugrue. 'We were back together on the eighth of September, fighting for Humbert at Ballinamuck – part of eight hundred and fifty men facing a force of ten-thousand Redcoats under Cornwallis and Lake.'

'Do you remember where you were on the nineteenth of November, seventeen ninety-eight – the day of Wolfe Tone's demise,' asked Jeb.

'Indeed, I do,' said Sugrue. 'I was thatching the roof of your mother's cottage in Tyrellspass, along with you and...'

Sugrue stopped his sentence abruptly.

'Me and Tom McAndrew,' stated Jeb. 'How is he keeping, Sugrue, poor auld Tom? What a soldier.'

I noticed the change in Sugrue's face.

'He's.... He's okay, he's grand,' he muttered, then said no more about him.

The drunker they got, the more romantic and daring their stories became.

'Seas suas, seas suas,' said Jeb, pulling Sugrue up out of his seat. 'Let's say the pledge together, once more for auld time's sake.'

'What pledge?'

'Tone's pledge,' replied Jeb. 'The pledge of the United Irishmen.'

The two old warriors stood to attention, placed their hands over their hearts, faced the ancient flag of Ireland and O'Connell's picture, and spoke in unison.

'I, in the presence of God, do pledge myself to my country, that I will use all my abilities and influence in the attainment of an impartial and adequate representation of the Irish nation in Parliament; and as a means of absolute and immediate necessity in the establishment of this chief good to Ireland, I will endeavour, as much as lies in my ability, to forward a brotherhood of affection, an identity of interests, a communion of rights and a union of power among Irishmen of all religious persuasions, without which every reform in Parliament must be partial, not national, inadequate to the happiness of this country.'

They hugged each other when they came to the end. Jeb remained standing, had himself a little wobble, and held up his glass of whiskey.

'I'd like to propose a toast,' he said. 'To Theobald Wolfe Tone.'

Immediately, the four whiskey glasses collided in mid-air and everyone, except myself, took a generous mouthful.

'To Munro and McCracken,' said Sugrue, and they repeated the dose.

'To Humbert and Defenderism,' hailed Jeb, and once again the glasses were joined and drained.

'To liberte, egalite, and fratermite,' shouted Sugrue, taking another turn in the toast.

'To Hoche and his fourteen thousand brave souls,' said Jeb, before another swig from the glasses.

'To William Drennan and his Emerald Isle,' continued Sugrue.

'Let no feeling of vengeance presume to defile; the cause, or the men, of the Emerald Isle,' they sang, arm-in-arm.

'To Bond, Emmet, McNevin, and Sweetman.'

'To Lord Edward Fitzgerald.'

'To Nielson and the Sheares brothers.'

The list went on, glasses were emptied and replenished and then emptied again. Eventually, at the behest of Jeb Turling, Sugrue regaled us with a beautiful rendition of *The Croppy Boy*.

When Roger Giles heard what happened he was mad. He never wanted Walter Pollach on the search to begin with. As far as he was concerned, Pollach was a glorified tax collector with no tracking experience who fancied himself as some sort of military genius. But Giles was even more annoyed with Teddy from the yeomen. He should have known better. Once the Sugrue Gang's bedding had been found, the rest should have been easy. Giles knew we had been hiding under the bed. He knew we had used the foul-smelling corpse to trick the trackers and escape the hounds. And Giles was proved right when he sent Pollach and the yeomen back to the house. They found no rotting corpse in the bed, just a long mound of fresh clay out the back with a cross at its head.

'That's twice now,' snarled Giles, 'he's got away from me. There won't be a third time.'

As the end of September drew ever closer, Giles stepped up security around the ships in dock. He ordered his militia men to patrol the waterways and check all canal traffic going in and out of Dublin. This was a mighty task, as travelling by canal had become so popular that up on one hundred thousand people a year were now using boats and sea vessels. It wasn't just Bianconi's drivers that were now on red alert, but the taxi-carriages and omnibuses of the city too – with the lure of the viscount's reward to sharpen their wits. All the fishing boats in the coastal areas were accounted for, checked and watched. Roger Giles was sure of only two things – the Sugrue Gang was heading away from the countryside and towards the anonymity of Dublin; and he could rely on nobody, besides himself, to catch its leader once and for all.

Thirty-eight – A Ship Waits in the Bay

The yeomen were fed up as yet another fly-boat headed their direction.

'Is all this really necessary,' snapped Walter Pollach, who had been demoted from his self-appointed position in the wake of his cock up with the rotting corpse. 'I mean, what are the chances of Sugrue and his maties taking a fly-boat into Dublin? They haven't two shillings to rub together, let alone the price of a jaunt up the canal.'

Teddy was taking no more advice from Mister Pollach. As far as he was concerned, Pollach had already caused him serious embarrassment – and very nearly his position as second-in-command in the Longford Division of the Irish Yeomen.

'I don't care if it's a fly-boat or a homemade raft, we're checking every single vessel until our shift is up,' he told Pollach in no uncertain terms.

As the fly-boat was waved down and stalled for checking, a barge drifted up from behind in perfect silence. It glided through the middle of the canal, slicing the water evenly.

'Ahoy,' shouted Teddy, from the shoreline.

The owner of the barge smiled and waved back.

'Pull over,' ordered Teddy.

The man steered the barge skilfully to one side.

'Check it out, Walter,' said Teddy, who was heading for the fly-boat.

Walter Pollach stepped wearily onto the barge. The ominous clipping noise of his boots sounded even louder on the wooden deck.

'Hullo. What's your business on the canal,' he rasped.

'Sir, I'm bringing timber poles to a city merchant,' answered the man in the barge, pointing to the black canvas covering.

'Show me your papers,' demanded Pollach.

The man took out his licence and handed it over.

'Jeb Turling, is that it?'

The old man nodded in agreement.

'What sort of a name is that? What's Jeb short for?'

'Sir, I don't know. I don't think it's short for anything. My mother liked the…'

'Okay, okay,' snapped Pollach. 'I don't want the history of your puff. Right, remove this cover and give me a wee look.'

Sugrue couldn't believe it as Walter Pollach's voice filled his eardrums yet again. He looked at me and shook his head. Jabber clenched his teeth with sheer determination. He fixed his gaze on the long rusty nail he had found earlier. He placed the nail between his fingers and made a fist. He wasn't going to be taken alive. In the few short days since they'd met, Jeb Turling had made a big impression on Jabber. If he was going down, then he really was going down with his shield or on it – and he was taking Walter Pollach down with him.

Jeb lifted the corner of the black canvas covering to unveil rows of neatly stacked timber fencing poles and two large clay jars with corks in their spouts.

'Everyone wants to fence these days. Sharing land is becoming a thing of the past,' said Jeb, as coolly as his racing heart would allow. 'But, I suppose, if someone has to benefit from it, it might as well be me.'

'What are those,' asked Pollach.

'Oh, they're just a couple of jars of whiskey that were given to me by the last man I delivered to on the canal. I wouldn't mind but I don't even drink the stuff. Ah, I'll give them away when I get into Dublin. Hold on until I show you the rest of these poles.'

Jeb made a half-hearted attempt to pull back a piece of covering.

'You'll do. I've seen enough. Show me up one of those jars,' said Pollach.

He twisted the cork free and smelled the tip of the spout. Then, he tentatively placed it to his mouth and took a sip. He licked his lips.

'That's gorgeous,' he said.

'Sir, I don't know how you drink it – horrible stuff. I'll tell you what, you can have it for nothing – if you want. Have both jars, why don't you?'

Pollach took another mouthful.

'Well, I am going back to my master's house the day after tomorrow. He loves a good whiskey. What's this you heathens call it – the water of life.'

'Yes, indeed. Uisce beatha – the water of life. Very well, sir. By all means, you are welcome to them. Have you been away from your master's house for long?'

'Myself and those fellas on the brae of that shore have been out now for about ten days. We're only waiting on a ship to sail for America on the first, and then we're heading back to the Midlands. My master is Viscount de Bromley. Have you ever heard of him?'

Jeb was securing the covering as Pollach was talking.

'Ah, I don't think so. Sir, I'm from just outside the Pale myself. You have my advantage – I was never in the Midlands.'

Pollach folded the licence and handed it back. Jeb replaced the cork in its spout and presented the two jars of whiskey to Walter

- 268 -

with a smile.

'By the way,' said Pollach, as he was about to disembark, 'you didn't happen to come across an old grey-haired geyser of seventy and two younger men, roughly mid-forties, on your travels?'

Jeb stroked his chin and began to think.

'They'd be fairly dishevelled-looking, I'd imagine, after nearly a whole month on the run. Anyway, they're very dangerous villains. If you come across three men fitting their age descriptions, it would be best not to approach them. Play it safe and contact the police immediately.'

'Thanks for the heads-up, I'll be sure to keep an eye out. If I see three suspicious-looking characters like that, I'll be sure to alert the peel...the police.'

'Good man,' said Pollach, and he gave Jeb a smile. 'There's a hefty reward for their capture, so keep that in mind. Thanks again for the whiskey.'

'Good luck now,' said Jeb, 'mind those jars when you're stepping off.'

As Jeb steered out towards the centre of the canal, he gave a big wave to the yeomen on the shore. He was breathing heavily, but trying to look natural.

'I'm next on the list for a massive heart attack,' he shouted, before taking into a fit of laughing.

The relief was palpable under the canvas covering. I was in a cold sweat. Sugrue, normally so cool under pressure, admitted he had almost lost it – especially when Jeb started to peel back the covering. Surprisingly, Jabber didn't seem a bit bothered. He just remained on his haunches in the semi-darkness, the rusty nail protruding from his closed fist and that look of steely determination in his eyes.

Once through the security barrier on the Royal Canal, it was plain sailing into Dublin for Jeb. He deliberately slowed our progress, so that there would be less time for us to kill. As we tipped along, a sign appeared on the bank of the canal. It read: *No health check, No entry.* It reminded Jeb of how suspicious city folk had become of country people and the diseases that were said to come with them. We finally sailed up the Liffey and moored at Wood Quay. Nearby, Christchurch Cathedral's bell told us it was three o'clock. Jeb's mind had gone into overdrive. It was still nine hours until the sailing – a long time to harbour three fugitives in the empire's second city. He said he had an idea, as he pulled back the canvas covering and we finally got to feel fresh air on our skin. I stepped out stiffly from behind a stack of fencing posts, while Sugrue's eyes blinked rapidly – adjusting to the brightness of the sky.

'Right lads,' said Jeb, 'we have to move fast. Put those shawls around ye.'

I watched Jeb finish with the black canvas covering and suddenly realised just how close we had been to getting caught by Pollach. We must have looked strange – stepping off the barge in our trousers and boots with shawls covering our heads. I surveyed the River Liffey for the first time in my life. It was full of sea vessels of all descriptions. The quays were all named. Merchant's Quay was a hive of activity, as a large group of men unloaded boxes from a boat. We scurried down a nearby street.

'Where are we going,' whispered Sugrue.

'This is Winetavern Street,' answered Jeb.

'I like the sound of that,' joked Sugrue.

'There's a brothel down here where we can stay for the remaining hours.'

Then Jeb turned and looked at Jabber.

'I don't want you getting any notions in your head. It's for hiding yourselves and nothing else.'

'That's a scurrilous remark,' said Jabber, 'I've had a lot of practise at celibacy, you know.'

Winetavern Street was dirty and overcrowded. We passed a boy who was begging on a step. He had only one leg. My heart went out to him. I stopped to give him some money.

'What are you doing,' snapped Jeb. 'Put that money away now. Do you want to get us all nabbed?'

We came to a tall Georgian tenement and Jeb rushed inside.

'He seems to know his way around,' mused Jabber.

Jeb made a beeline for the reception desk. An old woman sat there, looking sleepy.

'Four rooms please, one night,' gushed Jeb.

'Someone's in a hurry,' she said eventually, 'they're two pence each, money up front – and that's only the rooms.'

Jeb took out three thruppenny bits and the old woman fumbled for change in a tin can under her desk.

'Could I interest you in some of my girls,' she asked.

'Not just at the moment,' replied Jeb, throwing us each a key. 'We're going to have a wash and something to eat first. But we'll be looking forward to the company of your beautiful ladies later on.'

'Are you sure about this, Jeb,' I whispered, a bit concerned. 'I'm a married man, you know.'

'Relax,' said Jeb. 'Right now, this is the safest place for ye fellas to be. Give me that money, Jim. I'm going to need lots of it. Now, follow me up the stairs and we'll talk more.'

Jeb ushered us all into the one room and bolted the door. He went through his plan, then got up to go.

'Nobody leaves this room until I get back. And don't answer the door to anybody for any reason.'

Then Jeb was gone. Sugrue bolted the door again and collapsed into bed.

Jeb needed a walk to steady his nerves. He could feel the tension of the past few days in his muscles. He strolled around by Gardner Street and onto Mountjoy Square. He gazed up at the windows and thought of Daniel O'Connell. Any one of those red-bricked houses could have been the counsellor's old home. Although he was a regular in the city, Jeb rarely had the chance to look around. He spent all his time with the barge, loading and unloading goods at the quays. He was struck by the wealth and splendour of it all, and how it fitted in so nice and snugly with the worse slums in Europe.

Jeb had something to eat, then went shopping in Arnotts on Henry Street. A lady waited inside the window, a measuring tape in her beautifully-manicured hand. She offered Jeb her assistance and then apologised, showing him a chair and asking if he would prefer the services of a male attendant. He said he would far prefer if she waited on him. Then he set his rescue plan in motion. Firstly, he decked himself out in a black suit, complete with top hat and cloak. He used his new suit to guess the measurements he needed for Sugrue, myself and Jabber.

'My word, you are a busy man,' remarked the assistant delightfully, 'anyone would be forgiven for thinking you were preparing your whole household for the big ball in town tonight.'

'Ball,' said Jeb, 'what ball?'

'Go on ourra that,' she quipped in her beautiful Dublin accent, and playfully tapped him on the arm. 'What ball indeed, and it only the talk of the whole city this past month.'

'There are two balls on tonight. Which ball is the big ball,' continued Jeb, searching for information.

'Oh, I didn't know that,' she said apologetically, 'I was talking about the masquerade ball the Earl of Grantham is throwing in Fitzwilliam Square. It's only going to be the greatest social event of the year.'

'*Masquerade*,' returned Jeb. 'Well, well, well. I wouldn't mind gate-crashing the party you'll be attending. Are you married?'

She gave Jeb another playful tap on the arm and said: 'Would you go on ourra that.'

Suddenly the plan was taking a different turn in his head.

'I'm Jeb.'

'Annie,' said the shop attendant, and shook Jeb's waiting hand.

'I was only joking with you, Annie. Of course I'm going to the Earl of Grantham's masquerade ball. I'll need four face masks now, just to put the finishing touches on these costumes.'

Annie went away and got four white face masks. When Jeb was leaving, he gave her a large tip for all her help and loveliness.

After this, it was time for some serious spending. Jeb hired a taxi-carriage. His first trip was to south Dublin Bay, to the terminus building at Victoria Wharf, where he purchased three first-class tickets for New York. He went down to the port and had a look at the *Erin's Queen*. Then he headed back towards the city, where he parted company with the taxi-carriage driver at a house on Heytesbury Street in Portabello. The brass plate at the steps to the front door read *Annabrook House*. Jeb walked around the back and asked for the coachman, Mister Stapleton.

'He's below in the stables,' said a young fella. 'Will I give him a shout?'

'No need,' answered Jeb. 'I think I'll surprise him.'

Jabber watched out the window as a man lit the street lamps with a long pole. He was restless and fed up of being locked in the room. Then the street became alive with girls. They walked up and down, chatting and laughing. He recognised some of them from earlier. There was one girl with big red hair – it could have been a wig. She was pretty. Jabber suddenly felt an even bigger urge to be free. I lit an oil lamp and adjusted the wick. Sugrue sat on the bed, rubbing his eyes with one hand and biting the fingernails of the other.

All at once, a clatter of hooves had the three of us up at the window. The girls were standing around in groups, staring at the horse-drawn carriage which was now parked outside our *boarding house*. We heard footsteps on the stairs. There were lots of footsteps. Sugrue positioned himself at the door and put his finger to his lips.

'You can just drop those suitcases there,' said a voice from outside.

Jabber hurriedly quenched the lamp.

'The O'Ferrall county says hello,' said the same voice into the keyhole, and there was a collective sigh of relief.

Jeb was dressed like a lord. He was all business.

'Everyone to his own room,' he ordered. 'Chop, chop. Have a good soak and get spruced up. I want ye looking like gentlemen. Have a close shave. Put oil in yere hair and comb it back neatly. Yere new clothes are waiting for ye.'

'Ah here,' said Jabber, 'we're not a shower of fancy dans.'

If Jabber was joking, then Jeb wasn't laughing.

'You are what I say you are, until I get you safely on that ship,' warned Jeb. 'Sugrue, I got you a ticket. It's decided – you're going to America. Jim, here's the rest of your money. I only bought the necessities. I had to rent a horse and carriage. If ye lads are supposed to be gentlemen, then ye have to look, behave, and travel like gentlemen.'

Jeb gave me the remainder of the hundred pounds and the tickets. Then he threw a party mask at Jabber.

'Here you go, Cinderella. When you've finished making yourself beautiful, put this on – you're going to the ball.'

We scrubbed up so well that the woman at reception didn't recognise us on our way out the door.

'Are you fellas lost,' she asked, as Jeb threw the four keys down on her desk.

The transformation was startling. We could have passed for the three finest gentlemen in Dublin's fair city. Jeb danced attendance on us – carrying our suitcases and calling us all sorts of swanky titles. The girls rushed over as he held the carriage door open. They promised to take special care of us when we got back. Jabber reached out and placed a coin in the red-haired girl's gloved hand. She blew a kiss and he pretended to catch it and place it in the breast pocket of his black velvet coat.

'I could get used to this,' said Sugrue, fixing a gold pin in his cravat.

Jeb loaded the last of the empty cases onto the imperial and the horse clip-clopped his way out of Winetavern Street. As we got rolling, Sugrue was curious to know where the driver had attained a beautiful red Brougham carriage and the white Clydesdale mare.

'That's the canal for you,' answered Jeb, looking back from the perch, 'you'll always know a man who knows a man.'

'How far is Kingstown,' I asked.

'Less of your Kingstown. It's Dun Leary to ordinary auld eejits like us,' said Jeb. 'About six miles.'

On the way down Sackville Street, the carriage came to an abrupt stop. Sugrue reached for his walking stick, ready to use it as a baton. Jeb's head appeared at the carriage side-window.

'Get out and have a look, lads,' he said, pointing to a lamppost.

There was a wanted poster with *our* names on it – right in the middle of the city!

One hundred pounds, recoverable from Viscount de Bromley of Edgeworthstown in the county of Longford was written at the bottom.

Jabber was shaking his head in disgust.

'What's the matter with him,' asked Jeb.

'He thinks he's worth more than that,' answered Sugrue. 'He fancies himself as a bit of an outlaw.'

Jeb stopped again and said we were getting close – once we could see the beam from the East Pier lighthouse. He stressed the importance of arriving at just the right moment. It had to be a rush job – a last minute thing. That way there would be no waiting around on the pier. We needed to hit the gangplank running.

'Put yere masks on now,' he shouted from the perch, 'we're almost there.'

We sped into Dun Leary port at five minutes to midnight. It was like a fair-day carnival. A large crowd of well-wishers were cheering and whistles were blowing. Jeb alighted and began to unload the empty suitcases. Sugrue stepped out in his mask. He started shouting orders and scolding Jeb for being late. He flashed his gold pocket-watch. The hand had almost reached twelve. Jabber took hold of one of the cases. Jeb snapped it back off him.

'You're supposed to be a gentleman,' he barked.

I got out and looked for the gangway.

'Merciful hour,' gushed Jabber, struck by the enormity of the ship in the dock.

The hull was painted a beautiful dark green, with *Erin's Queen* written in large white letters. Her sails rose fifty feet into the air. There were ropes and mast poles intertwining. Men were running and climbing all over the place, doing last minute bits and pieces.

My face mask afforded me the comfort of a good look around.

'Sugrue,' I said, and nodded towards a group of men to the right of the pier.

There he was in all his glory – the man with the grey beard, in full militia regalia.

'Roger Giles,' Sugrue said to Jeb.

'Keep to the left,' ordered Jeb. 'And make sure yere masks are secure.'

Jabber was already over by the ticket checker and the man in charge of the gangplank rope. Some people were huddled around a burning barrel, close to the gangplank. A man in a green coat threw what looked like water over the huddle and made a sign of the Cross. They were reciting the Hail Mary. He blessed them again as the rope was opened and the huddle made their way up the gangplank.

'Would you like a prayer to help you on your way, my son,' asked the man in the green coat, as Jabber waited for the rest of us to catch up.

He couldn't believe his eyes.

'Father Murtagh!'

Father Murtagh was as shocked as Jabber.

'Do I know you, my child,' he said cautiously.

'It's me, Jabber Farrell.'

Jabber lowered his mask. Father Murtagh looked around suspiciously. The only policeman that he was aware of was still standing by the terminus, where he had been for most of the night.

'Now I recall, you're Milly's son – Joseph, isn't it? Fancy seeing you here.'

Remembering our situation, Jabber also looked around anxiously. Then he quickly put back on his mask.

'What are you doing here, Father?'

'I come here all the time, Joseph. I'm still a priest, after all. I minister to those who are about to depart for foreign shores. You wouldn't believe how many people become born-again followers of Christ at the sight of an emigrant ship. I find it the best place of all to sow God's seeds.'

Three masked men went running towards the gangplank rope. I had Lady Jane Teale's letter in my hand.

'Sorry for the delay, old chap. We were having such a merry night at the Earl of Grantham's ball that we lost all track of time,' I said, in my rehearsed gentleman's voice. 'We are bound for

America on the business of Lord and Lady Teale from Lacken House. My name is John Brown. Here you go. And this is my travelling party.'

I presented the letter to the ticket checker.

'That's okay,' he said, after looking at the red seal. 'Your tickets please.'

He examined the tickets more closely.

'Sugrue,' said Jabber, 'look who I found.'

Father Murtagh nodded nervously at myself and Sugrue. It was strange to see him in a green overcoat. It must have been just as strange for him to see us in white face masks. I was waiting impatiently for the checker to hand back our tickets. Jeb was keeping an eye on Roger Giles. He was a long way down the pier, looking towards the gangplank. Just like Sugrue, Giles had a pocket-watch. He had it in his hand. Midnight had come and gone. All of a sudden, a man on horseback galloped up to Giles and engaged him in conversation. Jeb recognised the rider as the same man he had given the jars of whiskey to the previous morning.

'Paddy,' he said, pointing out the man on the horse, who was now looking in the direction of the gangplank also.

'Pollach,' said Sugrue, and he turned to the ticket checker and told him that if he didn't hurry up the ship would be gone without them.

'Don't let anyone through that rope until I know exactly who's getting on,' said the ticket checker to the man guarding the gangplank. 'There are five of you here, but only three tickets. Are ye sure everything is above board?'

'Yeah, and have a good look at the same tickets before giving us any of your shite,' snapped Sugrue. 'Do you treat all your first-class customers like this?'

'I beg your pardon, sir,' said the ticket checker. 'But I'm merely doing my job.'

Pollach was riding towards the gangplank and waving furiously. The big crowd slowed his progress. The policeman left the terminus and walked towards the ship, trying to disperse the crowd with shrill blasts of his whistle.

'Hold those passengers,' shouted Walter Pollach, 'on the orders of the captain of the Longford Yeomen.'

Instead of dispersing, the well-wishers waved all the more and cheered even louder. Some rushed forward, sure that the whistling was coming from the ship. Pollach had come to a standstill, so he jumped off the horse and started to run.

'Pardon me, Brother,' said Jeb to Father Murtagh, as he placed the ticket in Sugrue's hand, 'it's time for this man to take his leave.'

Jeb pushed Jabber towards the gangplank. I followed close behind.

'I told you before, I'm too old for America,' argued Sugrue.

He held the ticket out to the young curate.

'Father Murtagh, would you do me the honour and go in my stead?'

'Patrick, I can't take your ticket,' said Father Murtagh. 'I have finally found my true vocation – administering God's message to the weary wanderer.'

The ticket checker gave the crew a signal. The last of the passengers had been checked through. The gangplank guard rolled up his rope.

'You won't administer much of God's message below in Kilmainham jail. You're wanted by the authorities almost as much as I am. Look, there's a peeler heading right this way.'

Father Murtagh almost jumped out of his skin. He looked at the ticket, then at Sugrue, then at the approaching policeman. He gripped the green overcoat around his chest in an attempt to hide his cassock.

'Father, listen to me. A wise man once said: "My grace is sufficient for you. For My power is made perfect in weakness."'

'Corinthians, chapter twelve, verse nine,' returned Father Murtagh.

'Jim and Jabber are going away, and I'm too old to look after them. Father, my weakness really needs your power now.'

Reluctantly, Father Murtagh took hold of the ticket.

'Hang on there, you must be mistaken,' said Sugrue to the ticket checker. 'This man is getting on – not me.'

Pollach was almost upon them. He still couldn't make himself heard, his shouts drowned out by all the excitement. Hats flew through the air. The policeman had stopped and was taking care of Pollach's horse – patting his nose and leading him back towards the terminus. The passengers were looking over the deck rails, waving and cheering back. Sugrue and Jeb waited until Father Murtagh was a good distance up the gangplank. Then they disappeared into the crowd.

By the time Pollach reached the ticket checker, the gangplank had been removed and the horn of the ship was signalling its farewell.

'I have been ordered to apprehend those men who just got on,' said Pollach, 'the ones with the masks. Mister Roger Giles, captain of the yeomanry, wants to check them out. We've spent the last week and a half on the hunt for three fugitives.'

'It's okay,' said the ticket checker. 'Those gentlemen were coming from the Earl of Grantham's masquerade ball – a Mister John Brown and a couple of his friends. They're going to America on the business of their masters – a Lord and Lady something-or-other from Lorcan House. I checked his letter myself. The seal is authentic. They're travelling first class. They were very lucky – any later and they could have stayed at the ball.'

Walter Pollach relaxed when he heard this. He was glad, after all the boats he had searched in the previous days, that he didn't have the hassle of delaying a ship.

'Mister John Brown,' repeated Roger Giles. 'Who told you that, Mister Pollach, the fellow in the mask who didn't board?'

'I heard it from the ticket man's own mouth. He checked them in personally – to the first-class compartment. What fellow are you talking about? I didn't see anybody else with a mask. Besides, those fellows were only wearing masks because they were coming from the Earl of Grantham's party. They must have forgotten to take them off in their rush to get here. You see, Captain Giles, I leave no stone unturned in my investigations. The Sugrue Gang may still be out there but, by hook or by crook, we'll bring them to justice.'

The ship pulled away from the dock as the decibel level increased once more. Jeb Turling sat in the perch, alongside an emotional Paddy Sugrue, and watched it slide away.

'Travel well, my auld sons of Eireann, I leave ye to God,' said Sugrue, as he looked up to Heaven, 'and don't forget to come back to us.'

'With yere shields or on them,' whispered Jeb, as he put a consoling hand on his old friend's shoulder.

Up on deck, Father Murtagh, myself and Jabber looked back at the cheering crowd. I sought out Walter Pollach. He stood on the pier, watching happily as we sailed away. I looked at Roger Giles, who was standing sullenly beside him. A boldness came over me. I wanted nothing more than to reveal my identity – to take off my mask and laugh in their faces. I was relieved and jubilant and exhausted. I hugged Jabber. I searched for Jeb and Sugrue. I scanned the whole shoreline. But I didn't see them anywhere.

'I never thought I'd hear myself say this, but thanks be to God for *Erin's Queen*,' said Jabber.

'Amen to that, Joseph. God be praised,' added Father Murtagh.

'I could do without the queen, but I hope it's not the last we see of Erin – or Sugrue and Jeb, for that matter.'

'Don't worry, Jabber, we'll see them again,' I said. 'We shall return.'

It felt strange without Sugrue, especially as I was expecting him to come with us. It was sad.

'I don't know about that,' lamented Jabber. 'We *are* fugitives after all – with a price on our heads.'

'Don't worry, Joseph, keep your heart up,' said Father Murtagh. 'We may be down now, but we're certainly not out. Even Jesus was rejected in His own land. But someday, maybe sooner than you think, we'll be welcomed back to Edgeworthstown with open arms.'

The people were becoming like dots on the shoreline. We could still hear them, but only just. It's strange the thoughts that go through your head as you're drifting away from Ireland. I looked and listened as long as I could, only too aware that in another minute or two there would be no more looking and no more listening. The fair land would be no more.

'Mostrim, Father, not Edgeworthstown,' Jabber declared. 'If we're ever welcomed back to Edgeworthstown, I won't be long about filling in whoever's doing the welcoming on a couple of home truths. I will state, quite clearly, that when I was growing up, this was Mostrim. This is Mostrim – forever and always.'

Acknowledgements

I would like to thank my parents, Sean and Mary Cassidy. To my auntie Kathleen, and James and Michael.

I would also like to mention Master Kenneth Sheridan, former teacher and principal of the Boys' National School in Mostrim, for his encouragement and training.

A big thank you to Eamonn Morgan, for all your hard work on the proofreading.

To the memory of Mrs. Margaret Devine, my old writing and reading colleague.

To my brother, Johnny, and my partner, Petrina, for all your help and support.

Go raibh mile maith agaibh to my brothers Glen and Daniel, for helping me with computer technology. And to Daniel for all his help with the cover design.

To my old colleague and friend, David McGurran, thank you for your help.

I would also like to thank the staff of the famine museum in Strokestown House, Co. Roscommon.

Thank you also to the staff at Longford County Library for your help. I would like to particularly mention Mr. Martin Morris.

I would like to extend my appreciation to Mr. Sean Kiernan, for his enthusiasm and words of encouragement.

Last, and by no means least, a massive thank you to the staff at Rapid Print, Longford, and Choice Publishing, Drogheda, for all your courtesy, hard work, and good advice. To Marita for her ideas and help on designing the covers. To Mary Fleming for all your help with the cover design

To the late John Cassidy, Kathleen Kenny, James Kenny, Michael Kenny, Kenneth Sheridan, and Margaret Devine – A Thiarna dean trocaire ar a n-anam dilis.

References

Edgeworthstown, Myths and Memories: Seo is Siud, Mostrim Heritage and Historical Society, Self-Published, 2007.

Edgeworthstown, Parish of Mostrim: O Theach Go Teach, Mostrim Heritage and Historical Society, Self-Published, 2003.

Fields of Home, Marita Conlon-McKenna, The O'Brien Press, 1997.

Helen, Maria Edgeworth, Sort Of Books Publishers, 2010.

Ireland and the British Empire, Kevin Kenny, Oxford University Press, 2004.

Ireland Since 1870, Mark Tierney, C.J. Fallon Ltd., 1991.

Ireland, 1815-1870: Emancipation, Famine and Religion, Donncha O Corrain and Thomas O'Riordan (eds.), 2011.

Ireland's Own, Channing House, multiple editions and years.

Ireland 1798-1998: War, Peace and Beyond, Alvin Jackson, Wiley-Blackwell, 2014.

Longford, History and Society, Martin Morris and Fergus O'Ferrall (eds.), Geography Publications, 2010.

The Elements of Style, William Strunk jr. and E.B. White, Pearson Longman, 2009.

The New Testament of Our Lord and Saviour Jesus Christ, The Gideons International, 1987 Edition.